SNAPDRAGON
Tears in Blood

SNAPDRAGON
Tears in Blood

To
Liz

8-29-24

BRYAN CHAMBERLAIN

For information regarding permission, write Bryan Chamberlain at
251 N DuPont Hwy, Suite 110, Dover, DE 19901

This book was originally published in paperback in 2019

Independently Published
I.S.B.N. 978-1-092-66284-0

Printed in the U.S.A.

Text type set in Adobe Garamond Pro
Cover art by Ernest Hoyer

Dedication

Alexis, Megan, Drew, Aliyah, Tyler and Makayla
To the treasured eyes of youth,
may you always see hope in the world.

Mary Chamberlain
A woman that loved more than anyone deserved
and loved more than she ever got in return.

Jackson Morgan III
With memories of a fallen friend.

R. I. P.

Table of Contents

CHAPTER 1

History or Legend

"I have found some property that fits what you've been looking for."

"Good, where's the location?" Hong Jin's face brightened as he responded to Morra Dok, a local real estate agent.

"It's located in Amphoe Ban Thi within the Lamphun Province here in Thailand. However, Mr. Hong, there is a small problem. It's been declared unfit for habitation and is considered haunted. No one has been allowed to go into the region for more than a hundred years or so without coming up missing. Furthermore, the only way to get there right now is by helicopter, unless, you feel like taking a forty-mile hike," expressed Ms. Morra Dok.

"That sounds very good, Ms. Dok. I could build lodging as a starting point for potential students. Then, send them out to find the school. They will secretly be given a GPS marker so we can track their progress. And then we can…"

"Mr. Hong," Ms. Dok interrupted. "Did you not hear what I said? The land has been deemed unfit for habitation by the government. We are going to have to get governmental approval before we can even see it. And there is still the issue of it being haunted. You know, like the Suicide Forest in Japan."

"You don't really believe in ghosts, do you?" Jin started questioning the

1

integrity of Morra's story.

"Ah, no, Mr. Hong, but the stories; the stories are a little too real. And much of them are based in historical evidence."

"Do what is necessary for us to see the property. If it is as you've previously described, I still want to see it, just the same. Okay?"

"Very well, Mr. Hong, I will see what I can do."

"Why?" Hong Jai, the eight-year-old son of Hong Jin, asked simply.

Hong Jin turned his attention to Jai, "Why what my son?"

"Why is it haunted?"

After a moment of silence passed between the father and son, they both turned towards the real estate agent, Morra Dok, for an answer.

"Well," she hesitated. "It's been said, over the last several hundred years or so, well over a thousand men have gone into the region never to be seen again."

"Why?" Jai asked again.

"Well, um, there are more than a few theories. Some say it was supposed to be the place of an ancient and powerful monastery. Anyone who dared to intrude upon their land was hunted down and killed. Another is about a woman who supposedly had lived in the fourteenth century. Legend says she was away preparing for her wedding when her school was attacked and the invaders killed the man who was to be her husband." She cautiously looked at the eight-year-old then continued.

"When she returned home and found everyone had been murdered at the monastery, her heart burned with revenge. It is said she searched decades for those responsible. When vengeance was finally achieved, she was left so cold and empty by her victory that some say she was somehow frozen in time doomed to relive her sorrow forever. Some stories say she never married and her spirit still searches for her beloved. Others, say she remained alone and killed anyone who tried to get close to her. It's pretty tragic if you ask me."

"Who was she?" Suddenly caught up in her story, Jin asked, understanding what it was to lose someone he loved.

"Honestly, I don't know what her name was." Morra replied attempting to smile.

"So, are there any other ghost stories we should be aware of?" Hong Jin asked as if still questioning the validity of the legend.

"Yes, actually, there is. About a hundred and fifty years ago a prince wanted to build a palace where you want to build your school. He went with a couple thousand men and enough supplies to build it. There was a massacre with only one survivor who died shortly after giving his report to the king."

"And what was that report!? They were ambushed by ghosts and goblins!?"

"No, Mr. Hong! A beautiful woman had appeared in the camp, so she was taken to the prince. When he saw her, he wanted her. When she turned him down he became very angry and tried to force himself upon her. Her response was simple. She killed him and everyone else without mercy."

"One woman?" Jin said maintaining his disbelief as if any group of women let alone just one woman could possibly do what was being said. "So, what did the king do?"

"He declared the land unfit for habitation and forbade anyone from going back into the area for fear of retaliation by the spirit world. And that's why some people simply believe it is haunted by the ghosts of the dead of that fateful day."

"That is a very fascinating story, Ms. Dok. Although, I do not fear the dead, however, I am still intrigued to see this property. You've made it so compelling. Just the same, I will honor the memory of the fallen. If this will appease the government, let me know."

"Why are you so interested in this property anyway? Morra asked searching for his reasoning.

"Because I am," Jin responded sharply, looking at Morra dismissively.

"Very well Mr. Hong, I will check with the officials again and see what they say. I will get back to you as soon as I hear something, okay?"

Jin said thank you as he shook Morra's hand. He then took his son by the hand and left the office.

"Papa, do you think we'll see it?"

"Maybe, my son, I believe there still might be a chance."

Hong Jin was an international martial arts champion from China. Very successful, he currently had endorsements worldwide providing him with great wealth. Jin was looking forward to raising his son and to retirement at the ripe age of thirty-one. His dream was to rebuild a school and train future champions undisturbed. He lives now for his son and to fulfill his dream. This was why he chose to move to Thailand. Ever since Jai's mother had died during childbirth, Jin has never really been the same.

• • •

The following week Jin's cell phone rang. It was Morra Dok from the real estate office. After three rings, not wanting to seem overly anxious, Jin answered. "Hello, Ms. Dok, what can I do for you today?"

"Well, Mr. Hong, we received an answer to our inquiry."

"And that is?"

"They said for a 'small donation' they will be more than happy to lift the quarantine on the land so you may see it."

"And how much is this 'small donation' supposed to be?"

"Three million five hundred thousand baht."

"Really!? Are you serious!?"

"I'll understand if you want to change your mind and see something else."

"The money is not the issue. It's the principle of the matter that bothers me. I am trying to buy land, not politicians. If the government had simply asked for a non-refundable deposit that would have been acceptable, but no, they are asking me to bribe them and that is not."

"What do you want me to tell them?"

"Exactly what I said, my integrity is not for sale. Yes, I may have endorsements, but I only endorse what I believe in. I'm sorry I ever came here!"

"No, please don't feel that way. I really think they're just trying to scare you away from the property, but I will get it straightened out, so don't worry. Okay?"

"Fine, but one more attack against my honor and I will be looking elsewhere."

"Yes Mr. Hong, I understand. This deal is very important to me as well. Aside from the financial gain, this is a deal of a lifetime. I want this done right also, Mr. Hong. Besides sir, like I said before, I really think they're just trying to scare you off."

"I'm sorry Ms. Dok. Sometimes I forget I'm not the only one who has to actually work at my career. And please, tell them I will place a deposit on the property."

"Thank you, sir, I'll send you the information you need right away. And I'll give you a call as soon as I hear something."

"I'll get my attorney and accountant on it immediately. And I'll also have a helicopter on standby for when you call, so be ready to go."

"I'll be ready. I'm looking forward to it as well." Each hung up their phone.

When Jin received the information, he reviewed it. He then had his secretary file all the proper paperwork and permits. He also told Jai they would be going to see where their new home would be built. Jai rejoiced happily at the news.

· · ·

"Papa, is riding in a helicopter the same as flying in a plane?"

"No, my son, it is very different. I would say it is more fun and has a much better view." Jin handed Jai a digital camera. "With this you should be able to get a lot of pictures and video." Jai smiled ear to ear.

They stopped to pick up Morra from her office. The door to the limousine opened and Morra Dok stepped inside. "Mr. Hong, thank you for picking me up. Hello Jai, how are you?" She asked with a smile to the little boy. "I believe you are going to love the property. Just in case you don't, I have some coastal property that is very secluded. I can show it to you in a couple days."

"I am quite sure I'll be very satisfied with this land, Ms. Dok, after all the hurdles you went through for me."

"Okay, I just thought I could interest you in a beach home."

"Nice try."

"Say cheese," Jai said as he quickly snapped a picture of Morra.

"What? No! You're going to delete that right!?"

Jai giggled and shook his head no while he tried to hide his camera. Jin snickered quietly as Morra protested against her looks. Shortly thereafter, Jin convinced her she looked fine by the time they arrived at the airfield.

Once there, they boarded the helicopter and took off. The view of the city and the surrounding area was breathtaking. They could see the waters off the coast. It was full of boats of varied shapes and sizes. Resort hotels filled with vacationers from around the world lined the coast. They seemed to be enjoying the sun, the beach, and whatever water sports they desired. The people of the city were energized with life unaware of the many mysteries growing in their midst. In the distance ahead of them, the mountains reached skyward with silent majesty.

Morra looked to the west remembering the morning forecast. A major storm system was coming up from the Indian Ocean into the Bay of Bengal and across Southeast Asia. It was supposed to bring heavy rain, lightning, and possible hail.

Morra reflected back for a moment to her childhood and why she was afraid of lightning. One afternoon a storm was brewing fiercely. She was told to come into the house. When she did, her dog ran out the door. Young Morra chased after him. As she was about to reach him, lightning struck and killed her pet right in front of her. The force of the sound wave from the lightning bolt knocked her back several feet. When her head hit the ground, it put her into a coma for eight days. Now, looking back, she realized she hadn't owned another pet since.

Coming back to the present and trying not to expose her phobia she said, "I hope we have enough time to look at the property and get back safely." Morra pointed towards the storm heading slowly their way. It was still several hours away.

"Of course, we will, Ms. Dok. We should have plenty of time. I don't foresee any problems for our trip," the pilot said with encouragement through the headphones.

"See, what could go wrong? We'll go see the land and I will make an offer by dinner," Jin said.

"Mr. Hong, what if they reject your offer?"

"Ms. Dok, you should know better. That would merely be the start of negotiations."

Afterward they sat quietly for a while until the pilot spoke up. "Sir, ma'am, we're coming into the region now."

"I would like to circle the perimeter of the property, both high and low. Would that be a problem?"

"Not at all, sir, just sit back and enjoy the view."

As they looked on, they noticed the lake seemed to be frozen over. They were very confused by this because it was over 90 degrees that day. Jai's face was stuck to the window with awe. He smiled, giggled, pointed and took a few pictures. Jin was glad to see his son so happy. He knew it has been hard on Jai not knowing his mother at all. Many nights, including last night, Jai had awakened in tears. Having some understanding, he blames himself for the death of his mother.

Jin knew it was too great a burden for an eight-year-old child to carry. He had his personal assistant find the letters his wife had written to their son while she was pregnant so he could read them to Jai. The letters were usually about how much she loved him and how she couldn't wait to hold him. The letters always ended with 'I love you, my little prince' and were sealed with a lipstick kiss. Jin made sure Jai had a picture of his mother so he could talk to her anytime he wanted. Jin thought to himself many times his wife would have been proud of their son.

As he was watching Jai, his thoughts were interrupted by the pilot, "Mr. Hong, we're here." He gracefully set the helicopter down near the lake among the tall wheat-like grass.

"Looks like a good spot. You've done an excellent job."

"Thank you, sir."

CHAPTER 2

Tortured Release

They saw much overgrowth while landing. Tall grass and thick trees covered the landscape as a whole. When Jin and Morra got out of the helicopter, they headed straight for the lake. They marveled not that the lake was several miles wide, but more that it appeared to be frozen solid. They were amazed at the phenomenon because of how warm and humid it was. It should have been water, not ice.

While the pair stood in awe, the pilot helped Jai out of the helicopter. He also put Jai's camera around his neck so he wouldn't have to hold it. The pilot then unloaded the rest of their supplies.

"Amazing, what could have caused this?" Morra had murmured rhetorically. She wondered what Jin thought as he stood speechless before they started walking around. After just a minute of wading through the tall grass a scream echoed into the air. Morra had fallen forward after tripping over something. As she scrambled to her feet she screamed again, this time out of fright. "M-M-Mr. HONG!" She pointed to the ground. "Mr. Hong!!"

The pilot and Jin both ran over to Morra. "What's wrong? What is it? Are you hurt?" Jin questioned intently.

"It's a skeleton!"

"What? Where?"

"There!"

Jin looked to where she had pointed and the discovery proved to be astonishing. A fallen warrior lay on the ground with its skull separated from the body. He appeared to have been dressed as an elite guard of some sort and a spear lay in the grass about two feet from him.

Over the next hour, they uncovered the remains of many more bodies hidden by the tall grass in an area immediately down from the helicopter. There were both soldiers and non-soldiers. While most seemed to have died of a separated neck, many others had a crushed sternum or met their demise from one of the many weapons that now lay idle. This appeared to be the site of a great battle. However, it looked to have been a slaughter because there was no sign of an opposing force.

Unless it was an armor of some kind, all uniforms and clothing were extremely weathered and tattered. In contrast the weapons were in excellent condition without any signs of rust or decay. While the adults were busy trying to clear the area to investigate further. Jai used his new digital camera to record what they found. They were all too busy to notice as Jai slowly wandered off out of their sight.

Walking along the edge of the lake to the tree line, Jai stopped where a small portion of the ice was rustic in color. He moved closer to see the stain. That was when he saw it. A statue was slightly hidden by the trees. About twenty feet from the edge of the lake was an earthen statue of a woman kneeling. It looked like crimson tears flowing from its eyes to the lake. As he reached the statue, he pushed off a small branch that lay across her. He stood back and stared at it for a couple minutes. Jai thought the statue of the woman was pretty.

After recording the statue, he wondered to himself, why was she crying? Although, he said aloud, "I wonder if you're the one Ms. Dok was talking about?" He stepped closer to touch her face and was abruptly halted.

"How dare you touch me", the statue spoke to Jai. Jai was startled and stumbled backwards. The head of the statue turned and glared at him. Its face went from great sorrow to extreme rage and hatred. "I am Zhe Duan Chi, defeat me or die."

Jai wanted to get up and run, but fear had gripped him. In spite of his fear, he still blurted out, "No! Papa said to fight girls is wrong. They are to be cherished not abused."

"What!? You do not challenge me!?" She sounded slightly confused.

"No!" Feeling more confident he asked. "Why are you crying? You shouldn't be crying. You are a statue. But why are your tears red?" When the statue did not respond, he got up and moved closer to it. "Please don't cry. I don't want you to cry anymore." He slowly reached into his pocket and pulled out a handkerchief to wipe the tears from her eyes. As he did, the bitterness that lingered in her heart for so many centuries was broken by the sincerity of the boy's actions. Her tears began to flow clear again.

The wind started to pick up. The cleansing scent of rain grew stronger as well. The approaching storm became more menacing and a silence shattering crack of lightning stretched across the sky. This caused Jai to lose his grip on the handkerchief which blew away. As he stood he followed it with his eyes. Jai noticed something was near where it landed. He went over to it. He saw a jewel encrusted tube about five inches thick and eighteen inches long. He picked up the tube and stared at it for a minute or so. Another thunderous flash of lightening brought him out of his stupor.

In the distance Jin and Morra called frantically for him. The boy faintly heard his name in the wind. He looked back and saw them coming. He realized he needed to go. He picked up the handkerchief and quickly went back to the statue.

"I have to go now." Holding up the tube he asked, "Can I have this?" She said nothing. "Please don't cry anymore."

Jai set down the tube and tied the handkerchief around her wrist. Then he said, "Use this to dry your eyes, okay? I am sorry you ever had to cry." With the camera still around his neck, he grabbed the tube and ran back to meet his father and Ms. Dok. Morra was relieved to see him coming because the lightning was almost paralyzing to her. She thought to herself, they could now go and she would soon be safe from the lightning.

Zhe Duan Chi quietly rose to her feet within her earthen covered form. She watched the boy return to his father. She thought about what had just happened. She was about to kill a boy in a blind rage for no reason. She was going to murder an innocent child and all he wanted to do was help her. The thought made her sick to her stomach. She leaned against a tree wondering what could have driven her to this. Zhe Duan Chi began to remember her life. After a few moments, she realized what it was. It had been her quest for revenge that made her so numb. She had gained great power and misused it. Plus, she never got over the death of Pin Ai Ren. She had put the blame on any man who tried to get near her and killed them for it. She now cried tears of remorse because she was never able to let go. She whispered out loud to those that met their end by her hand, "Please forgive me."

•　　•　　•

Jin was very upset, yet relief was on his face when he picked up his son and held him. "Don't ever do that again," Jin charged Jai for running off on his own.

"Please don't be angry, Papa." Jai said. "She's real. She's really, real. Papa, the crying lady is real, just like you said."

"What are you talking about? Wait, what?" Jin pulled his son back and stared at his son.

"What is that? It's beautiful!" Ms. Dok interrupted pointing at the tube.

"I don't know, but we need to get out of here. That storm looks to be sweeping in a lot faster than anticipated," Jin responded.

"I agree. We need to hurry. This place is scaring me."

"Papa, can I keep it?"

"It doesn't appear to be a weapon, but it does look to be valuable though. Since you found it, I don't see why not. However, I do think we should get it appraised and checked out first. At least to find out what it is."

When they finally arrived back at the helicopter, it was ready for takeoff. Once inside they were quickly fastened in and the pilot began to lift off. Lightning streaked across the sky. BOOM!!! Ms. Dok jumped in her seat with a shriek. The pilot even made a ducking motion with the helicopter while Jin remained calm and Jai just stared out the window looking for her.

Suddenly, lightning started flashing continuously all around them. Instead of the roar of thunder, they thought they heard the roar of a great beast. Morra sat frozen in fear not being able to scream. Then the sky opened its well and rain raced to the earth. The pilot did his best to get them out of the region as fast and safely as he could.

•　　•　　•

On the ground, Zhe Duan Chi finally conceded defeat to what she thought was a potential enemy. Hong Jai had done so without any act of aggression and bested her with something she had long forgotten. An eight-year-old boy, who reminded her of her beloved Pin on the day they met, did what thousands of grown men could not. He overcame her violent nature with love and compassion. Jai mended her broken heart. She no longer cried tears of hurt, bitterness, and rage. She now cried tears of hope.

Zhe Duan Chi slowly walked to the edge of the lake. She stood silently for a moment feeling the burden of hatred being lifted and replaced by compassion while it rained and lightning flashed thunderously across the sky. Her earthen casing began to crumble from her flesh as the warm rain washed it from her skin. Being freed of her own stigma, Zhe Duan Chi cried out with the strength and power of a dragon. She was once again truly alive. She removed the cloth from her wrist to dry her tears, in spite of the rain. She hoped it was for the last time, and then retied it.

Before her was her own Lake of Sorrow. Suddenly, the ice began to crack and erupted skyward. The ice fell back to the earth as clear water refilling the lake anew. Thunder and lightning raged all around her as the wind roared ferociously.

The dragon tattoo wrapping itself around her body instantly ripped itself from her flesh. It tore through her clothing and dove into the water. The pain was so great she dropped to the ground barely conscious. Blood flowed gracefully from her body. Fear squeezed her soul and the rain burned like acid. She knew that she had used her power for the wrong reason. The reckoning was now at hand.

"Long Tian Di, please forgive my transgression. Bring back the lives of the innocent slain in my ignorance. I am the one that deserves death, not them." Weak and trembling she whimpered and pleaded for their lives.

She was barely able to lift her head or eyes when a great dragon came up from the water. It burst forth with an earth quaking roar.

Glaring, he looked down upon her, "You grovel before me to change what you've done. How dare you! You are an ungrateful whore. You are a whore for power. You are a whore for revenge. And you, the chaste virgin, and yet, you are not innocent in the least. The blood of your victims pours from your hands, eyes, and your soul. You killed them all out of revenge because they desired you. Too bad it took you so long and cost them so much before you realized what was missing from your waste of a life. Such a dominating form you showed in killing your last suitor. Oh, but you didn't. Have you become so weak that a mere child was able to defeat you? How interesting I find you overcome by an insignificant, unarmed whelp. Yes, you deserve to die. Now what do you have to say for yourself!?"

"Great one, it's because of the boy I now understand my chosen path was wrong. It is my humble request, if it pleases you, that their souls be redeemed and their lives restored."

"It is not my place to redeem them but yours. If I were to exact a right

17

judgment, I would have to kill you, raise you then kill you again so many times I'd become bored. I might even forget why I was doing it. It would be simpler for you to do this. I will offer you a means of redemption. You may choose one of three ways.

"Your first means of redemption is for each life you have taken, that soul will be allowed to take full possession of your body for one week. They will be able to do as they please with you. You will feel and experience everything they do without being able to do anything about it. Do you think you'd still be pure or violated for pleasure? You may even be sold into slavery. I'm sure it will be humiliating.

"Your next option is to face the wrath of all those you have slain. You would be their prisoner and they would punish you as they see fit: one day for each person you murdered. I could just imagine the torture you might go through. The beatings would be bloody and the violations long. You won't even be able to defend yourself. Once your sentence was through, you would be free to seek out the hero of your nothingness.

"And finally, you could choose to save an equal number of lives you have stolen. For every life you save from death, one soul will be set free of the lake to live out their days. So, what do you choose?"

All she could do was whimper in pain while she lay without movement. "Thank you, great one. I will do all I can to redeem their blood and set their souls free. And thank you for the mercy you have shown them and the forgiveness you have given me."

Laughter erupted from Long Tian Di. "Forgive you; it's not in me, for you or anyone else." He laughed again. "You now understand the power you hold, so be wise with it. Until you have fully redeemed yourself, you cannot search for your champion. You may even get to see him die before you're done. Pity he has only one life and so short too."

"Thank you, great one."

"Go your way. I shall see you no more."

Long Tian Di kept his shape as he transformed into water. He then crashed down upon Zhe Duan Chi, washing over her and branded her anew. The blood loss made her too weak to scream, but the pain that wrenched through her was too great to lay still. Her whole body burned like she was drowning in acid. She let out a long scream to deal with the pain. This weakened her even more. Her strength was gone as she just lay on the ground even though her wounds were now healed.

"You may tell one who you truly are, however you need be careful. Two others will already know. One may forget, but the other has never forgotten. To all others, you shall now be known as Snapdragon."

He silenced himself as his presence also faded away from her. She quietly drifted off to sleep with thoughts of the boy. Then the storm slowed its wrath. The thunder and lightning grew quiet and a light drizzle remained in the land.

•   •   •

Meanwhile on the helicopter, nerves returned to normal as they left the area. They watched the ferocity of the storm in the region calm itself after several minutes. All were completely unaware of the events that transpired on the ground except one.

"You were right, Ms. Dok, I guess the land is truly cursed." Jin expressed to Morra.

"I tried to let you know, Mr. Hong, but you insisted. Would you like to look at a coastal property now or something else of interest? Perhaps you would like an island."

Looking back, Jai was at peace. It felt like he heard her say, "I will see you again my champion. Please don't forget me."

"Papa, it's okay now. It's not cursed anymore. She's free."

Afterward, Jai too drifted off to sleep with a peaceful smile. His father simply looked at him with a slightly confused, but reassured look on his face.

CHAPTER 3

Negotiations

As Jin watched his son sleep he realized Jai had left the camera on. He reached over and carefully slipped the camera from around the boy's neck. Jin saw his son continue to smile as he slept. He knew he would be happy here and he could begin his search. He started to look at the pictures on the camera when he noticed the camera was still recording. He pushed the stop button. Jin figured he would watch the video later. He wanted to see what pictures were taken. He laughed to himself when he saw the picture of Morra. Even though Jai had taken some good pictures, Jin was more impressed that Jai had been recording most of the time.

Remembering their encounter, Jin recalled how calm Jai was when he found him. He set down the camera and pulled the tube out of a satchel. After examining it for a few minutes Jin saw the tube was made of gold and encrusted with diamonds, rubies, sapphires and emeralds. He shook it to see if something was inside and he was right. He also found out that only one end opensed. Jin took a quick peak inside to find an old scroll in it. Knowing how fragile paper can be, he decided to wait, replaced the end piece and put it back in the satchel.

He then picked the camera up again and decided to fast forward the video to when Jai had wondered off on his own. After watching the video, he was never more proud of his son. However, it still terrified him with what happened at the statue. Jai had shown heart and compassion. Jin thought more about what his son said concerning the woman being real and the land no longer being cursed. He knew he had four things to do once they landed. First, study the video completely, then have container appraised, find out what was on the scroll, and finally figure out who this woman really was.

"Ms. Dok, I've decided that I will make an offer for the property."

"What!!! Are you serious? You can't be serious. Did you bump your head getting into the helicopter?"

"You know I didn't."

"What could possibly make you still want this place? After what we have found, I don't think the government is going to sell it. They will most likely have an investigation to decide what to do with the remains and what about all those weapons or for that matter, anything else they may find. They are going to want to know what's in there." She pointed at the jeweled container. "And it is probable they will want to put that thing in a museum or bury its secret in some unknown location. The government will want to know everything there is to know about this place. They've requested a full report on what's back there since you were willing to pay the fee to see it. They think you may have found a lost treasure or something valuable. And the truth is, we did and it starts with that thing in your bag."

"The reason I am still willing to make an offer is because of him."

"Mr. Hong, I don't understand. What are talking about?"

"I want him to grow up in a place where he wants to be. Even though what we found was frightful, he showed no fear. He was very courageous in his little adventure. Wrong that it was in him wandering off like that. I do honestly feel he was meant to find this thing." He said pointing at the tube then continued. "I could tell Jai was very comfortable being there. Despite, the weather and what we found. I've not seen him sleep this peacefully in a long time. Something or someone made him that way and I want to find out what it was."

Morra looked at Jai. "But, what do you think the government is going to do?" She questioned as she looked back to Hong Jin.

"I was hoping I could trust you."

"Sir, you can."

"Then why did you wait until now to say something?"

"Mr. Hong. I truly did not believe we would find anything there. However, a discovery of this magnitude is important. A massacre occurred there. The dead should be honored and not swept into a mass grave."

"How dare you. I've lived my life in honor. What kind of villain are you trying to make of me? If I did that, the land truly would be cursed and good for nothing. Do you really think I could or would do something that heinous? You insult me Ms. Dok. My intention is to check the royal registry and find out who those people were."

"Too many good intentions have become lies, Mr. Hong."

"Again you insult me. I come here looking to build a school and raise my son. My first thought after our encounter was for those who died, not some cover up. All I need is a favorable report to the government. Then I can take care of the dead the right way. If you want a mass grave, go tell the government what we found."

The pilot slipped in the conversation. "You know, ma'am, he's telling the truth. The government has become so corrupt that he had to pay just to see the land. You said yourself they thought Mr. Hong may have found a treasure of some kind and you know they are going to want their cut. They probably won't care about who was left behind, but what was left behind."

Silence filled the helicopter as Morra thought about what was said. She finally spoke. "Mr. Hong, I'm sorry for my behavior, but what we found really worries me. In spite of **all** that, and if you really truly want it, what is your offer?"

"I was going over the numbers in my head, but I will speak with my accountant to make sure I don't over extend myself. Then I should have a full proposal for you tomorrow. It will be a good one."

"When I get it I will look it over and give it to them with my report. If you have it to me by noon, I could have it to them by the end of the day. And maybe we'll have an answer a couple of days after that, ok?"

"That sounds good. One more thing though."

"What's that?"

"Jai wanted to know if you would join us for dinner."

Smiling to herself she responded, "Wow, really, and when did he say this?"

"This morning."

"I appreciate the offer, Mr. Hong, but I'm really busy. Anyway, I don't make a habit of going to dinner with clients."

"My son really likes you and thinks you're very pretty. He also said that you have his mother's eyes, whatever that means. All I know is he's happy when you're around."

"Do I really have her eyes?"

"Personally, I don't see it, but take a look for yourself." Jin took an old picture of his deceased wife from his wallet and showed it to Morra. After she looked at the picture, she too did not understand what he meant.

"Mr. Hong, in the case of Jai, I would not want to impose on the memory of his mother, whatever that may be. As far as you go, I will not compete with your dead wife."

"That's fair enough for me. I will tell him you said no, that you were too busy to have dinner with him."

"Mr. Hong that is not fair and not what I said."

"So what do you say, where would you like to go for dinner? Maybe you could still talk me into that shore property. But after dinner I will have to excuse my son and myself, I have a press conference tomorrow afternoon."

The pilot interrupted again. "Is it about the tournament this weekend? I can't wait to see it. They say it's going to be a real bloodbath."

"Actually, yes it is."

"Is there any big news or inside scoop on who's going to win?"

"There is no inside scoop. Whoever wins is the better fighter of the night. I do have some big news though. My fight this week, it's going to be my last. Win, lose, or draw, I'm going to retire. I will also announce my plans to open the school. I'm still relatively young and can teach the next generation of fighters. Hopefully, they too, will become champions. A win this weekend should help promote the school."

"What about all that money?"

"I really won't need any more money."

"Are you sure, I can always use some more cash. You know what I mean?" The pilot said with a big grin on his face.

"What I need is someone I can spend it on." He turned his attention to Morra. "So what do you say, Ms. Dok?"

"We barely know each other Mr. Hong."

"I'm not asking you to get married. I'm saying I like you and I want to see more of you. Jai even feels comfortable around you. All I'm saying is let's have dinner. That's all. Whatever happens after that just happens. And if it doesn't, we will let destiny take care of itself, if that's okay with you, Ms. Dok?"

"Okay, but call me Morra."

"Sorry to break up this romance, but we'll be back to the civilization in few minutes."

"Thank you. It'll be nice to get home. I'll need a bath after what we went through today." Morra proclaimed in response to the pilot's announcement.

"Can the two of you do me a favor?" Jin questioned Morra and the pilot.

Morra spoke first. "What's the favor?"

"I need to know if I can really trust the two of you to keep what we saw today to yourselves. I want this deal to go through. So no one can say anything to anyone, it is absolutely necessary."

This time Morra felt insulted. "I said I wouldn't mention it in my report."

The pilot responded a little differently. "That's all good and fine. You get the girl. What do I get?" His statement made Morra blush.

"Since I believe that this deal is going to go through I will need a few things. The first thing I need is a supply and labor manager. Basically I need a contractor I can trust. I plan to build a road to the location, aside from the buildings themselves. I will also need good contacts for supplies. Plus, on top of all that, I will need transportation everywhere I go." Jin lured him in, sensing his greed.

"I get it. You want a go-to-guy."

"You know anyone who could do the job?"

"Mr. Hong, I'm your man. I know everybody that can get the job done right."

"I'm sure you would be more than capable for the task. I think you'll like the pay as well."

"If this deal goes through for you, my services will be at your disposal."

"Thank you very much."

Their conversation ended as they landed. The pilot tended to the post trip inspection of the helicopter. Jin woke Jai to put him in the limousine. Morra got in behind them. The chauffer grabbed their things. Morra was dropped off at her office. She then went home, where she lives with her mother, to get ready for dinner. The limousine took Jin and his son back to their hotel.

Jin got Jai's attention from waving to Morra by tapping him on the shoulder. "Alright, now that we're alone, why don't you tell me what you really found besides this tube?" Jin asked holding up the satchel.

Jai's face lit up. "Well, papa, I found her; the one you and Ms. Dok were talking about. She is so pretty, but she was crying when I saw her. And then she got really mad at me and wanted to fight. I said no, like you said."

"Are you sure it was her? It could have been someone else that tried to pretend to be her and hurt you."

"Papa it was really her. She told me her name. She's not angry anymore and now she's happy. I could tell."

"She told you her name? And what was that?"

"Yep, Zhe Duan Chi, and she said I was her champion."

"She said what?" Jin started to laugh.

"I was her champion."

"How did you manage that?" Jai just shrugged his shoulders. "And one more thing, where is your mother's handkerchief?"

"I gave it to her because she was crying. I hope you're not mad."

Outside, the limo was pulling up to the hotel. When they got out they also went to get ready for dinner. A few hours later Jin took Morra to a quiet restaurant. Jai was happy that she decided to come along.

During dinner, Jin was asked for his autograph a couple of times, which he didn't mind. However, Jin became very annoyed when the promoter of his upcoming fight saw them. He didn't like him because he always tried to get big promotions to fight outside the ring for publicity. He knew this time would be no different.

"Hong Jin, I didn't know you were here. We could have shared a table with you and your son. And who is this lovely lady? Oh, you already, know your opponent, Sot Roo?"

"Hey, old man, how you doing tonight?"

Jin smiled politely, "We're having dinner and I'd like to get back to it."

"Since we're all together how 'bout a photo?" A cameraman came from around the corner.

"No."

"Why not, you afraid I'll look better with your date than you?"

Remaining calm, Jin replied, "We'll see who will be looking better come Sunday morning."

"Now there is no need to be rude. Hey, sweetheart, when you are done with your dinner, I can take care of dessert for you." Sot Roo said to Morra trying to goad Jin.

"It will be important for you to learn one thing tonight. When you keep trying to push your opponent into a corner there is only one direction he can go and that is forward. This will cause you to be laid on your back if you keep pushing." Jin then continued eating his steak.

Sot Roo became enraged and said for Jai not to grow up to be a coward like his father. Jai looked at his father and back at Sot Roo.

Morra spoke out of frustration. "Mr. Roo, it is a coward that tries to provoke a fight privately for sympathy when he knows he will lose openly."

Sot Roo stepped angrily towards Morra. "What did you say!? Bit...."

The promoter realized that things were about to go very bad very quickly, intervened. "Alright now, it's time for our dinner. Let's go champ."

They moved on to their table with Roo's entourage. Jin, still simmering, kept eating. They ate dinner quietly until Morra started talking about the real estate business. She reminded him of the shore property. They struck a deal over tea, provided everything else went as planned.

After dinner, Jin took Morra home to her mother. As he walked her to her door, Jin decided to ask Morra to go out again. He was pleasantly surprised when she said yes. He told her they would have dinner before the fight on Saturday and she would sit ringside with her mother and Jai, if she liked. He smiled and gave her a hug and told her good night with kiss on her cheek.

•   •   •

"My lord, Long Tian Di has visited Zhe Duan Chi again."

"I will go see her tomorrow."

"But what are you going to do about the staff. The incantation is not finished."

"Not to worry, the final portion of the incantation can't be started until one week before the alignment, which is still a few years away. For now the staff is safe."

"Yes, my lord. I will go prepare your things."

•   •   •

The following day, Snapdragon was awakened by the sunshine that broke through the heavy clouds. She slowly stood and looked around. She was confused by the clothes she now had on, and saw she was in an open field by the lake, not among the trees where was last. Snapdragon noticed the lake was larger and there was now an island in the center. And to her surprise, the very monastery she burned to the ground was standing erect, undamaged on the island. She remembered it should have been at the bottom of the lake. Her lake of sorrow had changed greatly. As Snapdragon moved closer she started to feel it. It was the souls calling out to her. The souls of those she had killed. With her heart filled with regret, she became weak with this understanding.

After meditating for several hours, she decided to redeem the Fallen

Ones. As Snapdragon approached the water's edge she spoke, "I will redeem you, life for life that your souls be released and you may live out your lives in peace."

The lake remained quiet before her. Small waves slowly reached her feet. The water was cool; sending a chill through her. After relaxing she took a step into the water.

Suddenly, the Fallen Ones vengefully reach out, grabbed her by legs and dragged her into the lake. They lashed at her while she was taken toward the bottom where bindings were waiting for her. She could hear them saying, "Murderer!!! We will have our revenge. Murderer!!! You will suffer. Murderer!!! Punishment and pain are yours."

As she struggled against her bonds, fear began to overwhelm her because she thought she was going to drown. Snapdragon saw the Fallen slowly move away from her. As the air was escaping from her lungs, what looked like a man approached her walking on the bottom of the lake. He was dressed in a tan hooded cloak that covered half his face. He placed his hand on her shoulder.

"Be at peace, my child." Then he whispered in her ear, "Breathe."

"Father?" As she went to look at his face he turned away from her. Even though she was still able to hold breath she had the sudden need for air and inhaled. The water burned as it filled her lungs forcing all air from her. The Fallen watched in amazement at what was happening. The man simply walked away while the woman struggled. Snapdragon slowly realized that she was now breathing water. She calmed down when the water no longer caused her pain. In her still weakened state, the Fallen quickly finished binding her and continued their assault.

They all stopped briefly when they heard the man speak before he left the lake. "You may punish her as you see fit, but you are forbidden from taking her life. If this is not heeded, I will return and none shall survive."

The last thing the man heard as he left was Snapdragon as she cried out, "Father! Why? Father, please." Her assault began again without mercy.

CHAPTER 4
The Scroll

'HONG RETIRES AFTER SWEEPING VICTORY' was the Sunday headline in all the papers from around the country. Hong Jin was not upset to see the morning paper. The picture showed the referee was standing over a defeated and demoralized Sot Roo, drooling as he was counted out. In other local news, a veteran helicopter pilot died in a recent crash. Authorities cited faulty equipment. Jin was also smiling because he was officially retired. He now had time to put into motion all of his plans and raise his son. After reading the paper Jin slept most of the day away. He had given Morra money to go buy new clothes for her and Jai.

The following day, Jin's assistant let him know of an antiquarian who was also a professor at a local university. She also informed him the professor might know of a restorer to help out with the scroll. Finally, she told him that he had an appointment on Thursday at two with Rattiban Jonatee, a government official, concerning the land.

•   •   •

Jin met with Morra shortly before their appointment with Rattiban Jonatee in the lobby of a large office building. Also with Jin were his personal assistant, his accountant, and two lawyers. Jai stayed back at the hotel with Morra's mother. After discussing the basic proposal, they went up the elevator to the eighteenth floor.

When the doors opened, they walked into a large room with offices that lined the outer wall. Cubicles filled most of the area. A woman sat behind a metallic desk with a smoke glass top. She looked to be a central receptionist. Beside her desk were two armed guards and two more gaurds flanked each side of the elevator.

"May I help you?" The receptionist questioned without looking up to them while writing down some information.

"Yes, my name is Morra Dok. This is my client, Mr. Hong Jin. We have an appointment with Mr. Jonatee at two."

Again, without looking up, she pressed a touch sensitive portion of her desk. "Sir, your two o'clock is here." There was a brief silence. "Thank you, sir. Please escort our guests to conference room eight." Before the two guards could take their first step the receptionist was taking her next call.

The guards escorted the group to the conference room. Each took their post beside of the door. One of the lawyers opened the door for Jin. Then it became clear why there was a need for the armed guard. Sitting in the room was Rattiban Jonatee and the young Prince Rama Jao Chai, of the House of Chakri. Also with them were their respective assistants and attorneys. There were also another four guards inside the room, one in each corner.

Once everyone was inside the room the door was closed by a guard outside. The Prince stood as did everyone else. The Prince then applauded Jin.

"Congratulations, Mr. Hong, on an impressive victory."

"Thank you, I'm sorry I intruded."

"No apology is necessary. You're on time. You see, I'm here to tell you personally that I'm very interested in your venture. I had gotten wind of this little enterprise at the fight when I overheard some people talking about your announcement. They said you were going to retire and try to build a school on prohibited land." He sat down. "Please, have a seat." Jin was the first to sit. Once all were seated, Prince Rama continued. "Now that I have your attention, please, tell me your plans."

Feeling betrayed, Jin proceeded after looking at Morra and Rattiban. "Great Prince, after having to make a considerable donation to national conservation just to see the land, I thought I made it clear that my intentions were pure." Jin said this to find who had committed treason against him. He took note of the quick glance Prince Rama made in Rattiban's direction. "I was looking for a place that was special, a place with character, secluded, and rich in *our* history. The lake is a plus for underwater training. This place met with what I was looking for. My plans however are very simple: build a school for martial arts and raise my son, nothing else."

"So you thought you could go ahead and start building this school of yours on restricted grounds without any resistance?"

Jin and Morra looked at each other confusingly. Jin spoke. "What are you talking about, your Grace? I haven't even talked to any architects yet, let alone contractors."

"Yesterday I had geologists go look at the land so I could see the condition of it for myself. He brought back this video."

After watching the twenty minute video, Jin and Morra looked at the

Prince with amazement. Morra said, "This can't be the same place we looked at."

Rattiban spoke up in a firm tone. "This is what you asked to see. This is the location of the Lake of Sorrow."

"I don't know what you're trying to pull but this is what we found at the lake." Jin handed over an edited version of what Jai had filmed. After watching for about ten minutes, Jin realized the tree line was the same. It was the only thing that was the same, but the same none the less.

"I have a few questions. First, the island and the monastery were not there when we were. Where did they come from? Aside from that, the question I really have is what happened to the remains? What did you do with them? And, how are they going to be honored now?"

Prince Rama now had a puzzled look on his face. "You're telling me you did not build this."

"No, Rama, I mean your Grace, I did not. Before I would have started I would have made public the findings and each given a proper burial and honored the deceased for the sake of their descendants. You know that."

"I have spoken to my father about the matter to see how it should be handled. He said for me to use my own discretion. He also said, 'to weigh a man's honor is wise, but not before examining one's own integrity.' With that being said and judging by your reactions, I have decided to permit this for you. After seeing the fight and meeting you in person, you have proven yourself honorable. I do not know how this transformation occurred or what happened to any of the bodies you're talking about. Perhaps, it may seem that there is something greater at work here that you and I may not yet understand. Perhaps, the path has been opened. It seems to me, you are destined to have this school of yours, especially since it has been mysteriously erected on an island that wasn't there before in the middle of a frozen lake. You have the royal family's blessing to proceed."

"Thank you very much, your Grace. I hope I don't disappoint you."

"There are some conditions. First, you will train the royal guard at a discounted rate. Then, you will pay the estimated value of the island within the lake and any structures on it for the property as a whole. And finally you will pay taxes on the property as it is now versus what it was when you first looked at it. Can you accept these terms?"

Jin looked at his lawyers and accountant. His accountant did the calculations on his laptop. His face showed no emotion. "Sir, you could manage this. It's more than you might like, but it is feasible."

After a few minutes, Jin smiled. "I will accept your terms."

"Good, I have the documents right here." One of the prince's lawyers handed out copies to all that were present. While this was going on the Prince looked over at Rattiban briefly and said, "I have also decided that your donation shall count with your down payment. If Mr. Jonatee would be so kind to redirect the funds towards that, our business here should be almost concluded." Rattiban definitely got the message when the Prince glared at him again. They got the message very clearly.

Over the next couple of hours all the documents were signed. Food was brought in for all to enjoy. The tournament was the topic of discussion over the meal.

"So what happen in the first round?" The prince looking slightly puzzled at Jin.

Smugly, Jin replied. "Master Sun."

"How so?"

"I merely played the coward."

Rattiban interjected. "How was that possible? You beat Sot Roo pretty bad."

"That was the point. I was out to dinner last week before the fight with my son, Jai. Sot Roo was very disrespectful in telling my son not to grow up to be a coward like me. But, it got me thinking. So, the first round was the key. I deliberately let him win it."

"Come to think of it, it did look like it was going to be over in the first. You know, the way he had you in the corner up against the ropes."

"Like I said before, that was the point. As soon as the bell rang, I looked him in the eyes, pretending to act intimidated by him and immediately took a couple of steps back. He took the bait and came at me like the bully he was, swinging and kicking at me all the way to the corner. Once there, I used the ropes for leverage to keep me up. That allowed him to get tired out faster. I was able to block almost everything he threw. I had to make sure I threw a couple back so the ref wouldn't stop the fight. With about twenty seconds left I saw my opportunity. He was tired and took a half step back to catch his breath. I grabbed him by the back of his neck and put my knee into his heart as many times as I could before the bell rang."

Prince Rama complimented Jin on his strategy. "It was beautifully orchestrated. And the way you opened the next round was nothing short of spectacular. You kicked him in the chest so hard, I felt it. I don't even think his feet touched the mat before his back hit the corner. I've never seen anything like that."

"But why didn't you finish him?" Rattiban inquired.

"I didn't want anyone to think it was a fluke. The world needed to know I was leaving on my own terms without any question as to who the best truly is. Granted, Sot Roo is a strong competitor. The way he talked to my son, he needed to be taught a lesson. With each round, I wanted him defeated mentally, physically and emotionally. I wanted him to quit on his own, but unfortunately for him, he didn't last that long."

"What did you use to practice your punches and kicks on?" Rattiban continued his questioning.

"Why do you ask?"

"Sot Roo will most likely never fight again."

The prince turned the questioning on Rattiban. "Why do you say that?"

"According to the promoter, the doctor said his left hip is broke or dislocated, as is his right shoulder. He has hair line fractures in his femur and two in his pelvis. He also has a separated sternum with six broken ribs on his left side and five on his right. Not to mention, that last upper cut in the fourth shattered most of his teeth as if he had no mouth piece in. Come to think of it, what kind of lesson were you really trying to teach him?"

"Looks like you will have to join the school to find out."

All Prince Rama could do was smile at Rattiban's fearful reaction. Shortly thereafter, everyone left satisfied except for Mr. Jonatee, who had to return the money he took.

•   •   •

In the limousine, Jin and his personal assistant, Ms. Zhu, talked about the deal as the others went about their own business. "Well sir, looks like you easily made a very powerful friend in Prince Rama Jao Chai."

"It wasn't as hard as you may think, but time will be the test, Ms. Zhu."

"Oh, that reminds me! Remember the professor I was telling you about?"

"Yes, I remember."

"His name is Prof. Bahraan Wattoo. He works as an antiquarian at the Bangkok University. He has a few published books on antiques and relics. I can call him to see if he is busy this afternoon, if you would like, Mr. Hong."

"That sounds like a good idea."

Ms. Zhu took out her phone and called the professor.

"Hello."

"Hello, Prof. Wattoo, I'm Ms. Zhu and I'm calling on behalf of Mr. Hong. We were wondering if you were not too busy, since we are going to be near the university, could we stop by?"

"Yes, Ms. Zhu, I remember now, we spoke the other day about a particular item. Will you be bringing it with you?"

"We do have it with us."

"I am looking forward to our meeting. I will have things ready. See you when you get here."

"Thank you, Professor. See you then." About twenty minutes later they arrived at the university. Once at the office of Prof. Bahraan Wattoo, they were greeted by two men. A balding, middle aged man with glasses introduced himself as Prof. Wattoo. He then presented Dr. Feun Foo the restorer he spoke to Ms. Zhu about just days before. In turn, Ms. Zhu presented herself and Hong Jin.

"Mr. Hong, it is such an honor to meet you." Prof. Wattoo spoke up. "My colleague and I are such huge fans. Could we bother you for an autograph?" Jin saw the enthusiasm in the men and happily gave it to them.

"Do you think that the two of you will be able to help?"

"Indeed Mr. Hong, we believe that we are able to give you all the answers you're looking for."

Jin smiled and then handed over the satchel to the professor. "How long do you think it will take?"

As Dr. Foo took the satchel he said, "To date the items should be simple and not take too long. However, properly restoring and translating it is another matter. It could be several years before that portion is actually finished. The restoration of a large document is a very delicate process. Although, the translation should only take a short time depending on the language and dialects of the script, the restoration, however, will be considerably longer."

Jin sat back for about thirty minutes as he watched the two men work very meticulously in their examination of the container and the scroll. The two colleagues carefully removed the scroll and placed it into a deep glass tray. Prof. Wattoo then took the empty tube to test the materials. Meanwhile, Dr. Foo clipped a few samples from the scroll for carbon dating. Afterward, he brushed what he called his 'special oil' onto the back of the scroll to help with its integrity. He also said that this would help with the restoration process without damaging the ink.

"If you like Mr. Hong, we can hold on to these items. That is if you feel comfortable with us doing the job." Prof. Wattoo expressed with a nervous, yet hopeful grin.

"I believe that they are in good hands, Professor. I will bid farewell. Please report all of your finding to Ms. Zhu. Oh, I just remembered, I would like to be able to put this on display at the school once it is done, and if it's possible, to have it published in book form with only three copies one in Thai, one in Cantonese, and one in English. The first is to honor the nation of Thailand for its heritage. Secondly, so I may read the story in my native language. Finally, I want a copy to give to my son, because I want him to have something special for when he goes to college in the United States. At least that's where I would like to see him go."

"We will do our best."

"That's all I ask."

Jin shook hands with the two men and left with Ms. Zhu, leaving them to their work.

CHAPTER 5
Culture Shock

Ten years later, the sun set for the last time on Snapdragon's watery prison. She lay limp and unconscious at the bottom of the lake. Her body was swollen from years of imprisonment along with the many cuts and bruises covering her. Her hands and feet were still ensnared by seaweed cut deep into her wrists and ankles.

While her last assailants were still striking her, their strength left and they began to fade away. Of all those she killed, there were twenty-four that chose to have mercy on her. Because they did this; their lives were given back to them. As their spirits rose in the water they became human again. They rejoiced in the darkness for being alive. As they waded in the water two realized she was still bound. Both felt an overwhelming need to release her so they went back down while the others left the water. When they got to her, there was a water-like being already releasing her. To their surprise the creature handed her over to them. They took her and left as quickly as they could for the surface. Once there they saw on one shore a monastery and on the other a lone figure walking from the tree line toward them. The moon had given them ample light to see this. One of the men suggested going to the monastery for help. The other insisted that the place was evil and they should get as far away as possible. They decided to get away as quietly as possible.

A heavy cloud moved in front of the moon causing the area to become very dark. The two men took advantage of the opportunity to get out of the lake. As they carried Snapdragon out of the water, they looked back at the lake. Suddenly, they heard a woman's voice.

"My name is Nak Kian. I am here to help her, but who are you?"

"I am Guo Tahaan. This is my lord's school. Lord Chai is a very dangerous man. He will kill us if we're caught."

"No, his majesty the Prince had this built." The other man spoke up.

"And you are?" asked Nak.

"Oh, I am Kwan Mankong, but how dare you speak to the royal guard, woman!"

"If you let me I will explain what has happened." Guo and Kwan looked at this brazen female that dared to speak out of turn. Nak covered Snapdragon with her cloak as they laid her on the ground.

"My ancestor was with her the day she burned down the monastery and killed your master, Lord Chai. And another was nearby when she laid waste to your prince and his army. My family has chosen to watch over her through the centuries. Until ten years ago she was left undisturbed for more than hundred years. Now that she is free my family will no longer watch over her. I do have a couple of questions though. Why are you still here and who were the others?"

They looked at each other. Guo spoke. "I believe we were given a second chance because we had chosen not to punish her. As far as the others, I'm not sure who they were or where they went."

"Why?"

"Lord Chai decided to have her as his bride. When he found out that she was to be married to someone else he sent everyone at the school to hers. He said to kill everyone and bring her back. So that's what happened, except she wasn't there. Then decades later she showed up and killed everyone looking just as young as the first day I saw her."

"As for me, I thought the Prince was going to help her when she wandered into the camp, but I was wrong. Much like your Lord Chai, he decided to make her his. He was a man without mercy. He told us, while she was getting changed, once he was done with her that we could have our turn. He also said to dispose of her when we were done. A few minutes later, after he went inside we heard him screaming and went in. The last thing I remember is seeing the Prince with his chest caved in and a spear coming towards me."

"I see. I do think it is peculiar that each of you come from a time period when great battles were fought here at the same location. Both of you seem to have been killed believing she was justified in her rage. Still each of you chose not to punish her for taking your life."

"It seems that it worked out better for us this way," Kwan expressed joyfully because he was alive again.

"Yes it does. However there are some things you need to know. Like the worlds you've come from are long gone. The world is a more dangerous place than when you both were alive before. There are now people and creatures with strange abilities and great power because of things that have occurred in recent years. They are called genetic mutates, g-muts or muts for short. Some may be stronger than her.

46

"There are things that you may think is magic, but isn't; like electricity, cars, and machines of all types. I would suggest that you two go to the monastery in the morning. There is a new master now. They may be able to help you to adjust to this new world and I will take her so she will not try to kill you again. As a woman, I will be able to talk to her without her thinking I am trying to harm or even take advantage of her. You may also decide to adventure on your own and discover the world you are now in. You are now free to start your new lives, whatever you choose."

They looked at each other and back at the school. Guo speaks. "I say we shall go to this place to start our new lives. Maybe we can be of some help and teach a better path." Kwan nodded in agreement and the two walked away quietly.

Nak picked up Snapdragon and carried her into the forest to a small cottage with a stream nearby. After she cleaned her, Nak put a salve on her to help with the cuts and bruising. She was severely wounded from the years of abuse. She then carefully laid her in bed. Snapdragon slept violently for the next few days while she healed; in the meantime, Nak took care of her as best she could. She had even gotten her some new clothing.

When Snapdragon's ability to heal herself finally kicked in, she woke with a jump when she was fully restored. She quietly got out of bed. She was very confused by her new surroundings. She saw Nak sleeping in another bed. She looked around again and picked up a knife and put it quickly to Nak's throat.

"Where am I!?"

In fear, Nak shakily said, "You're safe in my home."

A moment passed and not sensing any danger she slowly pulled back the knife. "Who are you?"

"My name is Nak Kian. I am a descendant of the boy that wrote down your story and I am here to help you adjust to this world as it is today. The world has changed a lot. There are many things that might confuse you, but you don't have to be afraid. You're here so you don't have to feel overwhelmed all at once. I also do not want to see you go into another rage and be back in the same position you were just in. Plus, there are a lot of things that you will have to learn about."

"Is there anyone else here?"

"Sometimes my brother, Zeng Sun, is here, but he is not here right now. He's in another country."

Over the next several hours the two women talked about the world and current events while Snapdragon got cleaned and dressed. Nak explained that there were others like her with abilities. She expressed the need for someone stand against those that would use their powers for the oppression of others.

"I must now use my power to help improve the world. I have hated for too long and need to make amends for that." Snapdragon spoke with great sincerity then continued. "I have a new mission in life and with that a new name; Snapdragon. You will no longer speak of my former life or breathe my true name from this moment forward. That part of me is now gone."

"Snapdragon; I don't think I want to know why you chose that name."

"I didn't. It was given to me."

"There must have been a really good reason."

"I don't know but I'm sure there was." Out of the corner of her eye she saw her handkerchief on the table beside her bed. She quietly got up to retrieve it with thoughts of her champion.

• • •

Meanwhile, Guo and Kwan adjusted quickly to their new home. They each had proven their worth as fighters. Guo demonstrated his intense fluency in unarmed combat with muay baron especially in his advanced years. Kwan showed off his superior skills with various forms of weapons. Master Hong was so impressed that he offered each of them a teaching position at the school.

In the short time there they learned a great deal about the new world around them. Guo and Kwan grew to become friends. In the evenings they talked about their respective homes and time periods. They even talked about Snapdragon, going into detail about their respective encounters, and why they chose not to punish her. Guo mentioned one day he will need to go to Chi and ask forgiveness for all he did to her. They even pondered about the others who were restored to life and who they were.

At that moment, a couple miles west of the Paed Cud Tay School, the rest of the Fallen started separating into three groups. The first group was led by a young man named Cea. Six men followed him remembering him from before. In like manner, four men were loyal to Thi Tai, who was their leader when they were last alive. The last group consisted of the Burazai brothers who lost their lives fighting Chi in the arena. They were Sam, Klum, and Phu Chay. Aside from the seventeen men to rise, seven women who met their end at the hands of Chi also received another chance.

The groups of Cea and Thi formed an alliance. The brothers decided to distance themselves from the others quickly. They concluded they would rather not seek any form of retribution against Chi as was the intention the others. The brothers just wanted to go home, not fully understanding how much time has actually past since they last lived.

"Let them go. They are foolish to believe they will survive without us. They'll be back, if nothing else, for food." Cea stressed to Thi.

"What makes you think that?"

"First, they don't even speak our language. Second, I don't believe they even know the area, judging by their reactions as we were traveling. But, if you like, I will have Tam follow them."

"That won't be necessary. Besides the only thing good about that group was the woman."

Both men laughed as they looked over at the remaining women. They viewed women as property as they would livestock, used and sold as necessary. Of the six, only one woman would not be man-handled so easily, Lahan, the granddaughter of Lord Chai. She was trained harder than any man under Lord Chai. She was his greatest achievement.

"Tomorrow, we will go to the school as refugees seeking help. It will allow us to gather resources and set into motion our vengeance."

Of all the Fallen, there is one among them completely loyal to Chi. He is crafty enough to play his part to find her again.

•   •   •

A week later the sun rose quietly on a gentle morning breeze. A light mist was on the water. A young man stood near the edge of a lake next to a replica of the statue of Zhe Duan Chi where yellow snapdragons grew naturally around it. The memory of their only encounter remained with him. From time to time, he would come here to talk to her. This day was no different, except this day he came to say goodbye.

Hong Jai was leaving for America to go to school at Miami International University. He was going there to get a degree in business communications. Hong Jin hoped he would grow to be involved in international affairs. Jai had a lot of studies because of this and wasn't given the opportunity to learn martial arts. While there, Jai learned many languages to prepare him for his future.

Master Hong approached his son and sat down on a stone bench by the statue. "Morra told me if I find you to let you know your breakfast is ready."

"Thank you, father, will you tell mom I will be in shortly?"

"Yes, but I would like to talk to you first."

"Sure, what about?" Jai turned and sat next to his father. He saw a box on his lap.

"I just wanted to tell you that I love you and I'm very proud of you. You have worked very hard to get where you're at and a couple of hours from now you will be on your way to a new life in America. So I want to give you something that will remind you of your heritage and our time here and a little something to help get you settled." Jin handed Jai the box with a smile. As Jai opened the box he continued. "Do you remember when I took the scroll in to be restored?"

"Yes, a little.

"Well I decided to have them make three copies of her story. One was done in Cantonese for me, one in Thai for Prince Rama Jao Chai, and one done in English for your journey. As you already know the original was put in the foyer of the main house, however this is your copy. I hope you like it."

Jai looked into the box and saw the book and an envelope. He picked up the book to examine it then smiled at the statue. "Thank you father, I will treasure it always."

"Don't forget the envelope." Jai then looked inside and saw a credit card. "Just in case you need something or not, but you will have to wait until you get to America to find out how much is in your new account."

Jai held up the card, "Mom, right?"

"Yes." They both smiled. "Come my son, let's eat and get you ready. Besides all the new recruits we got last few days seem to be getting more than a little restless. I also need to talk to Prince Rama about a new recruit named Thi Tai." The two got up and went in. Jai looked back one last time.

•   •   •

Meanwhile in Bangkok, Nak kept Snapdragon busy and away from the monastery by taking her shopping for new clothes and to teach her about the world. They were eating lunch when a bus went flying through the air and down the street. Immediately, the two women got up to see what was going on. Outside people were running scared.

What surprised Snapdragon more was not what was thrown, but what threw the bus. It was an eight foot tall human-like black scorpion with a stinger that was another couple of feet above its head. There was also a centaur with a golden bow drawn and a nine foot Minotaur wielding a large morning star. Off to one side seemed to be a large man with the head of a ram pointing. The ram-headed man looked to be in charge.

At the other end of the street she saw a woman on the ground and a man floating in the air. The woman was of African descent and the man had a dark olive complexion on his face. She was dressed in a grey body suit with black boots and he wore all black. What tore at Snapdragon the most were the innocent people caught in the middle. She knew she had to do something to help them.

"Stop them!" Nak shouted to Snapdragon pointing towards the group of four. "They're the bad guys!"

The two sides started charging at each other. The centaur shot his bow and the arrow went straight through the man floating in the air, however the man appeared to be unharmed. Unfortunately the arrow pierced a woman running with a child. In an instant, the woman and child were vaporized. This was more than Snapdragon was willing to take. Enraged she charged the centaur with a battle yell that captured everyone's attention, because it sounded more like the roar of a dragon. She hit the centaur with a flying roundhouse kick so fast and hard; he flew backwards into a building across the street which surprised all. The humanoid scorpion was the first to react with a strike from his stinger to her chest. With Snapdragon's superior reflexes, she was able to grapple his tail and threw him into the Minotaur. They went tumbling down the street.

The centaur slowly staggered out of building shaking his head. The ram-headed man started to speak as the other two were getting up. To her surprise, Snapdragon was able understand him because it was one of the gifts she received from Long Tian Di, but never had to use before now. Empowered and fully restored, she was more than ready for the fight ahead of her.

"Sagittarius, let's go! Taurus, Scorpio, move now! Tetra, we will meet again." Aries turned his attention to Snapdragon. "I don't know who you are, but you have just made yourself a very powerful enemy." He waved his hand to open a portal. When the others were through he slowly backed in before closing it.

Nak ran over to her. "Are you okay? That was amazing!"

"Yes, I am fine."

Tetra walked over to Snapdragon and Nak while Placer flew over. "Hello, my name is Tetra Stack. This is Placer. We are from the Stack Foundation. I would like to thank you for your assistance. And yes, that was amazing."

"Yeah, that was awesome." Placer also contributed.

"You're welcome. What were those things?"

"They are from a group called the Zodiacs. They are powerful beings of supernatural origin. No one knows where they are from. It is believed they are the 'true' Zodiacs of Greek myth. If they are or not, these monsters wreak havoc wherever they go, wanting to be feared and worshipped by humans. But you handled them rather nicely. Their leader is known as Constellation. We could really use someone with your talents on our team. It could be a rewarding experience for you as well as profitable."

"Snapdragon, this is the opportunity you've been looking for to help you fulfill your goal. On top of that they'll definitely be able to teach you a lot more about the world than I could." Nak expressed.

"Let us help these people first. Then we can talk later." Snapdragon insisted while walking to help the people.

After about twenty minutes, Tetra told Placer to continue assisting the people any way he could since the police, fire department, and ambulances began to show up. Then she tried to lead the women inside the restaurant where they were before, but Snapdragon refused and kept helping where she could. The owner of the restaurant came over to thank them for what they had done. He also said their meal was on the house. Nak thanked him for the kind gesture but insisted on paying.

After a few more minutes, a royal limousine turned onto the street. Two men got out. Nak recognized one and Tetra recognized the other. They were the crowned prince, Prince Rama Jao Chai, and Marcus Ruger, but they were not alone. Also coming around the corner were two units of soldiers, one from the royal guard trained by Master Hong Jin and the other unit from the Super Human Assault Recovery Program, also known as a S.H.A.R.P. team, came with Ruger.

The S.H.A.R.P. team was wearing standard armor. Each was equipped with a jet pack, a forearm laser blaster on one arm and neuro-cannon on the other. The neuro-cannons were design to shut down the powers and abilities of a genetic mutate by knocking them out long enough to put a neuro-collar on them. The guardsmen were dressed in light-weight riot gear.

Tetra quickly went outside to confront Marcus. Nak followed. Placer landed prepared to fight. After she lifted the bus from its side, Snapdragon looked on to see what the people were excited over.

CHAPTER 6

By Royal Degree

"Well, look who decided to volunteer for a demonstration. If you would like, we can now begin." Marcus Ruger said to the Prince after seeing Tetra and Placer approaching.

The Prince glared at Ruger who seemed all too eager to put his people in more danger. As Prince Rama looked around, he saw the damage that has already occurred. People that survived were still being helped out of the bus. A short distance away, he heard more sirens getting closer.

"Alright, men, get ready." Ruger shouted to alert his team. The sharpshooters as they like to call themselves, surrounded Tetra's group in a half circle formation with their laser blasters charged and ready.

"So, Marcus, you finally decided to commit cold blooded murder out in the open?" Tetra said sarcastically.

"If you surrender peaceably we can take care of those formalities in private, my dear." He said in rebuttal.

"How is it that the two of you know each other?" The Prince questioned.

Ruger replied first with a smile. "Ex-lovers."

"In your dreams!"

"Tell your men to stand down, Mr. Ruger, or the consequences could be severe." Prince Rama commanded. Ruger became frustrated, but complied. "Why are you here, Miss?"

"Tetra Stack, your grace. My associate and I were here to help your people against the Zodiacs. We heard that they were in the region, so we tried to capture them but were unsuccessful. More to the point, our sources discovered that Mr. Ruger here was supposed to meet with their leader, Constellation."

"Now who's dreaming? You have been trying for years to link me with criminals. Are you trying to imply that the good Prince is Constellation? He is the only person I am having a meeting with in this country. The only thing that we have been talking about was the S.H.A.R.P. units."

"Do you have problem with that, Ms. Stack?"

"No, dangerous mutates need to be apprehended and the units can be affective. However, it is my strongest opinion if you order any units from Mr. Ruger, use your own men. I do not trust him and it would be my advice for you to do the same. It has been reported that Mr. Ruger is believed to experiment on mutates that he has captured so he can build his own personal mutate army."

"Is this so?"

"Not at all, your grace, she is just jealous of my success."

"I'm jealous! YOUR nuclear reactor caused this mess in the first place! It is because of YOUR shortcuts that millions died and who knows how many were infected! Wherever YOUR reactors are the population of genetic mutates jumps astronomically! It's because of YOU these people live in fear of the monsters that YOU'VE CREATED AND INVITED INTO THIS WORLD!"

Placer immediately jumped in front of Tetra in the middle of her rant. "Tetra! Enough! You know he's not worth it."

Marcus applauded with laughter at the outburst. "Well done, Tetra, you can pick up Oscar on your way home."

"You son of a…"

"Ms. Stack, please wait." Prince Rama spoke up calmly. "Mr. Ruger, please get into the car. I believe that our business here has ended. Mai, please escort Mr. Ruger and his team to the airport. By royal decree, I have revoked their visas. Goodbye, Mr. Ruger." He then shut the door.

As the car drove away, they heard. "Tetraaa!" The S.H.A.R.P. team slowly followed behind the limousine while the royal guard stayed.

"Prince Rama, I would like to apologize for my outburst. It was inappropriate. It's just that my father had taught all his children to protect the earth and its inhabitants from monsters like him. But don't get me wrong, his units are still very affective. He did something a few years back, I know can never trust him."

"Apology accepted. You must have a very proud father."

"One can hope." The others, including the royal guard, helped where they could while Prince Rama and Tetra entered the restaurant to talk.

"Are you the oldest?"

"No, actually I'm the baby of the family." Tetra smiled sheepishly.

"I would like to ask you something. Do you have any armored units that can help with my problem? I believe I have the best trained men on the planet and I want to protect them the best I can."

"We have been working on flexible mesh armor back at the Foundation. It will allow for better movement than the tin cans you saw today. We can offer you lighter forearm weaponry, simpler stun technology and a body forming shield generator. However, if you still want a jet pack, we will have to do some modifications. Each unit will also be custom fitted, where Ruger Enterprises only offers a standard one size. We believe at the Foundation that everyone is important because of who they are, not what they have to measure up to. Granted, there are specific qualifications for certain jobs though. And, we at Stack Foundation do understand this."

"How soon do you think I could get about one hundred of my guardsmen fitted?"

"If we were to have a facility here, we could possibly get started immediately. If we take them to America, I would say on a revolving basis, we could produce two a day after about a three-week process. That's counting the fitting and training of the equipment."

"Sounds like you have a solid plan. You have a deal, Ms. Stack, and I will give you permission to build a facility here as well, if you like."

Suddenly, a dozen flashes spotlighted them as they were ambushed by reporters with twice as many questions.

"Thank you, I will take you up on that offer only if by royal decree. We can take care of the paperwork tomorrow, but for now let's finish helping the people so they know they are cared about by their Prince."

The two finished their drinks, shook hands, and then move through the reporters out of the restaurant not answering any questions. "You should be in public relations, and yes the deal will be by royal decree." For the next couple of hours they helped the people side by side.

• • •

"Master, there is a new threat to your plans." Aries knelt down before a mystical doorway. "Ren's daughter has a new ally and she is extremely powerful. I think she may be a dragon in disguise. I would dare say she is as powerful as us, my lord."

"You dare come before me in failure." A cosmic being in human form standing about fifteen feet tall with stars for eyes appeared on the other side of the portal. He was dressed in a hooded robe with moving star patterns on it. He was also holding a staff that looked to have a galaxy floating at the top. "Wait, you think she's a dragon? Perhaps I should summon Megoon Dracul, the Black Star Dragon."

"No, my lord, we can handle her. I just wanted you to know what has happened."

"Fine, then use the twins to contact the man, Marcus Ruger. If you fail me again, you will suffer greatly and I will bring forth Megoon Dracul to put an end to things. Do you understand me?"

"Yes, my lord."

"Are you sure?"

"Yes, my lord."

"We shall see."

The portal closed before Aries and he rose. He then summoned GemIni. They appeared in front of him. "Your assignment is to meet Marcus Ruger at the airport. You're his ride. Bring him here."

Gem is a beautiful human female with godlike power much like her brother, Ini. They share a psychic link where they can mentally communicate with one another. Powerful psychics individually, but if they are within an hundred feet of each other, their power is amplified.

"Sure, no problem, are there any specific instructions?" Gem asked.

"Don't mess this up!" With that, GemIni left for the airport to wait for Ruger.

•   •   •

After the long afternoon, Tetra, Placer, and Snapdragon had time to sit down and talk back at the hotel where Tetra was staying. Snapdragon decided to take Tetra's offer of going to America. Nak, no longer bound by her family's pledge, began her journey back to her cottage. Prince Rama held a press conference to talk about the day's events. He shared with the people of Thailand that measures to help secure the safety of the people had begun, but it would still be a work in progress.

Meanwhile, at the airport two planes had collided on the runway that caused a ten hour delay, which infuriated Marcus Ruger even more. Marcus was still fuming that he lost millions from a possible contract with Thailand because of Tetra. He hated her so much he was seeing red. And because of her, he also missed his meeting with Constellation. To top it off, he had to take a commercial flight because his plane was unavailable and would not be ready for another day. He thought to himself, he should have killed everyone and worried about damage control later.

At the same time, a young man sat anxious, but quietly. He was nervous because he just did not know what the future had in store for him. He thought about Zhe Duan Chi. Jai wondered if she was real or a figment of his imagination. He hoped he would do well enough to make his father and mother proud. He took out the picture of his natural mother and began to feel guilty again even though he knew her death was not his fault.

Suddenly the flight attendant announced the flights would begin boarding in ten minutes and that everyone should calmly get in line. Everyone knew that was just too much to ask.

Marcus and Jai reached the line at the same time. Jai stepped back knowing how upset the man had been all day.

"After you, sir." Jai said with a smile. Ruger looked at Jai as if he owed him the spot. At the gate, Jai showed his boarding pass and entered the tunnel to the plane. On board, he went to a first class seat next to Marcus Ruger. He knew it was going to be a long flight, so he did not say anything to Ruger.

An hour later, they were in the air. "Mr. Ruger, would you like a glass of champagne?" The flight attendant questioned.

"Yes, I would like that."

"Mr. Hong, what would you like?" Jai was not used to being called 'Mr. Hong' so he did not answer when she spoke.

"Hey kid, I think she is talking to you." Marcus reluctantly intervened.

"Oh, I'm sorry. Water please."

"Thank you, sir." She then went to get their drinks.

"Let me apologize for being rude earlier. My name is Marcus Ruger of Ruger Enterprises, Inc. Please, call me Marcus."

"My name is Hong Jai, but in America it will be Jai Hong. My father is Hong Jin. He is a retired Muay Thai champion."

"Really, I made a lot of money betting on him. Did he teach you anything?"

"He taught me that this is my greatest weapon." Jai pointed to his brain.

"Excuse me, but I have to ask. Is your father the one that trained the Prince's men?"

"Yes sir, he is."

"Your father has done an amazing job."

Everyone received their food and drinks, then watched a movie. Since it was a long day, most of the passengers went to sleep during the movie. Jai was one of them. Marcus had another drink while flirting with the flight attendant before going to sleep himself.

The next day they landed in Hawaii for fuel. After waiting his turn for the restroom, Jai got out his books to study.

"You're serious about your studies aren't you?"

"Yes sir. My father taught me to work hard so I can aim high."

"I like your father more and more."

Jai smiled and said thank you. Jai and Marcus talked about his career goals. Marcus was so impressed that he offered him a job at his office when he was not in class. Marcus saw great potential in him and wanted to be the one to hire him after college.

After leaving Hawaii, Jai finished reading his book <u>Tears in Blood</u>. The cover showed the face of an Asian woman with crimson tears. Marcus finished his call with his daughter, Jessica. She was also going to be a freshman at the Miami International University.

"Wow, that was incredible."

"What's that?"

"It's something my father gave me. Would you like to read it? It shouldn't take too long to read." He said holding up the thin book.

"Sure, aside from plotting corporate revenge I have nothing else better to do." Jai laughed because he thought Marcus was kidding, but he really wasn't. Then he handed Marcus the book. He looked at it for a minute then began to read it.

•   •   •

Nak, unaware of her special visitor, returned to her home late that evening. Initially, she was startled, but was pleasantly surprised.

"I wasn't expecting you until next week," she expressed to her surprise guest. "It's nice to see you were able to get away from your doormat."

After sharing her bed with him, she got up to get them something to drink. On her way back he began his interrogation.

"Why didn't you tell me she was released from the lake?"

Nak stopped suddenly. "I was going to tell you next week when you came. But since you're here now, I figured we could have discussed it after we finished, hence, the drinks." She made a funny face while holding up the drinks.

Becoming agitated, he slowly rose. "Where is she now!?"

"She's on her way to America. I'm free of my obligation to her. Now I can move in and be with you. You can finally get rid of your wife. So what's the problem?"

"You knew how important it was to me to know when she was released from that lake!!" He yelled at her with increasing anger.

Nak realized she was in danger of the one man she thought was an ally in her cause. She then dropped the cups as she turned to run when her lover picked up the very knife Snapdragon had put to her throat. Nak only got two steps toward the door while reaching for a shirt before being blocked by two men with very evil intent on their faces.

Fear overcame her. She felt the warmth of his body as he spoke softly into her ear. She took in a slow deep breath as he started to drag the point of the blade over her back; softly and methodically pushing into her flesh.

"Let me introduce them to you, my love. This is the lost prince, Prince Thi Tai. The building of his palace was interrupted when that abomination killed him. And this good man is my greatest grandfather and the original grandmaster of Paed Cud Tay, Master Cea."

Cea stood face to face with the last granddaughter of his slave, Raya. "If you tell me what I want to know, I will end your nightmare quickly. Where in America did she go?"

Nak Kian was tortured to her last breath. Without uttering another word, believed she betrayed her charge to a lover who betrayed her the whole time.

Without receiving any answers the three men decided to leave before dawn, leaving her body to bleed out and rot. Her hands were tied behind her back then strung up to hang from the ceiling. She died from her cuts and being stabbed repeatedly. Living in the middle of the woods with no one to hear her scream, she died slowly and painfully alone.

CHAPTER 7

<u>Tears in Blood</u>

Part 1

This is the story of a lonely and tortured soul. She was a woman who lived most of her life in regret without knowing love or compassion. Memories that she shared with me are here. Meet her through this story, maybe one day her soul might receive forgiveness and have peace for her broken heart. This is her confession.

Raya

It was a clear day when a young girl was walking along a path with her father through the mountains. He decided that his daughter had the talent to become a great fighter. He knew of a place willing to train her. They were on their way to Rohng Rian. Rohng Rian was a martial arts school, they taught Muay Baron. It is a fighting style designed to kill or incapacitate an opponent as quickly as possible. It focused on pressure points and killing blows. Being a female, the young girl was considered of a lower status and did not get any respect or much consideration. If she wanted to learn it was okay, but she still had to do the chores of her station first and she was only four at the time.

"Papa, why do I have to go?"

"Because I have some things I need to take care of and I want you safe while I am away."

"Will you be long?"

"I don't know, but while you are here you will be treated fairly. I have spoken to the grand master. He has agreed to train you with the males. It is a great honor. In addition, when you grow up, you will be able to help protect this world and its people. When you get older I want you to seek out the World Dragon."

"Who is that, papa?"

"He is a friend. He is very hard to find, but you must seek him out."

"Okay, papa."

The next day they arrived at the monastery. Waiting there at the gate was another prospect. His mother accompanied him. Once the gate opened, the grand master of the school, Master Pi, greeted them all.

"This young man must be Pen Ai Ren."

"Yes, Master Pi, this is my son and this is his payment." His mother said while handing over a small pouch of silver. In tears, she walks away.

"Well, Zhe Duan Chi, how are you today?" She just smiled. "I will take good care of her, my friend." He said to her father.

The girl's father placed a larger pouch in the grandmaster's hand then turned to speak to the woman crying. Master Pi took the children inside.

"Hello, my name is Ren Lasar and I was wondering why are you crying? Are you not happy for your son?"

"The reason my son is here is because a seer told me that my son will be murdered and would not be able to defend himself. I just want him to be as ready as possible."

"That's interesting. A seer told me my daughter will have to avenge her husband." They both looked back at the children as the gate closed. It was the last time she would ever see her father as the young girl looked back.

•   •   •

"If you think you're going to win, think again."

"Chi, just because I let you win for the last twelve years doesn't mean I will always."

"Pen Ai Ren, if you ever want to taste my lips, you should think about winning instead of my lips." Chi said playfully with a big grin.

"Fine, if you are so eager to lose, choose your weapon. I will choose my Bo staff."

"My choice is the feathered spear."

The school came together to watch as they sparred for over forty-five minutes with neither able to get a real advantage. Neither held back, they fought as if they were mortal enemies. Their passion to win blocked out any pain they were feeling. Suddenly, they heard the gong of Master Pi. They froze in mid strike and came to attention.

"Master Pi," They said in unison.

"Enough, what has caused this thing between the two of you? You have trained together since the day you walked through that gate." Master Pi interrogated Pen and Chi. They looked out the corner of their eyes at each other.

Pen hesitated then confessed. "Well, Master Pi, she bet her lips that I couldn't beat her."

"You're killing each other over her lips? I pity anyone with a real reason to fear you. And yet, you are so willing to lose your heart over them?"

"Master, I never owned it."

"Then, proceed." He said as he walked out of their way.

Pen was quietly transforming his Bo staff while being questioned into a three-section staff. He was only able to unscrew one section. When Master Pi said to proceed, he swung his staff under Chi's hand. At the point of contact, the staff broke apart. The chain section wrapped itself around her hand, catching her off guard. He was able to snatch the spear from Chi's grasp and knocked it away from her.

As they continued, the crowd watched them intensely. The challenge came to an end an hour later when Pen managed to get Chi's elbows locked behind her with his three-sectioned staff and held her in the air. While everyone else applauded Pen's victory, he could not help think about what Master Pi had said. As he looked into her eyes he knew, she owned his heart for real. When he lowered her, Pen let go of his staff.

"I believe these belong to you." Chi wrapped her arms around Pen's neck and kissed him. After a couple of minutes, they staggered away hand and hand.

Master Pi proclaimed with a smile, "It is about time."

• • •

After a two-year courtship, Pen asked Chi to marry him. She more than happily agreed. However, as it was customary, Chi and the other woman of the monastery went to the local village to get extra supplies because Chi was going away. She was leaving for a month to prepare for the wedding.

While Chi was there, she met a man. He was Lord Chai. He was a young warlord in charge over the region. He also ran a rival school in a valley several days away. Lord Chai had a reputation for being ruthless and taking whatever he wanted. When he saw Chi, she was no exception.

Chi had grown to be a beautiful woman. She was strong, poised, and confident. The villagers at the market loved Chi, because she was always so happy. She was constantly talking about Pen, how she hoped to be a good wife for him. She was in the middle of one of those conversations when Lord Chai's servant interrupted.

"Excuse me; I come on behalf of the great Lord Chai. He would like to know if you would honor him for lunch."

Chi responded politely. "Please inform your Lord Chai that it would have been an honor to join him for a meal, but it would come at the cost of dishonoring my betrothed. So, I will have to decline."

"Thank you. If I may, may I have the name of your betrothed that my lord may gift him for capturing such a beautiful lily."

Not sensing any malice, she told the servant. "He is Pen Ai Ren, of the Rohng Rian School."

"Thank you again. Lord Chai will want to visit him soon." The servant returned to report to his master.

Shortly afterward, the women returned with the supplies to the school. Two days later, Zhe Duan Chi left for a month of purification for her wedding. She took four women with her.

Lord Chai was outraged by Chi's response. When they returned, he had the messenger whipped and his wife and children beheaded for his incompetence.

•   •   •

A week later, Lord Chai was still infuriated by Chi's rejection. "Bring Commander Guo Tahaan to me." Lord Chai ordered a servant.

"As you command, my lord." The servant ran to the training area to get the young commander and gave him the message.

"My lord, what is your bidding?" Commander Tahaan said as he knelt before Lord Chai.

"These are my orders. I want you to take every available man and go to Rohng Rian School. Spy out who Pen Ai Ren is. Then, in the cover of night, make an example of him, I want him bound with his arms and legs spread. I want him stripped, whipped and castrated until he bleeds out. I want him to know that he died because he stole what is going to belong to me. In the morning when he is found, invade the school and kill everyone. And then bring the girl to me."

Two and an half weeks later, Lord Chai's orders were carried out with one exception. They could not find Chi. The following day, she returned with music playing, flowers thrown into the air. She had no idea what happened. When she saw the people upset and crying she stopped and asked why.

The women at the market told her what happened. She fell to her knees crying uncontrollably for some time. Anger slowly burned inside her. Suddenly, Chi got up and ran to the school. Once there she pushed pass the men trying to protect her from what she was about to see. All she could see when the gates were opened was Pen's bloody body hanging limp in the courtyard on two poles.

At the sight of this Chi screamed and ran over to him. She cut him down and held him crying. There was a note stuck to his chest with a knife. **'Now are you free to have lunch?'** She pulled the knife from his chest and continued to hold him.

Several minutes later, more villagers arrived. Many saw the massacre for the first time. Bodies laid almost everywhere. Many of the men cleaning up tried to drag Chi away from Pen. Her clothes were soaked with his blood. The women that attended her took her to be cleaned and redressed.

Some villagers tried to take her in, but she refused and remained at the school with her attendants. Zhe Duan Chi fell deep into a great depression that lasted many years. She didn't speak much to anyone, but mumbled about with the memory of Pen. Slowly, over time Chi's attendants left until she was completely alone. In spite of this, she continued to train and maintained the monastery.

The villagers left her alone; believing she had gone mad because of what happened. From time to time, would-be thieves came and found themselves hung as ornaments outside the gates as a warning to any who would be foolish enough to trouble her.

One day. when she was in the village to get some rice, bandits invaded as she was walking back to the monastery. The bandits only saw a dirty vagabond girl. They thought they'd have some fun by running her off the road. Chi heard the horses charging, she simply stopped and stared through them with a glassed over look in her eyes as if waiting for them to kill her. When they realized she wasn't going to move and fearful of them, they halted. She then started walking through the horses dragging her bag of rice.

Their leader got off his horse. He bent down and picked up the rice. Chi stopped when the string got tight.

"I am Tufei and these are my men, the Khoon Tai and we will take what we want!"

"Please, let her be. I will get a bag of rice for you and your men, just leave her be, she has been through so much." One of the merchants pleaded as a small crowd of villagers came out to see the commotion.

"Where do you think you're going with this?" He said ignoring the merchant. "I decided not to run you over. That means I saved your life. You owe me and that means this bag of rice is mine!" He then turned to the merchant. "My men will need a bag of their own!" With that he cut the string and tied it to his horse.

Chi didn't say anything and started to walk away. Tufei refused to leave her alone and stood in front of her. He then had his men get jugs of water and pour them on her. As they continued their laughter, the villagers attempted to intervene only to be beaten down. Chi still refused to cry out or defend herself. Impressed and infuriated by her will and defiance, Tufei was determined to break her. He had his men beat her with bamboo canes. Her only expression was a blank look with tears rolling down her face. Even when her legs eventually gave out and she lay on the ground, all she did was close her eyes and focused on her beloved, Pen.

Suddenly, Tufei stopped his men. He demanded the merchant to tell him what was so important about this girl that the village was willing to suffer for her. After the merchant explained everything about Lord Chai and his men, Tufei untied the rice from his horse and dropped it beside Chi and told his men to grab three young women. They screamed for Chi to help them. Some of the villagers died trying to protect the women. It was all she could take. Within minutes, of the 14 men that rode in, only three lived to leave. Without another word, Tufei and his two remaining men mounted their horses and left defeated and afraid. Even the people trembled at what they saw.

From time to time the Khoon Tai would return but they never harassed the people again. On one of those visits Tufei saw Chi once more sitting by a tree. He had his men find a bamboo cane. He took it to her and placed it in her hand. Then he knelt before her waiting for Chi to strike but she never did. She laid it down and walked to the monastery. Even though, Chi could have killed Tufei and his bandits, she simply chose not to.

His men never understood how a mute, dust girl caused him to change his ways. Little did anyone know how Tufei and the rebuilt Khoon Tai would become heroes of renown, but that is another story.

The last time he saw Chi was the day Lord Chai's men came demanding tribute. She awoke to screams and fighting coming from outside the monastery. After rushing to prepare herself, she opened the gates to see the soldiers beating the people. No one was left unpunished, even the women and children fell victim to the horde of soldiers. Fueled by renewed rage,

Chi was unwilling to allow Chai's men to ravage the village and monastery again.

After more than an hour of fighting her way to the village, with dozens of soldiers having met their end; Chi's strength was starting to fail her. Before she lost the ability to even defend herself, she slew more than a hundred men. Taking advantage of her weakened state the soldiers stomped and kicked her mercilessly until they were stopped by Commander Tahaan.

He looked down upon her with admiration. He had one of his men get a count of the number of men she killed, then ordered her to be stripped and strung up as Pen had been and whipped one lash for every man she killed. Two men doused their whips in oil and set them on fire. They preceded a slow walk around her with each lash burning into her flesh. The whips cauterized a fresh scar with each lash. The strikes were deliberate and without mercy. Even after she passed out, they continued.

While they were in the middle of whipping her, the Khoon Tai arrived to save her. Being fresh, they were strong enough to fight back and force Commander Tahaan and the rest of his men to retreat. After giving chase for half a day, they returned to the village.

Tufei listened to the villagers recount the heroism of Chi. They cleaned and tended to her wounds every day. Each day Chi would be awake long enough to be fed something and go back to sleep. Tufei never left her side for over a month until he received word Lord Chai's men were returning.

That night, while sleeping, Chi dreamt of her father and their journey to the school, and how he told her to seek out the World Dragon one day. When she woke the next day, she went back to the dormant school to say goodbye. As she went to leave, she saw the note among her things. She picked it up. She said with full hatred, "I may not be ready now, but when I am, you and I will have your lunch, Chai, and you will suffer for what you have done."

Chi left the school after setting it on fire. As the people came to put out the fire, they were surprised when Chi said to let it burn as she walked away. From that day forward, Zhe Duan Chi lived only for vengeance.

•   •   •

Almost twenty years passed and Zhe Duan Chi still had not found the World Dragon. Her search has made her become even more bitter and lonely. Any man who has ever tried to get close to her, she rejected. Death visited any who tried to force themselves upon her.

Over time, Chi lost her touch with humanity. Her depression became worse. Her scars made her feel like monster. There were moments where she would wander for weeks and months at a time. Then, one day, she came to a stop on a high cliff. Chi sat and let her feet dangle. She thought about walking off the cliff.

When she went to sleep that night, she felt hopeless and lost. She did not know where to turn for help and thought of herself as a complete failure. She believed she let her father and Pen down.

While again sleeping, Chi had another dream about a pair of eyes in a cave. Then she was pulled backwards through the cave out the opening and saw a waterfall flowing from the side of the mountain. Around her the same mountain erupting with lava flowing down the side, except around the waterfall. Her dream showed her an island. Chi saw the eyes again and heard a great roar as she continued to fly backwards from the island back into her own body.

Chi woke the next morning full of hope and determination. When she looked around, she saw a white tiger laying a few feet away. Chi got up slowly looking at its pale blue eyes.

A ruckus coming from some trees nearby cause the tiger to sit up quickly. Through the trees came a group of slavers. There were two men with pale skin, three dark-skinned men with several young women chained together. They looked like they were taken from the surrounding area.

"Look at the pretty lotus flower." One of the pale men said sarcastically.

"A little old and dirty, and not very pretty with those scars, but we could still get a fair price. I'm sure someone could still get some use out of her." The other one said.

"Hey fellas what do you think we can get for that hide?" One of the dark-skinned men said.

"He's probably worth more alive." A second dark skinned man said.

Chi stood a little scared. The tiger stood facing the men with a low growl. The first man drew his cross bow. The others got down and readied a net for the tiger. The tiger then stood on its hind legs and roared at the men.

"Lotus Flower, tell your kitty to get down or this arrow is gonna be for him!"

All of a sudden, the wind picked up and got stronger. The men were having trouble standing and the one with the cross bow could not hold it straight.

"What is she; she must be a Wopu!?" This was the last thing the man on the horse screamed before a whirlwind touched down on top of him. The funnel vacuumed the other four men as well, but left the women and the horses alone. After a minute, the whirlwind dissipated sending the men flying in different directions. Two went over the cliff.

All the women shook in fear because none of them had ever seen anything like it before. The tiger sat down again. He then walked over to the women and bit their chains to set them free. Once free, each of the women grabbed one of the scattered horses and fled.

Then he went back to Chi and nuzzled her side. He even placed his paw around her as if he was hugging her. Chi was still in shock, but petted his head and scratched behind his ears anyway. For a little while, Chi became playful again, even if it was with this strange tiger.

Around midday, the tiger stood at the cliff and looked out to the sea. Chi did likewise, she soon felt at peace. At that moment, she saw a clue as to where to go. Smoke rose on the horizon. She looked at the tiger and it looked back. Chi noticed the tigers eyes were now amber in color. She remembered they were green and tan as well. She couldn't figure it out. However, there was something familiar about this tiger. The tiger then walked away from her. Zhe Duan Chi now focused again on her search for the World Dragon more than a desire for revenge.

Chi's mind was clear of depression. She left the area in search of a boat to find the island. After a few more days of traveling, she found her way to a harbor town. Once there, she had to beg for food and her depression began again. The locals started to call her 'Foon' because they considered her to be lower than the dust on the ground.

This continued for a while until one day while sitting outside of a restaurant eating a bun, a local bully entered. He scared the customers and rushed them out the door. Chi looked inside to see him demanding money from Chui Shi Yuan, the owner of the restaurant. As she slowly walked in the floor creaked.

"Foon, get out and mind your own business," yelled the would-be thief. He got so annoyed because Chi stood there and watched. He pushed Chui backwards and went after Chi. As he went to swing a punch at her with all the strength he processed, Chi's training came flooding back to her. She easily maneuvered out of the way and proceeded to brutally demoralize him. She punched and kicked with such speed and precision that he was paralyzed to prevent her from dislocating or breaking all his major joints. He never had another chance to even land one hit. The last thing Chi did to him was jump up and locked her legs around his head and flipped him through the front door into the street.

She ran out, stood over him and screamed, "MY NAME IS ZHE DUAN CHI AND YOU WILL RESPECT IT!!!"

Chui went to the door to see the street filling with others coming to find out what was going on outside the restaurant. Chui motioned for Chi to come back inside. She stood just inside the door as he cleaned up. He prepared a table and sat her down. As the crowd came in they saw Chui bring her food and drink. He practically had to beg her to eat and the people just watched and stared.

Chui addressed the crowd as they were pointing and whispering. "Sit down or go on your way. This is not a freak show."

Things settled down for a while when four men came in asking what happened to the man being carried away outside. No one said a word, they all looked at Chi. What the men saw was a dirty looking older woman with her head hung over her plate as she ate with her cup of water in hand. One of the men sat in front of her.

"Aren't you the one they call Foon?"

"Her name is Chi," Chui spoke up.

"Chi, ok, Chi, did you do that to Qifu?" Chi slowly raised her head to look at the man in front of her. "What you may not know is I am Zhanshi Guowang, and around here they know me as the Warrior King. And Qifu was one of my up and coming prospects, very promising indeed. And you did that to him?"

Chi sat quietly as he spoke keeping an eye on the three men with him; ready to strike if necessary. The men were fighters working for Zhanshi also.

"What I really want to know," he started to say as he got up and walked away, "is can you do it again?" Once he was past the men, they attacked. He stepped to the side of the counter to watch the outcome.

Chi pushed the table forward and rolled between the men to face them in a better position. With a fury of hands, elbows, knees, and feet, she made short work of the fighters. To exclamate the point, Chi jumped up and locked her legs around the neck of the last one standing, flipped backwards slamming him down in front of Zhanshi. She broke his neck, killing him instantly.

Zhanshi applauded her and offered her to fight for him in the weekly fights he sets up in the region. She knew it was a means for her to earn some money to buy a boat so she agreed.

She fought for two years and in that time he made sure she had money, clothes, and a place to call home. Chui made sure she never missed a meal. She trained religiously again. It also allowed her time to work through her feelings.

Once she obtained enough money to get a boat, she set sail for the next several years in search of her island. Chui went with her, along with some fighters who were ready for something different. Zhanshi Guowang was not happy. He also knew he could do nothing to stop her.

•   •   •

After many years of island hopping and fending off pirates, her boat ran aground one night during a monsoon. Many of her crew had already died fighting pirates or succumbing to malaria. Those who survived were few. Chi only had four remain with her, three men and a woman.

Ba Duo, the last surviving crew member from her fighting days and her first mate, hoped to get back out to sea as soon as possible. Ti Neung, a young woman in her late twenties looking for adventure was very happy to be on land for a while. Chi's favorite cook, Chui Shi Yuan and Nuli Bentat, a strong slave Chi picked up at their last port. Once on board the ship she offered him his freedom and to join her crew of his own free will. She would treat him like the rest of her crew. He agreed to her offer. She let him know, if he tried any funny business, he would die. She said this more in jest because she felt she was no longer desirable.

Zhe Duan Chi's reputation had stretched a great distance because of her

83

fighting skills. Too many times, she had to prove herself. The last port was no different. The one she outbid for Nuli was so upset he drew his sword and challenged her. She accepted the challenge regardless of her age. The crowd made a circle around them. They just knew she was going to lose. Her opponent swung first. Age had slowed her, but still being faster than her opponent, she blocked his hand and punched the inside of his wrist. This caused him to drop the sword. She then hit him twice in the chest, first with an elbow then with a sidekick. As he turned to run, she kicked him with a roundhouse kick to the back of his neck so hard it gave him whiplash and his false teeth spewed out of his mouth. The man fell thinking he was paralyzed because he couldn't move his head. Chi knew at that moment life for her was almost over. Her strength was leaving. Her speed slowed. More importantly, it hurt too much to fight anymore.

The following day the men set up shelter, while the women explored the island and gathered food. She thought this might be the one when they saw smoke bellow slowly from its peak. After they searched a couple of days, they found it. The waterfall was majestic. It went half way up the mountain and at the bottom was a lagoon that overflowed as the island's only river. This confirmed for Chi she was in the right place. Chi remained hopeful, even though she knew time for her was running out. They also discovered a cave behind the waterfall. It was large enough for everyone to stay when the weather was bad. So Chi moved the camp to the lagoon. It provided shelter, food and freshwater.

Her crew was talking one night at supper about Chui's cooking. They laughed about how his cooking had improved significantly.

Ba started a different conversation. "Since it looks like we are going to be here a while, at least until we fix the boat, what are we going to call our new home?"

Chi responded quickly. "Long Dao, however, once the boat is fixed, all of you will be free to go. I am going to stay. I believe my destiny ends here."

As the others looked at each other, Ti spoke first. "Chi, do you really think this is the place?"

"I do. I just have to wait it out to see if I am right."

"As for me, when the boat is done, I'm leaving. What do you want to do, Chui? You want to stay on this rock or fish in the sea?" Ba proclaimed and questioned.

"I like it. I think I will stay." Ti and Nuli both agreed they would enjoy living on the island.

"Suit yourselves, I already miss the water.

Over the next few months, everyone worked hard to get the boat finished. Nuli and Ti had gotten closer. Ba became frustrated because he wanted Ti for himself. Chui stayed busy gathering food and cooking. Chi began meditating a lot when not working. She continued her intense training. One of the things she did was practice climbing up and down the waterfall; falling many times into the lagoon. She grew more and more tired and everyone saw her frustration. She did her best not to let the chronic pain stop her. She cried most nights because of it. Arthritis was setting in and her joints were starting to lock up on her.

Then the day came when the boat was finished. Ba was anxious to get going. He was still the only one. The others said their goodbyes with heart felt wishes for his safe journey. None of the others had any regrets in staying. He said his goodbyes and waited for the next high tide and left. He was saddened for Chi. She was the greatest fighter he had ever seen. Ba Duo felt the island was killing her. He thought he would never see her again.

CHAPTER 8

Tears in Blood

Part 2

More than a year passed when the tremors started. The smoke at the peak of the mountain stopped. During that year, Ti became pregnant. Nuli was very happy about that. When the weather was extreme, they all stayed in the cave behind the waterfall. Otherwise, they stayed in their own hut shelters. Chi stayed in the cave most of the time, because she wasn't able to work anymore.

After the tremors kept getting worse for another month, everything remained calm for a few days. Everyone gathered around Chi believing she was at the end of her days. Then around midnight the island started to shake violently. Three hours later the volcano erupted skyward. The eruption made the night sky glow red through the waterfall from inside the cave.

Chi knew it was time. She slowly got up. She quieted the protests from the others in telling them it will be okay. They feared for her. She made sure the others were safe, especially Ti because she was more than eight months pregnant. Chi made Nuli promise to take care of Ti and the baby. She hugged them all, even Chui. All were in tears as she turned and slowly limped to fulfill the only promise she made to her father.

Ti buried her face into Nuli's chest and cried harder. He held and reminded her, this was something Chi had to do even though no one wanted her to leave. Chui sat down and cried for his friend. Chui regretted not telling Chi how much he cared for her. None of them really cared about what was going on outside until Ti went into labor. They knew they had to live for the baby.

Chi began her very slow and painful climb to the mouth of the waterfall. While climbing, she noticed the lava flowing on both sides. Too afraid to let go, she pulled through the burning pain in her joints and muscles. If it weren't for the waterfall, the scorching air from the lava would have choked out her lungs.

Once inside the mouth of the waterfall the water pressure dropped considerably. Chi also noticed the air was surprisingly easier to breathe than she expected, but fear still filled her just the same. Exhausted and aged, she slowly dragged herself forward with an intense pressure in her chest and numbness beginning in her left arm. She started to descend when suddenly a sharp drop took her unaware. Chi slid and tumbled down the rocky tunnel for a while until she found herself free falling into a large underground cavern and lake.

The heat of the water burned and caught Chi off guard as did the sudden impact knocking the wind out of her. She struggled to come up for air out of the hot water only to discover the air was just as thick and suffocating. The ceiling illuminated by phosphorus allowed her to see as she swam to an embankment. Chi slowly got out of the water and cleared the hair out of her face.

Breathing heavy and holding her chest, she began looking around the cavern as if it was the last thing she would do. She saw the water started to move on its own in a circular motion. A whirlpool formed as the water drained from the basin, exposing a sleeping dragon. Zhe Duan Chi looked in awe at a great dragon lying at the bottom of the basin. She fell backwards as he opened his eyes and raised himself to let out a fearful roar. It was powerful enough to be felt vibrating through her bones, but shook the island as well. Then the dragon looked down at Chi who was trembling and shaking in fear.

"I am Long Tian Di. Rise and be not afraid. I am not going to harm you; for I have been waiting for you."

Weakly, Chi rose still trembling and speechless, staring into Long Tian Di's eyes, at that moment, she recognized them. They were the same eyes she had seen in her dream. She then became very calm. Her breathing slowed to a normal pace.

"Your father came to me and asked me to bless you."

"My father, you know of my father?" She asked weakly.

"Yes, your father searched for me for more than a hundred years. He wanted you protected and asked that I lead you to the Pool of Dragon Tears. You are much like your father."

"Where is my father now?"

Long Tian Di paused for a moment then said, "That is of no concern to you."

"Hold on, how old is my father?"

"Not as old as I, although because of his years, he is counted among the protectors of this world, but enough about him. As for you, you must survive the pool or perish."

"What is the Pool of Dragon Tears?"

"The pool is filled with the last tear of every dragon that has ever existed. You must submerge yourself into the pool, drink in as many of the tears as you can, and if you survive, you will be blessed with great power."

"I am old and weak. It took so long to find you. How will this help me now?" She pleaded, feeling the tightness in her chest again. She lowered her head to the ground knowing her life was slipping from her.

"You needed to prove yourself worthy. You had to be willing to search the course of your life for me and now I smell the stench of death upon you. You needed to be willing to give up everything in your search. You even gave up your quest for vengeance to where you only wanted to find me. In that, you have shown yourself worthy."

"Where is the pool?" She gasped weakly feeling her chest tighten more. She no longer had any feeling in her left arm.

Long Tian Di raised his clawed hand for her to crawl on. When she did, he lifted her to a ledge with two openings and helped her stand.

"Take the correct path to the pool. You will be filled with great power and a rejuvenated life. If you take the wrong path, you will end up in a pool of acid and your destruction. I am sure you will take the right path. Do not test it. Run and jump in. Your life will end with one and merely begin with the other, so do not hesitate too long or you will be consumed by both."

Imposing her will against her failing body, Zhe Duan Chi made her choice and pushed headstrong into the opening. She hoped she made the right choice. She entered seeing a glow ahead of her. As she reached the pool, she grabbed her chest as her heart exploded within. As she hit the pool, she sunk quickly. She swallowed what she could. With no air to breathe, she had no choice but to breathe in the liquid as well. She knew she was dying. Then all of a sudden, her clothes dissolved away. Her skin began to burn, as did her eyes, lungs and stomach all in the middle of a heart attack. She thought for sure she jumped into the acid. Regardless of the pain, her last thought was of Pen as her heart failed her and everything faded into nothingness.

• • •

Chi woke abruptly when her body smacked the water. With blurred vision, she struggled to get her bearings. Surprised to be alive, she found it hard to swim because of a thick crust that covered her. In the distance, she saw what was left of the island. There were now two of the islands with the volcano falling in on itself creating a massive caldera. The island was split at the river. It glowed from the layers of lava. Huge chunks of fiery rock free fell from the sky all around her. She feared the worse. She believed her crew was gone.

After she hit the water, her casing cooled quickly and sealed. This allowed her to float and drift around the island. After a brief time, she fell asleep. Her transformation now complete, she awoke to what she thought was the next day. The sun was high in a blue sky. Then she heard muffled talking and a baby crying.

"What is that?"

"I don't know."

"Poke it with a stick." A woman's voice said.

Three familiar voices came into view through a crack over one eye. It was her crew. She was happy to see they were safe and to see the new baby. What they saw looked like a scaly rock in the form of a person. However, inside the rock casing, Chi suddenly felt extremely claustrophobic. She started to panic. As she struggled from inside, the rock began to shake then crack. With a surge of strength, she roared out of her cocoon. The rock covering went flying in all directions.

Ti screamed and turned to cover the baby. The others tumbled backwards. Chi stretched and then realized she was without clothes. Immediately, she jumped into the water before the others recovered. When they did, they saw a *young* woman's head sticking above the water.

"Miss, are you ok!? What happened to you and where did you come from?" Chui asked.

"It's me, Chi. Get me something to wear. I need some clothes!" Chi yelled.

"That's not remotely funny. I don't know who you are, but you're not Chi. Chi is dead!!!" Ti yelled angrily out to the girl.

"She doesn't look like Chi." Nuli expressed.

Chui laughed holding his hand to his ear. "Come out of the water so we can hear you better, little girl."

Ti smacked him in the gut. "Go get her some clothes, you too." She told Chui and handed the baby to Nuli, but kept the blanket.

"Come on, old man. Let Ti figure out who this girl is." Nuli grabbed Chui and the two men left to get something for Chi to wear.

After they were gone, Ti opened the blanket and encouraged Chi to get out quickly. Not seeing her old friend, but a very beautiful young woman in her late teens, Ti knew she still had to help her. As Chi got out of the water, Ti noticed the dragon tattoo that wrapped itself around her body. She was amazed at the artwork, but Chi couldn't tell her how she got it. She didn't even know until Ti mentioned it. After they both looked at the tattoo for a minute, Chi decided to cover herself before the men got back. Ti questioned the young girl and her claim to be Chi because of the tattoo and lack of the whipping scars among her other wounds she knew Chi had. Ti found it difficult to believe the girl before her.

She had to convince them she wasn't one of the many visitors they now got after the eruption. It was difficult because the change in her appearance was so severe. The nearly seventy-year-old woman now possessed the body of her youth when she was around twenty. The men left again after they brought the clothes, but not before commenting on how amazingly youthful Chi currently looked. Ti held the blanket while Chi got dressed. They went to a grove to get something to eat. On the way there, Chi thought the vegetation had somehow grown very quickly. Chui had a meal ready when they arrived.

Chi explained what happened to her over the meal. She told them about the dragon, Long Tian Di. Moreover, she told them what she learned of her father, in addition to how wonderful it was to see them all again.

"I do have one question though. How did you survive?"

Nuli and Ti looked at each other, and then Nuli began. "Well, a while after you left, another large earthquake occurred. The cave started to collapse at the opening and was covered with lava. We were all scared. Then after what seemed like an eternity, another earthquake cracked the back of the cave. This was when Ti went into labor and during an aftershock she gave birth. At that time, the crack opened to a tunnel that lead us to a hidden grove on the other side of the island where we were safe and are now. These two almost didn't make it." Nuli made the last statement while putting his arm around Ti and the baby.

"Are you okay now? And what did you name the baby?"

"Yes, we are. As far as the baby's name, we decided on Ying Chi Bentat."

"She seems big for a newborn. How old is she?" She said not understanding the lapse of time.

This time Chui spoke up. "Didn't you know? It's been almost a year since you left. We thought you died. We saw your cocoon floating around the islands for a good six months or so. We decided to build a small raft to see what you were."

"No, I did not realize it's been that long. I do believe I am ready to go home though."

Nuli said. "You're the boss, but we have no real way off the island."

"Don't worry we'll figure out something. Maybe we can build another boat."

Later that day, Chi wandered off to be on her own and learned that one third of the island was indeed destroyed by the volcano. The original island was about twenty miles long and thirteen miles wide. Now there were three islands. The largest was now longer in its width at about thirteen miles long and nine miles wide. The island on the other side of the caldera was a mere seven miles long and six miles wide. In the middle is the formation of a brand-new island, Long Dao Xin. It was about nine miles long and two miles wide.

On the large island where they stayed Chi went to the beach to meditate on her new abilities. She learned she was recreated with the powers of a dragon. She received the supernatural strength of a dragon. Her skin became as tough as one. She was now able to fly and understand different languages. Instead of breathing fire, she was given the ability to expel energy from her hands. She effectively became immortal.

She spent several weeks training. When she wasn't training, she and Nuli worked on building stronger shelters. Building a boat wasn't a priority any longer because Chi realized from her meditations and training that she could leave the island at any time she chose. She did her best not to display her new abilities openly so she wouldn't scare anyone.

•   •   •

Meanwhile, in a fishing village on the tip of the Malay Peninsula, Ba was playing a game of tiles. He was about to win as a crew of sea rats came into the restaurant talking about the eruption on Long Dao. He watched the three men sit at a table near the corner. After a few minutes, Ba got up collecting his winnings before walking over to the men.

"Gentlemen, buy a round for a tale of Long Dao."

The crew looked at each other and offered a seat to this stranger. Over the next hour of drinking and a delicious meal, they spun their yarn of Long Dao. Ba was truly happy for Nuli, Ti and their baby. He was glad to hear Chui was okay and saddened because he believed Chi had died since they didn't mention an elderly woman. What surprised him, a young woman on the island went by the same name. He was told she has a tattoo of a dragon covering most of her body.

His spirit perked up more as they told him of a treasure they came across called Heavy Iron. It was an ore with twice the density as normal iron and half the weight. It could be found in areas after a volcanic eruption. They continued and told him for every 100 lbs. of iron ore one might come across only half a pound of Heavy Iron.

"What do you do with it once you have it?" Ba asked.

"We sell the iron to whoever and the Heavy Iron to the people of Nihon. They are willing to pay for it."

"Do you know what they use it for?"

"It's going to be used to make swords. Have you ever seen one of them? They're amazing. The people of Nihon have this process of folding metal to make their weapons. Yeah, the strongest I have ever seen even with regular iron."

"We got there late one night, so they invited us to stay a couple days to get some rest. The next day we went to the smith. He looked at what we had and noticed a difference in the metal. He bought what we had and began to work with it. We left a couple days later after getting enough supplies. When we returned, the smith came looking for us. He said he was the Emperor's favorite smith because of his sword making ability. And he makes high quality swords, usually a five-head sword. And every so often, he may make a seven or eight-head sword."

"Hold on, what is that, a five-head sword?"

"Oh, it's the way they measure the strength and quality of a blade before it needs to be sharpened. You line up war prisoners and criminals and behead them. The more heads taken with just one swing the better the sword. Anyway, he was telling us he felt there was something special about this sword after he made it. He wanted to set up demonstration of it for the Emperor and present it to him as a gift from the village."

"So, did he like it?"

"The Emperor brought his executioner and all the war prisoners and the worst criminals. They drew lots to see who would be executed first. Those that survived would be granted their freedom. After the first day of testing all twenty-three were beheaded, so he sent word to the surrounding areas to bring their prisoners for the testing. Each night the sword would be cleaned but not sharpened. Over the next two weeks, the testing continued until a group of bandits tried to free one of their own. Most of the bandits were capture or killed, only a handful got away. Even the executioner had been killed bringing an end to the testing. The Emperor declared the sword had claimed over a hundred lives, therefore, he named it sword the *Hundred-Head;* the symbol of the true strength of Nihon.

"By the time we returned to trade, the sword was in route to be delivered to the Emperor when it is believed to have been stolen by the bandits who got away. So, when we arrived the smith was looking for us and more *heavy iron.* We were taken before the Emperor and he demanded we find more of this *heavy iron* so the smith can make another sword to combat the other. He said the Hundred-Head had no equal and was cutting through other weapons as a knife through a meal. They even believe the *Heavy Iron* has special magical properties because of it. However, as the story goes, we went back to where we got the ore from before. When we returned it wasn't enough.

"When we returned this last time, we found out the bandits had raided another village and took some of the villagers. One was a cook who poisoned all of them. Before you ask no one has seen the sword or the cook since. The worst part is we have to leave for Nihon in the morning so the smith doesn't have to stay in prison."

"Why is he in prison?"

"Because he made the first one and the Emperor doesn't want anything to happen to him before he can make another."

"And you found this stuff on Long Dao?"

"Yep. At least what's left of it."

"Is there any left?"

"You will have to go and search for yourself." With that final statement, the three men got up and left Ba sitting with his thoughts.

Ba got up the next morning to set sail for Long Dao, only to discover several boats had been burned and the crews' killed. He was relieved to see his boat safe and his crew ready to leave. Ba did not stick around for questioning. After several weeks of searching for Long Dao and fending off a few pirate attacks, Ba located the island. He knew he had the right location but the island was vastly different. After the eruption, the volcano had blown the island apart into three separate islands. One large and two smaller one now exists.

Ba saw a small boat on his approach with two men fishing. He realized it was Chui and Nuli. Ba steered his boat over to greet them. After talking to them for a while he found out the young woman was indeed Chi. Since the eruption they had an influx of visitors and a growing population. An hour later they all docked and headed back to the little village. There were less than fifty people. All worked together to build structures for housing and storage. They cultivated the rich soil for crops. They even built a small fleet of boats for fishing. Zhe Duan Chi herself was in charge. She had set up villages on all of the islands.

Ba was very impressed with the community. When he met Chi again he was in shock by how young she looked, not recognizing her at all. They talked for a long time about the island and why Ba chose to come back; heavy iron. Chi showed Ba where the other crew had gone. Ba gathered what he thought he needed and was ready to cast off after a month. Chi and Chui decided to leave with Ba. Chi left Nuli And Ti in charge as king and queen of Long Dao.

•　　•　　•

"We'll be in Singapore in the morning, Chi."

"Sounds good to me, you turned out to be a good captain."

"Thank you, have you thought about what you're going to do now that you're back?"

"I'm going home to find peace for myself. Chui wants to open a restaurant again. I was a little surprised that Nuli and Ti still wanted to stay on the island and raise their daughter."

"Yeah, me too, I can't get over how much younger you look. You truly look amazing. Would you like to have dinner sometime?"

"No."

"Fine, I get it. You're still not over Pen, yet, are you? It's been what, fifty plus years?"

"You're not my type." Chi responded feeling a little disrespected.

"You're over seventy years old. Everybody should be your type by now unless Chui or Nuli finally got to you. If not, you are definitely everyone else's type now."

Not completely understanding the full value of her new strength, Chi slapped Ba so hard she shattered his face. He didn't even have a chance to yell out in pain before he dropped dead. The current crew became very afraid and called her a devil and a witch. She terrified Chui too. He had instant flashbacks of when he first saw her fight and he now feared her. Knowing she had gone through some incredible changes did not make it any easier for him.

Even though she did not mean to kill him, Ba was no less dead. Chi kept to herself for the rest of the trip after burying Ba at sea. At port, everyone quickly went their separate ways with his or her own cut of precious stones. Ba's second in command kept his boat and the iron ore.

•   •   •

Zhe Duan Chi went back to her village. It was there where she hid the precious stones she collected. Only one person was still alive from when she was there before. A woman, who was a teen at the time, recognized her. When the woman saw her, Chi did not let on that she was the one she remembered, but convinced her she was someone completely different.

Over time, Chi became friends again with Mae and started to work for her. She found out that Mae married Tufei. She also learned Tufei was heartbroken over her. He died a hero protecting the village on the night his granddaughter Sunnu was born.

Chi also learned her old adversary was still among the living. A much older, Lord Chai had become an even more powerful warlord than he was before. He now expected tribute from anyone who entered his territory. If he felt cheated, he would have villages raided and burn them to the ground. She also found out there was no new monastery. This sadly left the village without any defense after the death of Tufei when the Khoon Tai moved on.

One day while Chi was out, six of Lord Chai's men came for tribute. Chi was at the river getting water. Mae sent her fifteen-year-old granddaughter Sunnu to the mill before they had arrived. Sunnu was visiting for two weeks.

"Alright, old lady, where's the tribute?" Tam Lai, the leader of the men, questioned Mae.

Mae became fearful because when they were there last, they broke up her shop. "Please, don't break anything."

"If you have our, ah, Lord Chai's tribute, everything will be okay."

"I'll go get it, just don't break anything." Mae went to the back to get it. While she was in the back, Sunnu came in.

"Grandmother, I'm back from the mill." Sunnu was carrying two bags of flour.

"Hey boys, I think we found our tribute." The other men started laughing as Sunnu entered the shop. Not realizing she was the joke, she smiled back to be polite.

"Hello, I'm Tam Lai, what is the name of this beautiful lily before me?"

"Sunnu, get in the back now!"

"Yes, Grandmother." She did as Mae told her. She smiled back at Tam Lai as she closed the curtain.

"Here's your blood money. Take it and get out!"

"You better watch what you say old woman." He looked at the amount. "You're short."

"What are you talking about? It's all there."

"You forgot the tribute for her."

"That's all I have."

"To bad, it's not enough. We will just have to take her with us."

"No, you won't. I'll kill you first." Mae grabbed a knife.

"Take care of her and get the girl."

Two of the men attacked the old woman. One of them stabbed her with her own knife in the stomach. The other three grabbed the girl from the back. They left Mae lying on the floor and took Sunnu.

When Chi returned a short while later, a crowd was around Mae's bakeshop. Chi asked what happened as they carried her body out. The villagers told her Lord Chai's men killed Mae and took her granddaughter because she did not have enough tribute. Chi became enraged. All the memories of Pen came flooding back into her mind. Her hatred rekindled itself. Zhe Duan Chi was full of bloodlust. She got off the wagon that carried the water jugs. Chi got on a horse and rode off heading towards Lord Chai's school.

Chi raced down the dirt road for half a day, until she came to a clearing. It was here where she made a gruesome discovery. Off in the distance, hanging from a tree by her neck was Sunnu. Chi charged over to her and cut her down. Sunnu was barely alive. Chi saw she was beaten and suffered from great abuse. Chi gave her water and cleaned her wounds. Sunnu laid in a fetal position trembling and shaking. When the young girl fell asleep, Chi took her home to the bakeshop. Sunnu woke the next day, long enough to thank Chi for helping her and to tell Chi the name of her assailant before she died. Even though Sunnu lay before her, all she saw was Pen's face.

Chi cried tears of rage because she could not save her. A woman saw her face and became afraid. Chi's eyes were full of blood and so were her tears. When Chi screamed out because of her loss, the sound of a roaring dragon came forth. She turned and ran outside then leapt into the air and flew in the direction of Lord Chai.

What would have taken a several days on horse or foot only took Chi a few minutes in the air. She landed about a mile away where she saw Tam Lai and his men. She attacked them without mercy, restraint or compassion. All the men were dead within a minute. Tam Lai was last to die. Chi dragged Tam to the bottom of the valley to the school by his crushed neck.

"Open the gate and bring me Chai, NOW!" Archers immediately took their positions.

"How dare you. Men, fire!" The gate captain commanded. The archers fired their weapons. Chi used the body of Tam as a shield then threw him through the gate with an exploding force. What happen next was a blur to Chi, but I witnessed all that happened.

Chi came through the gate ferociously. Something like a cross between fire and lightening came from her hands. Her war cry was a great beast. She flew around like a bird without wings. Her strength was amazing. Chi ripped up whole buildings. Her one and only goal was to destroy everything in her path to get to Lord Chai.

Chi left no one alive; man, woman, or child, all perished except for me. I do not know why she let me live, maybe it was because I was in chains, but for whatever reason I am grateful. I did not know why at the time, but when she saw Lord Chai she said, "Now, we can have lunch." When she said that, Chai turned pale. Before he could even move, she proceeded to kick him so many times I lost count because of her speed. With every kick, a bone snapped. The last thing she did was she jumped up with a twisting flip and planted her foot on the top of his head and drove him into the ground. Chi was amazing and terrifying. To be honest, I think Lord Chai was dead before she was finished her assault.

No one had the ability to harm her and when she was done, she burned what was left of the school to the ground. Afterward, she took me to the top of the valley. Together we watched the flames. Suddenly, she knelt and started to cry. All her anger was gone. She now hated herself for losing control. She hated the power she gained. She hated her father for not being there for her. He abandoned and left her alone because of it. Most of all she, hated Lord Chai for taking her beloved Pen away from her.

I asked her why she was crying. So she told me her story. Now I understood, she was alone because of who she was, who she is, and who she will always be. That night I fell asleep under the stars. I guess remorse set in again and likewise she started crying more.

When I awoke the next day, she had become stiff as if she died, but she was not cold but frozen in time. When I looked at her, she was still crying. I looked at the valley and saw a small pond where Lord Chai's school was.

When I got up to leave, I told her I would learn to write so I could write her story. As I walked away, I looked back. I swear I saw a white tiger walk over and lay down beside her.

I managed to find her village. They were relieved to hear Lord Chai was no more and would never be a threat to them again. When I told the people, Chi had avenged Sunnu's death; they told me she was still at the bakery. Sunnu did not die as Chi believed but fell into a very deep sleep. When I met Sunnu, we talked for a long time. I told her everything I knew and Sunnu said she now understands why her grandfather, Tufei, loved her so much.

Sunnu and I fell in love and got married. We had two children, a boy and a girl. We named them Pen and Chi after the love that started Chi's journey. Everything Chi did, she did for love, from fighting for Pen to saving Sunnu. I swear generation on generation my family will watch over her and keep her safe until the day love sets her free.

I was ten at the time; I am now thirty. In the twenty years since that day, the pond has grown into a lake. Zhe Duan Chi is still in torment by her loss and her vengeance. I pray one day she will allow someone to love her for her, even if she does not know how to love herself. What she will never know is how grateful and loved she is by the people that had the chance to know how much of a hero, warrior and friend she truly was. Thank you.

CHAPTER 9

Taking Possession

"That was interesting and a little tragic." Marcus proclaimed.

"See, I told you it was good." Jai said enthusiastically taking back the book.

The flight attendant spoke over the intercom. "To all passengers, please return to your seats and buckle yourselves in. Someone will be around to make sure you are secure. We will be landing in Miami soon. We hope you enjoyed your flight. Thank you for flying with us."

Jai enjoyed his flight and his conversation with Marcus. He had a chance to study. He read the story of Zhe Duan Chi. Jai missed his home already. He left his father, mother, and little brother, Hong Shan Tong. He knew he was going to miss his morning walks most of all.

When the plane landed, Marcus was relieved. He was home and could get back to business. He reflected back on his trip and realized it was not as bad as he thought. He liked the story he read. He also enjoyed the conversation with Jai and was pleased with his new prospect. As they left the plane, Marcus reminded Jai to give him a call after he got settled in.

As the two men were leaving, they saw a redheaded woman with green eyes standing about six foot holding a sign that read 'Marcus Ruger'. She was dressed as a chauffeur.

"Are you waiting for me?" Ruger asked as he walked up to her.

"Yes sir."

"I hope you did not have to wait long."

"No sir. If you will, follow me to the limousine so we can go. You have a busy day ahead of you." Marcus thought to himself that he would follow her anywhere. Gem smiled to herself at his thought.

Marcus was about to offer Jai a ride when they heard his name called. They said their goodbyes and separated. Jai looked up to see Ms. Zhu standing next to her car, a jade colored convertible Mercedes. He was happy to see a familiar face.

"Ms. Zhu, it is so wonderful to see you."

"It is good to see you as well, but please call me Michelle."

"Okay." Then they got into the car.

"Jai, we have a lot of things to do today. We need to find you some place to live, get you registered at the university, and stop by the bank. Where do you want to go to first?"

"The bank, I definitely want to go to the bank first. I want to see how much is in my account." They went to the bank to check his account. Jai was joyfully surprised as was Ms. Zhu to find that he had eight million in the bank. He took out five thousand in cash. Then they went house shopping. Ms. Zhu called a local real estate agent. They looked at houses a few miles from the university until one captured Jai's attention. It was a one-story unit with five sleeping rooms. It had a workout room, a small theater, and a screened in heated pool and a Jacuzzi. It included a garden and pond on the property which had about seven acres. Jai offered eight hundred thousand for it.

Finally, they arrived at the university. It took the rest of the day to get registered and signed up for his classes. Jai was very happy so far. He even met some of his fellow students that were to be in his classes. Michelle took him out to dinner to celebrate his new-found freedom.

"So why did you want such a large house, Jai?"

"I did not want to feel alone in a small home. With the larger one, I could eventually have a roommate or two for company."

"Sounds like a great idea. Once all the inspections and paperwork are finished, you'll be able to take possession of it in about four weeks. Until then, you can either stay with me or get a room at a local hotel."

"Thank you, it will be nice to have someone I know nearby."

•　　•　　•

Meanwhile, Marcus Ruger's day was very different. Once inside the limousine, Marcus felt at home. He was surprised to see Gem get in the back and sit across from him.

"Mr. Ruger, I would like to introduce myself. My name is Gem and this is my twin, Ini." The glass separating the driving and passenger compartments lowered.

"How do you do, Mr. Ruger?" A man with equally red hair and green eyes spoke to Marcus. He was also dressed in a uniform. Ini then raised the partition.

Gem continued. "We are here to take you to your meeting. Constellation is very eager to meet with you."

"I am eager to finally meet him as well."

A short while later the limousine had come to a stop in front a large mansion. Ini opened the door. Gem stepped out after Marcus.

"Well, Mr. Ruger, this is home sweet home." Gem said playfully.

"It is very beautiful."

Ini closed the door and followed behind as Gem led. As they entered, Marcus was impressed with the décor. It had Greek marble everywhere.

"Ini, please tell the master of the house that Mr. Ruger is here to see him." Ini left. "This place is known to us as 'Gateway Mansion'. Each room is like being in a different world." Gem leads Marcus to the library. He marveled at its size. He thought to himself that there must have been over a million books in the library.

"Actually, there are 32,458,937 books in this library from many different worlds."

"That's amazing, but how did you…"

"Know what you were going to say, it's in the script."

"Script, what does that mean? 'It's in the script', what's the 'script'?" (Yes, Alexis, this is for you.)

Gem put her arm around Ruger and guided him over to the massive fireplace. (As she did, she looked back over his shoulder at you with a shrug and smile on her face.)

"Never mind, isn't this the most beautiful fireplace you've ever seen?"

Suddenly, flames erupted from it capturing Marcus' attention. The flames turned black. It appeared as if the night sky came forth from the flames in the form of a large man. Marcus stood in awe in the presence of Constellation. He could only stare, polarized with fear. Marcus suddenly realized he was no longer in the library. He was floating in space as Constellation spoke.

"Marcus Ruger, your body is now mine. I am taking possession of it and you shall drift within the constellations forever."

"Nooo!!! You can't do this to me!" Powerless to do anything, Marcus's consciousness floated away. In front of the fireplace, the mind of Marcus Ruger was vacant. His eyes were blank with a look of horror on his face. Constellation took possession of Marcus through his eyes.

"Now that I have returned, this world will feel my wrath."

"This body suits you well. This man's very presence commanded respect and fear. So, if *we* can keep this body safe from harm, you can use it. Remember what happened with the last one."

"Barely, if it weren't for Ren and Charlemagne, I would have succeeded." When he faced them last, they trapped him into an exorcism circle and banished him for millennia. It happened too quickly for him to react.

"My lord, here is your scepter."

Gem presented Constellation a walking stick. It was a black cane with a silver cap on the bottom and a demonically withered hand holding an orb at the top. The orb was the color of night and looked to have a nine-layered galaxy slowly turning within.

"The Demon's Claw, you found it?"

"It wasn't easy to find. We had to go through six dimensions. Then, we found an ambitious and greedy young woman by the name of Esther Anwan and her friends to retrieve it for us."

"Can we still use them?"

"Yes, her ambition will be of significant use to us."

"Good, in any case, I'm glad to have it back where it belongs. Now go summon the others. It's time everyone sees the new me."

"I shall have everyone together shortly."

•   •   •

In an apartment, not too far from the university, six friends were gathered. Esther Anwan and five of her friends went through an experience that had changed their lives forever. Over the last several days, they entered a magical comic book called 'Terror by Night'. A well-dressed woman she met in the college library gave it to Esther in a sealed package. She said to follow the instructions explicitly. There was only one instruction, to read only at midnight.

At midnight, they were drawn into the comic book and at dawn, they would come out. Now with their adventure complete, all of them kept the powers gained from the comic book. What they did not know was how dangerous the scepter was they brought out. They got a lot of blood on their hands to get it, but it was the greed in Esther's heart that was too great to show mercy.

"So, did you get the money from that judge lady, my beautiful Jamaican queen?" Duncan Eirze asked of his girlfriend, Esther. She and Duncan had been together for a year. He was on the basketball team. After going into the book, he was now able to grow three times his natural size of six feet, eight inches making him an even twenty feet tall.

"Yes, I did, my prince. Now that I'm back, we can continue our discussion. I think we should call ourselves 'The Royal Court'. The book came to me so I will be the Queen. Since you are my boyfriend, Duncan, you will be the Prince. Jessica, you've been my girl since forever, with your psychic abilities you can stand by my side as the Royal Advisor. Traci, you can teleport which means you would make a great Herald. You can pop in and out at will and deliver my decrees. Boys, I haven't forgot you, you two are going to be Guardian Knights. What do you'll say?"

Chase Fielding responded first. "Guardian Knight sounds cool, but only if Traci is down." He looked at his girlfriend, Traci Lane. The two of them got together after they joined the track and field team last spring. The power he chose was to be able to run as fast as the speed of sound.

"You're going to be a true scream queen with your abilities, Esther. I don't mind being your advisor in all, but the name is going to be Psychosis. However, I believe I can speak for everyone. We're in, but we want our cut of the money now." Jessica pointed to the bag Esther was holding.

"Scream Queen, I like it and Psychosis. Anyone else want a different alias?" Esther asked while handing each of them their cut. Jessica Xin and Matt Pennington received twenty percent each while the others got thirty percent of the hundred thousand because they were couples.

"Psychosis sounds awesome but Jessica how 'bout you be my 'Geisha' instead?" Matt said right before he went flying backwards and was held against the wall by Jessica's mental powers.

"I'm not Japanese, you idiot. I'm Chinese. Another thing, I'm not a prostitute, you moron. Say that one more time and we will find out if you can be hurt or not." Jessica hated Matt because he was always disrespectful to her. Matt, on the other hand, only thought of her as a score he couldn't get. And now he knew Jessica knew it.

"Jessica, that's enough. We need him. He's our tank. And that will be his name, Tank. So let him go."

"Fine." Psychosis twisted Matt upside down and dropped him on his head when she cancelled her powers. Hence, letting him go as Esther requested.

As Matt/Tank got up, everyone roared with laughter. Chase decided he wanted to be called Sprint; Traci, Blink; and Duncan, Tower.

"Now that we all have our names, as my first royal decree, find that book. I want to know where it went. If anyone gets it, whoever it may be will know what we are capable of doing. If we are able to get the original again I, uh, we will be able to become even more powerful and while you're at it get me some tribute." At that moment, the pizza delivery came.

"Don't worry I got it covered." Matt held up a fifty and walked toward the door. Everyone erupted in laughter again. Except Jessica, she thought to herself 'finally'.

•　　•　　•

After taking some time to get to know the memories and life of his new body, Constellation entered a large room. At the top of this room was a star burning. The walls and ceiling were space. The floor was made of obsidian. At the center of the room was an oval table made of a solid piece of ivory. The centerpiece was a scale replica of the earth floating inches above the table. Surrounding the table were thirteen obelisk chairs, one for each Zodiac and a larger one for Constellation. Each of the chairs contained the star pattern of its respective sign, except Constellation. He sat down and observed those before him.

Starting with Aries, he glared at each for their failures. "I am very disappointed, when you were here before you were worshipped even by the gods themselves. Now you're nothing more than a group of cowardly peasants."

"My lord, man has evolved. They have become powerful. Some have even gained godlike power." Aries explained.

"You were greater than the gods and now you have proven yourselves weak!"

"My lord, the people don't fear us anymore."

"That's no excuse, MAKE THEM!" Infuriated, Constellation yelled.

"My lord, each of us is in our station. No one is failing in his or her tasks because of incompetence. The people have grown stronger in their arrogance. Their pride has weighed against you." Libra defended them against his wrath.

"Then it's time for them to remember why they should. You have catered to your pets for too long. Now you fear them. With the memories I've gained, this man had the potential to create havoc at will. He wanted to create an army of gods to command so he could rule this world. With what he has already set up, he may have been successful; for a mortal. What have you done? YOU HAVE DONE NOTHING! That ends now! The world will fear us again. All who dare to stand against us will find death embracing them. By the way, where is my pet?"

"Megoon Dracul is in a museum in Jacksonville, FL." Sagittarius responded.

"Is it yet possible to destroy the Nova Star?"

"No, my lord, it's a mystery still. It was made from the core of a supernova, but if necessary, we can have it sent to another dimension or world. Or perhaps, it can be sent to one of the Nine. However, we will still need someone who is honorable and naïve to remove it, maybe another Pandora. Once it's removed, it can be cast away and Megoon will have someone to take his wrath out on."

"Then find someone to free my pet, the Black Star Dragon, but in the meantime, let us remain silent for now. I will plan our next move. Until then use those that are at our disposal. Who all do we have?"

Libra reminded Constellation of Esther and her friends, and another group from the completed version of the book that came with the one she gave Esther. "It tells the story of a group that calls themselves, the

Elementals. However, they have not shown themselves as of yet.

"Put the girl and her friends to work and bring in these so called 'Elementals'. I may have a use for them. And I will contemplate how to bring Mr. Ruger's *Project GODSEND* to life. It's almost a shame I took possession of him. I would have enjoyed watching him bring his dream to fruition. It had the potential to be more effective than the twelve of you combined. It would've been more entertaining. Should have let him live." He looked at each of his Zodiacs with disgust.

CHAPTER 10

Elementals

"It's been a month since you've come to Miami. I hope you have adjusted well. I also see that you've been training very hard. The power you have demonstrated is incredible. You've met some of the others and seem to be getting along with them well. I think you're ready for your first assignment.

"Red Palm and Placer, as you know, are helping Seraph with her fight against the Shadow Realm. Terranika, Calebro and Rom-El are on assignment in the Caribbean looking into a young man named Nevo Marteen. And Crimson Reign is dealing with an issue before heading to Greece.

"I want you and Steel Hawk to investigate reports coming from Miami International University. There are claims that a group calling themselves the 'Royal Court' is extorting the students there. They seem to be genetic mutates, but they are also looking for a comic book called 'Terror by Night'. This is where Steel Hawk said he received his special abilities. Go clean up and be ready to leave in an hour. We need to find that book and figure out what's going on with this new group."

Tetra left Snapdragon to her workout. She thought back over the last month and realized her life has truly changed. For her it was a completely different world. It was the second chance she was looking for. She was given a place to stay and a means to help. The precious stones she hid had lain undiscovered when she went back for them. Tetra helped her liquidate them, which gave her a considerable amount of money at her disposal.

Snapdragon liked the other members of the team. They had accepted her as she was without any whispering behind her back. They gave her privacy and allowed her to adjust at her own speed. She knew she still had a lot to learn.

Snapdragon also learned to trust Tetra and let her get away with calling her Snap, but not the others. Snapdragon felt that she and Tetra were more like sisters instead of members of a team, although she wasn't sure why. After going to her quarters, getting a shower and dressed, Snapdragon went to meet Steel Hawk and Tetra in the briefing room.

She was dressed casually in a V-neck t-shirt, jeans, calf boots, and a Chinese sunrise jacket. She had her hair pulled back in a ponytail. She also wore a faded handkerchief on her left wrist. Tetra made sure she got a new wardrobe of the finest clothes from her culture.

"Woooe, you look amazing." Josh Hawkins a.k.a. Steel Hawk exclaimed when he saw Snapdragon. Josh was seventeen when he got his powers. He gained the abilities to turn to steel and grow wings to fly. He is also able to heal quickly and is incredibly strong.

"Don't mind him, he just turned eighteen."

"It's okay. It is something I am still getting use too. Before, I would have already killed him."

"What! Is she kidding? You are kidding, right?" Josh questioned.

"I think she's just messing with you. You wouldn't have really killed him, would you?" With the dead eye stare she gave them both, there was no question. Even Tetra thought it was a little extreme, but continued. "Anyway, I need you two to go the university in the guise of student reporters interviewing for an article. This is merely for recon, so no fighting. I don't want you two to blow your cover in case you need to go back. Okay?"

They both agreed and left. Josh had driven quietly to the campus. He suggested that he ask questions if she felt uncomfortable. She said she was okay with it and they went on.

Meanwhile, Jai Hong was walking to the eatery known as Let's Eat while talking to Marcus Ruger. "Yes, Mr. Ruger, I'm glad you remembered me. Now that I am settled in, I want to thank you again for the opportunity. I just finished signing the papers to my new home. I'm so happy. I will see you in the morning at ten o'clock."

At that same time, Jessica Xin coming down the adjacent side of the corner was talking at Esther on her cell phone. "I am really getting tired of Matt harassing any guy I talk to because I won't give him the time of day. He is a bigger jerk now than he was before he got his powers. I am sick of it! I gotta to go. I'm going to get something to eat so I can calm down. Bye." She hung up before Esther could even say a word. They were putting their phones away as they bumped into each other.

"Dui bu qi." Jai apologized in Chinese as a reaction to seeing Jessica also being Chinese.

"What did you call me?" Jessica responded.

"Oh, um, I'm sorry. I just thought."

"What because I'm Chinese I speak the language? Well, I don't!"

"I did not mean to offend you. Is there a way I can make it up to you? I am on my way to Let's Eat."

"That's a start." Even though she was only five feet tall, Jessica's attitude could be very intimidating even without her powers.

The two walked together to the eatery. They sat at the last table when they were spotted by Matt and Chase outside heading towards the restaurant. Suddenly, they turned the corner. Over the next hour, they had gotten to know each other a little better and Jessica wasn't hostile anymore.

Jai told her about his home in Thailand. Jessica scanned his mind from time to time to see if he was lying to her. He proved to be honest with her. She was very happy about that and started to let her guard down. They were enjoying each other's company when Josh and Snapdragon made their way to the eatery and started asking questions about the Royal Court. This made Jessica a little nervous.

"Maybe this weekend you might want to come over to my place and go swimming? I'm thinking about, what you call, a house warming party. I just bought my first house this morning."

"Sure, but I got to go. I'm running late for class." Jessica got up to leave.

"I'll walk with you if you like."

"Fine, let's go." Jai got up, dropped fifty dollars on the table and left.

They vacated the restaurant as Josh and Snapdragon reached their table.

Unfortunately, they were not able to find out too much about the Royal Court even when they spoke to the owner, Max. He claimed he had only heard rumors about the group. But, he would keep his ears open for any leads and give them call. None the less, he told them what he knew.

"The only thing I can remember hearing about was that the victims couldn't remember any specific details. A group of faceless students had surrounded them and then they were laid out on the ground. They were beaten and robbed. Three students are still in a coma."

Outside, Jessica thought she was making a hasty get away, but she was wrong. Around the corner of an alley came Matt and Chase. Matt looked at Jessica and smiled at Jai.

"Matt, I don't have time for this crap, get out of the way."

"Alright then, you can go. I just want to have a little chat with your new boyfriend." Jai had a very confused look on his face.

"You say you need a lift?" Before she could react, Chase picked her up and ran away with her.

"Now, how about that chat?" Matt grabbed Jai and held him in the air by his shirt. "I want you to stay away from my girl if that's alright with you?" Matt then threw him down the alley.

Snapdragon and Josh were exiting the eatery. Jai's yell caught her attention and she ran toward the sound. Josh followed suit. As they turned into the dead-end alley, they saw Matt was holding Jai by his neck in mid swing. Snapdragon charged at Matt, but did not reach him before he struck

Jai in the chest. Jai went spiraling backwards about ten feet until he hit the side of the building. Snapdragon hit Matt in the chest as he turned to face them with a running knee with the force of ten strikes. He went flying backwards through the air past Jai. When he hit the building at the back of the alley, his body was embedded into the wall. The bricks were pushed into the adjacent apartment. Josh knew he couldn't transform so he just ran over to Jai. She stood between them and Matt.

"Hey Geisha, you can't hurt me, but if you want, I'll let you scream my name." Matt arrogantly proclaimed as he slowly pulled himself from the wall and stepped down. Shocked, because he more than felt the hit by Snapdragon. Suddenly, sirens rang out. "I will have to play with you later. Right now, I've gotta go." Matt weakly pushed a dumpster toward them to block their path. He slowly went through the hole to make his escape. Matt looked back at her as he went out the door holding his chest struggling to breathe and coughing up blood.

Snapdragon turned her attention to the young man lying on the ground. As she knelt, she took her handkerchief off her wrist to wipe the blood from his face. Josh turned off the siren on his phone and called for an ambulance. Jai looked at her as Josh gently sat him up. Dizzily, he took the handkerchief from her and looked at it. He looked at her again.

Before he passed out from the pain, he whispered to Snapdragon. "Chi, is it really you?"

"Champion?" A look of horror came across her face as she looked on.

The words of Long Tian Di came mockingly back to her. *"You may even get to see him die before you done."*

123

"No, no, no, no! Not again." Snapdragon started crying, held him close, and started rocking.

"Snapdragon, are you okay? Do you know him?"

She was oblivious to everything around her. She kept muttering, "Champion, please wake up. I'm sorry, please wake up." She started wiping the blood from Jai's face again and glared at Josh with blood red eyes when he tried to get her attention.

"Holy crap, what's wrong with your eyes. The ambulance is on its way. You have to calm down. Take a deep breath. Breathe. Snapdragon, just breathe. It's me, Josh." Fearfully scuttling away, Josh spoke to her not wanting to upset her more.

Two paramedics eventually arrived with a gurney. Even though she had calmed; she still refused to let him go.

"We have to let them take him to the hospital."

Reluctantly, Snapdragon let him go with Josh's reassurance. After the ambulance left, the police cleared the crowd and tried to questioned Josh and Snapdragon. She walked away enraged while wiping her crimson tears. She too looked back at the hole in the wall anticipating their next encounter.

•   •   •

"My lord, you seem pleased that she has returned unharmed by her ordeal."

"No, she has changed. She has grown from her grief."

"Does she recognize who you are?"

"My guise as Red Palm is stable. Even Tetra does not know it's me. It's kind of funny that two of my daughters are working together and don't even know they are sisters and I am their father." Ren Lasar smiled to himself.

"It must be difficult for you."

"How is the grove?"

"It is good, my lord."

"I will be returning soon. The conclave is to begin with the full moon. I plan on attending this year."

"That's fantastic, I will see you there."

•   •   •

"You bastard! Why did you do that?" Jessica screamed as Matt entered the apartment.

"I don't know what you're talking about. Besides, he wasn't your type anyway. He was weak and pathetic."

"I really liked him and now he's in a coma thanks to you."

"Get over him. I'm here, that's all you need." Matt tenderly started to laugh. Matt tried to get a high five from Tower. He just shook his head.

"Alright you two, I've had enough of this between you. If Tank harasses anymore of Psychosis's boyfriends, Blink, you are going to send Tank to the Caribbean, the hard way." Scream Queen ordered.

"Hey Babe, don't you think you're taken this too far. He is just having a little fun." Tower tried to help Tank.

"I have spoken! Or did I not make myself clear! Tank has gone too far this time!" Esther yelled in response to Duncan.

"Sure, I was just saying." Scream Queen looked at Tower and he understood.

"Fine, I won't do it again. By the way, where's Chase?" Matt said brushing off the conversation, but not the pain he was still feeling.

"Don't worry about it unless you want to join him." Psychosis answered walking over to the window.

"She told him to 'Sprint' to Boston to get some lobsters." Tower said.

"And he went?"

Tower pointed to his head. "He had no choice." All of them looked at Psychosis. After changing the subject and talking about class work, Chase arrived with the lobsters about an hour later. Still angry, Jessica decided to leave.

Scream Queen waited until the lobsters were finished before she spoke. "I have a feeling; we are going to have a problem if the boyfriend dies. Psychosis may go rogue and if she turns on us, we will put her down. Either, Blink, you go to the hospital to eliminate the distraction and we see how the dust settles, or we eliminate Psychosis and the distraction."

"What about your contact with the Zodiacs? Can they do something to help the boy? We really can use Psychosis's abilities, plus she is a loyal member of the Court." Blink advocated. "Instead of that, I can teleport

Dumb-dumb here a mile underground and eliminate what caused the problem in the first place." She said glaring at Matt and placing her hand on his shoulder.

"Fine, I'll leave her alone." Tank quickly moved away.

"Then it's settled. Tank, you screw up again, you go bye-bye. If Psychosis does not let it go, she's gone. Otherwise, I'll see if the Zodiacs will help the boyfriend."

"Oh, I almost forgot. I think I have a lead on the comic book. I was asking about where I could find rare comics. Some geek told me about Sage Comics. It's owned by two guys named Daemon Sparks and Adam Stone." Blink added.

"I know where that's at. I get all my graphic novels there. D. B. Keplen is the best. The one he did about the marionette is my favorite." Chase expressed happily. "He's supposed to be in South Beach next month, can't wait for him to autograph all my copies."

"Oh-K," Esther said as she looked at Chase. "Da-da-da, never fear, Super Dork is here?"

Traci busted out laughing with the rest of the group. "She totally nailed you." Chase was a little red in the face, but he knew they were just playing. He hoped.

"We'll check out Sage Comics tomorrow, but right now, let's crack open these lobsters."

•   •   •

"Hey hon, did we get any mail today?" Daemon Sparks asked his wife Erin as walked in from work.

"We have a problem."

"What's wrong now? Let me guess, we're having fish and you drowned dinner?" Daemon laughed as he looked at the fish on the counter.

"No, you idiot, someone knows who we are. We got a letter in the mail today. It said, 'we know who you are' and sent a copy of the cover of the book."

"Let me see." Erin got the envelope for Daemon. A business card was also with the letter. It only had a number on it. "Did you talk to anybody about this?"

"Just my sister and she got one too. I'm scared."

"Hon, there is no need to be scared. We have powers now. Besides, if they're looking for a fight we can give it to them. Between you, Katie, Adam, and me, we are the Elementals. When we opened the comic from the shop, none of us knew what would happen. Now, we can be unstoppable. There is nothing for us to be afraid of."

"You're right."

"I'll call Adam, you call your sister, and we'll have them come over so we can discuss this."

An hour later, Katie was pouring four cups of coffee. Erin got the sugar and creamer. They sat at the kitchen table. Each had the mail they had received that day. All had the same contents. They placed one of the business cards at the center of the table.

Daemon started the conversation. "Any suggestions?"

"I say we call the number and at least see what they want. They apparently know who we are and where we live. It couldn't hurt." Adam mentioned.

"Have any of you used your elemental power outside your homes?" Katie wanted to know.

"I was too worried S.H.A.R.P. agents would come after us to do so." Erin expressed her concern.

However, Adam confessed. "I caused a small tremor to see if I still had my powers a few weeks back. It wasn't anything we should have to worry about. I don't think I set off any alarms."

"I think we should call the number as well. What's the point of having what we have, if we don't use it?" Daemon looked at his wife and her sister. "What about you two; call or don't call?"

After looking at each other, they smiled and said in unison to call. Daemon grabbed the phone and dialed the number. It rang four times before someone answered.

"Hello, Mr. Sparks, I hope we did not alarm you too much with your packages. We merely wanted to get your attention."

"You do. Who is this?" Daemon demanded.

"Your new employer, we want to meet with the Elementals."

"I don't know any Elementals."

"Come on, Mr. Sparks, don't be so naïve. We have the proof you are looking for. No, we are not going to expose you. We want to hire you for your services and skills."

"Who is this?"

"I represent a very powerful organization. We offer you your secret in exchange for your loyal service and there will be a monetary compensation as well."

"A monetary compensation, is this a prank?"

"Yes, compensation, be at Ruger Enterprises tomorrow at three p.m. and dress professionally." After saying this, the man hung up the phone. Daemon stared at the phone.

"Apparently, we have an appointment tomorrow at three."

"With who?" Erin inquired.

"I don't know, but we have to be at Ruger Enterprises at three." Now Daemon looked nervous.

"Hey, man up. We are Elementals. I think we should have stronger names than what we had in the comic. Take you for instance, your name is Pyro. That sounds like some-kind-of petty criminal. If your name was like Inferno people would be terrified of you." Adam started to become very animated about the idea.

"Inferno, I like that. So, what's your new name?" Daemon interjected.

"We talked it over. He is going to be Quake and I'm going to be Tsunami. We just couldn't come up with a good name for you, sis."

"There are so many choices to choose from. Come to think of it, I'll be Monsoon."

"Hey, that's pretty good, Babe." Daemon acknowledged that his wife chose an awesome name for herself. He also gave her a high five and a kiss for it.

CHAPTER 11
ICU

"We need to talk about what happened today."

Tetra entered the room. Snapdragon was at her desk with her hands in her hair. She appeared to be staring at her handkerchief with drops of blood gliding down her cheek. Snapdragon looked at Tetra.

"Oh my god, Snap, are you okay? I thought Josh was kidding."

"There is nothing to talk about." Snapdragon wiped her tears smearing blood across her face.

"Do you need to see a medic?" Tetra started to run out of the room to get help when Snapdragon spoke.

"No, I don't need to see anyone." She answered quietly trembling in rage. "It will be better if I am left alone, but what I want to know is, why. And then I want to beat him to death."

Tetra pulled a chair over and sat. "Please, tell me what's going on. Josh said when you saw that kid; it was like you saw a ghost. Who is he?"

"He's my champion and seeing him like that reminded me of my Pen and Sunnu."

"How is he your champion?"

"He is the one that showed compassion to me and released me from my torment. When he did as I told you before, Long Tian Di blessed me with his presence again. He told me that I might be able to see him die before I was redeemed. Now he's gone because I'm not redeemed. I wasn't able to save him."

"Snap, he's in a coma. He didn't die."

"He's not? Where is he?" Snapdragon looked very surprised.

"Josh mentioned he was at University Hospital." Tetra gave her a reassuring hug.

"I want to see how he is doing, even though I can't tell him who I am."

"Not like this, get some sleep tonight and see him tomorrow."

Tetra left her alone. She went to her office and sent Josh a text. He was at the hospital sitting down the hall from Jai's room. He was there to check on Jai. He had found there was a young woman asleep in a chair holding his hand. Jai was in an upper body cast including his head.

Suddenly, Josh heard a clopping coming down the hall. It was another young woman. She was a light-skinned black woman. She stopped in front of Jai's room and looked both ways down the hall before entering.

"Jessica, wake up." In the hall, Josh quietly moved closer. "Jessica, wake up." The woman checked to see if she was still breathing. "Girl, if you don't wake up." She started to shake her until Jessica came to.

"Traci, if you don't get your hands off me!"

"I thought you were already dead." Traci got another chair.

"What are you talking about?"

"Esther thinks if this boy dies, you'll go after Matt."

"I will."

"She said to prevent a fight, kill the boy and let you get over his death or take care of you and the boy. Then I said instead of that, teleport Tank a mile underground since he started it. Then I pointed out that the Royal Court is the strongest when we're all together. So, she gave an ultimatum, either Tank stops harassing you and you get over this incident or one of you gets eliminated."

"Did Tank agree to this?"

"Yeah, so if he apologizes to you at least act like you're willing to accept it, even if you're not."

"Fine, I'll let it go this time. If it ever happens again, I'll make his brain mush."

"That's fine by me. How come I couldn't wake you?"

"I was meditating. I was trying to figure out a way to help him."

"Oh, the other reason I'm here is because little miss Scream Queen has a plan to get our comic back. We need everybody at the guys' apartment tomorrow morning to go over it. One more thing, the lobsters were awesome. I gotta go, later." With that, Blink teleported out of the hospital room and back to her apartment.

Jessica was angered by Blink's visit, but was more so by what she discovered in Jai's mind. He kept searching for a girl name Zhe Duan Chi.

He believes her spirit saved him.

This made Jessica a little jealous, led her to believe he was in love with a ghost. However, the only image she could pull from his mind of her was a statue at his home in Thailand. She thought to herself that she needed to find out more about this girl. Then she held Jai's hand and drifted off to sleep. Josh left to report to Tetra. He told her what he overheard when he got outside.

The following morning, the nurse woke Jessica. "Sorry miss, you'll have to go now. We have to change him."

As she was leaving the room, another woman tried to enter. Each was surprised by the other. "You can't go in now. He's being changed." Jessica snapped at the woman.

"Who are you?"

"His girlfriend and you are?" Jessica surprised herself by what she said and with the ease in which she said it.

"My name is Michelle Zhu. I am Mr. Hong's personal assistant. He never mentioned a girlfriend."

"Wait, he has a personal assistant?" She shook her head in disbelief.

"Alright ladies, take your catfight in the hall. I have to work to do."

They moved into the hall out of the doorway. Michelle took the initiative.

"How is he doing?"

"He's in an induced coma so he can heal."

"How long have you been here?"

"Since last night."

"You go home and get some sleep. Here's my number. Give me a call later for an update. Maybe, you'll get a chance to meet his father later this evening."

"I have some things to do, but I'll give you a call."

Jessica turned down the hallway. As she left, she passed Jai's doctor, Dr. Rasa L. Hague. He entered the room with Ms. Zhu as the nurse exited. Snapdragon and Jessica did not recognize one another as they switched places on the elevator, because of the several people present.

Snapdragon made her way to Jai's room. She stopped before entering because she heard talking. The doctor was going over Jai's condition.

"Perhaps, I should wait until his father gets here." Dr. Hague initiated. He was a young doctor. At the time, when he graduated med school, Dr. Rasa L. Hague was introduced as the brightest star of his graduating class.

"His father is on his way from Thailand. In his absence, I can speak on his behalf. I have a POA in the event of any emergencies. As is the case, what is his condition and what are his real chances for a full recovery."

"If I had to roll the dice, I say he's got a fifty-fifty shot for survival. After that, a full recovery is unlikely. Mr. Hong has suffered severe injuries. He has multiple fractures and internal damage. Mr. Hong will never be the same if he even survives."

"He's strong, I'm sure he will be okay."

"I hope so."

Suddenly his heart rate began to drop. Dr. Hague asked Michelle to move out of the way. He called for the nurse to bring a crash cart. Snapdragon moved away from the door. She saw three nurses racing down the hall to the room. Two were steering the cart. Another was carrying a small portable circular saw.

Dr. Hague took the saw to cut the casting from his chest. As he began, Jai flat lined. Other nurses rushed to the room. One asked Michelle to stand in the corner of the room. When she did, the nurse closed the curtain. For the next two minutes, the only sound heard was the saw.

"Pull!" Dr. Hague ordered the nurses to remove the cast. Another nurse handed over the charged paddles. Michelle was in the corner in tears hoping for the best. Snapdragon was also crying as she leaned against the frame of the door begging Long Tian Di to help him. After jolting Jai four times, his heart started beating again. The doctor came from behind the curtain to talk to Ms. Zhu.

"His heart stopped for three minutes and forty-two seconds. There may have been some additional brain damage, but I don't think anything more than he has already suffered. However, I will have a neurologist come by to check him out later this morning when he gets in. The good news is we have him stable in the coma for now. The problem lies in that if we try to reset his ribs again, he may go into cardiac arrest again. I don't know if we could save him next time."

"Keep him stable as best as you can. When his father gets here tonight, he can discuss with you any further decisions."

When Snapdragon heard this, she left immediately and returned to the Stack Foundation to talk to Tetra.

•   •   •

"After one, we are all done our classes today. We will go to Sage Comics and confront Sparks and Stone. Find out if they have our book or know where it's at. If they give us any trouble, we will have to demonstrate to them why it's important to us. If they still refuse, then we kill them." Scream Queen explained her plan. She believed they held the key to understanding the comic and how to find it.

"So, let me get this straight. Psychosis gets everyone to leave. You want Sprint, Tank and me outside in case S.H.A.R.P. shows up. And, the three of you are inside looking for the book." Tower questioned because he was actually upset that she told him to be outside.

"Do you have a problem with that?"

"Uh, no."

"Everybody knows what you're supposed to do. I expect a positive return, so don't screw this up. If S.H.A.R.P. appears, we are going to have a real fight on our hands. Now let's get to class."

Walking out, Tank approached Psychosis. Scream Queen watched closely to see how she was going to react. She wanted to make sure Psychosis was still willing to be loyal to Royal Court and put aside her grudge with Tank.

"Hey, how's your boyfriend?"

"First off, he's in ICU, you moron. Second, he is not my boyfriend I just met him. And thanks to you, I may never find out if he could have been."

"I talked to Chase last night. He said you said you really liked this guy. He even told me you looked really happy when you were telling the girls about him even after what happened. I'm really sorry. I didn't know you really liked him."

"You didn't give me a chance to tell you either, did you or the reason I was in hurry in the first place? Nooo, you reacted without thinking as you always do. You're stupid. You are the perfect example of all brawn and no brains. I'm surprised you don't have everyone on this team hurt already."

"If you just stop and think sometimes instead of always jumping to conclusions and being so dis-re-spect-ful, maybe you could get a girlfriend. It won't be me. It will never be me! The sooner you realize that the better off you'll be. You have made me hate you. I cannot stand the sight of you right now. I use to like you as a person. I even thought you were funny."

"We're here now because you can't take a hint or rejection. You know what is bad, the entire time we talked he never thought of me wearing anything less than what I had on, even when he invited me over to his place to go swimming this weekend. That's what you call respect."

"Now he's in a coma and all I want to do is humiliate you the way you humiliated me. Then I want you to feel the pain he's feeling right now. Then I want the last thing for you to know before you died is nobody ever wanted you."

"Wow, you really like this guy."

"Yeah, I did."

"Jessica, seriously, I'm really sorry. I promise you. I won't ever do that again."

"Don't worry about it. If it ever happens again, I will find a way to break you in half. Then I will tell everyone the real reason why they ended up in the hospital was because they told you no and you were afraid they would tell everybody."

"You wouldn't?"

"You'll be lucky if I don't do it anyway."

"You know I'm not like that."

"Yeah, but I won't be the one you will have to convince. You're on the wrestling team for a reason, something about grappling with other men."

"You know it's not like that."

"Do I?" Jessica turned, leaving Matt to stand alone feeling self-conscience.

Esther was actually pleased with how Jessica dealt with Matt. She knew everyone was still loyal for now, but she still worried if the boy died. She was almost curious to see what would happen. She thought to herself that it might even be amusing, although she knew she needed everyone for now. What she didn't know was her thought did not go unnoticed by Psychosis as Jessica walked past.

•   •   •

"Tetra, I need your help."

"How can I help you?"

"I found out where the boy is, like you said, but there is a chance he will die. I want to know is there anything that you can do to help him."

"I know of someone that might be able to help. However, he lives in Madagascar. His name is Charlemagne. He is a very powerful sorcerer and a friend of my father's. For his age he's quite young looking."

"So how do I find him? Wait, how old is he? You know what, never mind."

"Honestly, I don't know. My father mentioned that he is somewhere on the peninsula north of Antsiranana in Madagascar. It may be useless to search for him though. It could take week or so to find him. Did they say how long he has?"

"How long does a coma last?"

"It depends; it could last a couple of days or years."

"Then hopefully I will have enough time, but I would like to leave as soon as possible." Snapdragon smiled to herself, because of the decades it took to find Long Tian Di. This quest should be relatively simple by comparison.

"Everything has been quiet for a while. Now would be the best time to do so. Go get ready. I will have a plane ready for you this evening."

CHAPTER 12
<u>Terror by Night</u>

Snapdragon went to see Jai one more time before she left. No one was there this time so she sat with him for a while. As she left the hospital when a S.H.A.R.P. team arrived. They were bringing in one of their own. Snapdragon saw a young girl in the back of the transport when some of the S.H.A.R.P. units got out. They had her hands encased in iron. Her feet were also shackled together. She was held in place with poles attached to a collar she was wearing. These poles were then attached to the walls of the truck. Snapdragon also noticed a crown of electrodes on the girl's head and that she was crying. Then one of the men shut the doors to the transport. Snapdragon approached them.

"Why do you have the child?"

"Her parents turned her in. Not that it is any of your business. What are you a sympathizer to those little monsters?" One responded to Snapdragon harshly.

"No, I'm just curious. What's going to happen to her?"

"Euthanized, just like any other unwanted mut."

"Don't you think that's wrong? What crime did she commit?"

"You guys go on. I'll handle this one." The others went inside. "Look lady, if you have a problem with the laws, write your Congressman and quit bugging us for doing our job. As far as her crime, she was born, that is crime enough for me."

"I'm sorry. I am a reporter or at least trying to be. I was hoping to do a story on the heroics of the S.H.A.R.P. units. If I could get a scoop on this story, maybe I'll be promoted to field reporter. I hate just being a copywriter." She smiled; all the while, she hated this person.

"Well, why didn't you say so in the first place? I'm Lt. John Samson." He took off his helmet and held it proudly.

"So what is this girl, supposedly, able to do?"

"Her mother said she shot fire from her hands at her sister, because she was teasing about beginning puberty. Then she couldn't control it and started burning down the house."

"Does she have a name? Did she hurt anyone? And the last question is will she have a trial?"

"Her name is arsonist, attempted murderer and resister of arrest. Her sister is here with third degree burns including one of my men. As you can see, he just went in. Her mother barely made it out alive. As far as trial, it will be quick. They are even thinking about televising her trial and execution. These things need to learn what will happen to them if they mess with real humans."

"Do you think there is any possibility for rehabilitation?"

"They are animals. She needs to be exterminated with the rest of her kind."

"Is that the final word?"

"Yeah, that's the final word."

"Thank you, for your time. I have to go now." The two parted ways. Lt. Samson went into the hospital and Snapdragon walked away to be out of sight. Snapdragon counted to ten then turned around and flew to the transport. With her strength, she ripped the doors apart in seconds. She jumped inside, with one punch, knocked out the guard and rescued the girl.

"Please, don't fight me. I am trying to save you. Just try to remain calm."

"Okay." In seven seconds, the girl went from death row to flying free with Snapdragon. While in flight, she removed the electrodes, shackles, but left the iron box on her hands. She flew straight to Stack Foundation to see Tetra. She landed on the Stack Foundation roof. Snapdragon spent the next hour with Tetra helping Allison get settled into a room.

"What's your name?" Tetra asked while freeing her hands.

"My name is Allison Burns."

"That's funny. Allison, you will be safe here at the Foundation. I have some things to do as well as get ready for a banquet tonight, but when I get back we'll talk tomorrow, okay?"

Allison simply nodded. Tetra and Snapdragon then went to Snapdragon's room. Once there, Tetra released her frustration.

"What the hell were you thinking!?"

"I was trying to help her."

"You should have called me first. I could have gotten her a lawyer, and a good one at that. Now, I have to get one for you too. I don't even have time for this right now."

"Was I supposed to let her die?"

"No, but next time call me. There are always better ways to help. I will have to turn her in tomorrow and do this the right way. No worries, like I said, I have a good lawyer on retainer. His name is Lawrence Anderson Wilson. By the way, don't you have a flight to catch? Oh, what was the name of that officer you talked to?"

"He said his name was Lt. John Samson."

Tetra stared at Snapdragon blankly upon hearing Lt. Samson's name. Suddenly, she left the room mumbling and shaking her head. "I swear my life feels like a damned cliché. Him? Why him? Anybody, but him." The door closed.

Snapdragon left for the airport shortly thereafter.

• • •

Tower and Scream Queen drove into a parking space in front of Sage Comics on a motorcycle. Matt parked next to them in his new car. Blink popped in and Sprint ran up behind her. Psychosis was already there using her mental powers to plant the idea that the customers needed to go home. She was working on the last two when the others arrived.

"You boys keep your eyes open, but look casual. Talk about Tank's new ride or something, while we check this place out. I'll *holler* for you if we need you." Scream Queen commanded her comrades. "Come on ladies;

let's show these boys how we handle our business." They were about to enter the store when Psychosis stopped.

"Hey, I would like to talk to you about something really quick." Psychosis mentioned to Scream Queen.

"Is it that important it can't wait?"

"Actually, yeah. When we go in here, you should introduce yourself as just Scream instead of Scream Queen."

Blink engaged herself into the conversation. "Do you know why two of the guys are in comas?"

"They refused to pay tribute."

"No, Tower put them there. When he confronted them about tribute for you, they made fun of your name saying that you must be a real whore to be called Scream Queen."

Psychosis continued. "It was said that the only tribute they wanted to give you was, well, you know."

"Yeah, and since then no one has taken us or you seriously. Even Matt and Chase have been giving Duncan a tough time over it."

"Are you for real? People really said those things." Rage started to build inside Esther. "Fine, they want to make fun of me. Scream will do nicely. Scream will be my name and what they will do when I'm done with them. I'll deal with those two idiots later. You know, I have a sudden craving for Alaskan snow crabs, but for now let's go." The other girls began to laugh.

Tower came over. "Hey babe, is everything okay?"

"It is now. I love you. Now get back over to those fools before they screw this up."

"Alright then, I love you too." Tower shrugged his shoulders and walked back over to the guys.

Psychosis feigned reaching for the door and used her psychic powers to open it for the couple coming out. She kept it open for Scream and Blink, then entered herself.

"I'm sorry, ladies, but we are about to close." Adam pointed out.

"That's even better. We don't want anyone disturbing our business with you." Scream rebutted. Psychosis locked the door.

Daemon stepped forward. "And, what business is that?" The proprietors of the shop were dressed in some form of business attire very unlike the laid back clothes they normally wore.

"We hear, you deal in extremely rare comics."

"Yes, we do, but we have an appointment we have to be at in an hour." Daemon grabbed a pen and a sheet of paper. "If you would, give us your name, a number to reach you, and the name of the comic you're looking for, we will look it up tomorrow and get back with you."

"That won't be necessary. I'm Scream. These are my associates Psychosis and Blink. We believe that you might know the whereabouts of a comic called Terror by Night."

The Elementals looked at each other. Erin a.k.a. Monsoon responded first to the statement. "You're the ones that got our book?"

"Scream, I think they were in it too." Psychosis got the information after focusing on Erin's mind after her outburst. "They believe we have it and therefore know who they are and what they can do."

"Do they?"

"Wait a second, you said 'too'. So that's why you have those names?" Katie came from behind the counter. "Who was in the other one?"

"What other one?" Blink asked in curiosity.

"You didn't get two comics?"

"What are you talking about?" Scream was becoming agitated.

"That's the way it works. You get two books. One for you to enter so you can go on your quest. The other is from the last person or persons to enter the book. Once you complete your quest, you keep whatever powers you have gained, but I believe you already know that. But, why did you only get one comic?" Adam concluded.

"The judge lady; she only gave me one." Scream remembered.

"Then she has the other one." Daemon insisted. "I wonder if it's ours or someone else's. See, once you have completed your quest, you get one chance to read your comic book then it disappears. You are left with the other one. So whoever gets Terror by Night after you will receive your story and secrets."

"You must be psychic." Tsunami said to Psychosis.

"It's apparent that both of us have been in it. We are the Elementals. What is the name of your group?" Daemon continued.

"We are the Royal Court. There are six of us including the three men outside. I am the leader. What about you?"

"I think I'm the most outspoken of our group. I am Inferno. This is my wife, Monsoon. Quake is my partner in crime and she is my sister-in-law and his girl, Tsunami. It's been a pleasure to meet you, but we really have to go since you don't have our comic."

"If you don't mind, may we come with you? Psychosis has already told me about your meeting at Ruger Enterprises."

The Elementals agreed. They thought it may be wise to have a little back up. On the ride over to Ruger Enterprises, the Elementals and Royal Court decided to join forces. They would keep their individuality and be allies. As they pulled up, they found themselves surrounded by a multitude of people going about their business. The ten of them entered the main building. Security check point stopped them before they could go any further.

"Where do you think you're going?"

The security guard was speaking to three young women in their late teens.

"You know who I am. I'm here to see my dad. Now, let us through," argued the fiery teenager.

"I am sorry, Miss Ruger, no can do. Your father left very specific orders. No one, without exception, gets in without an appointment. Period. You will have to call and make an appointment like everyone else."

"I haven't seen my dad since he left for Thailand. So you better let us in or you're going to be looking for another job."

"That may be the case, but you and your friends are NOT getting in."

Jessica Ruger stormed off with her friends, Sarah Pennington and Parker Madison in tow.

"Hey, Bro."

"Hey, Sis. Call me." Sarah and Matt exchanged pleasantries as they passed each other.

"We have a three o'clock appointment." Daemon stated as they stepped forward.

"What are your names?" After giving their names, security let the Elementals in, however, told Royal Court they would have to leave. Daemon argued that they were all together, but security would not budge. "Sir, you will be ejected from the building, if you persist."

At that moment, Libra was exiting when she noticed Esther. "Hello, Ms. Anwan, how are you today?"

"Your Honor, can you help us?"

"What's the problem?"

"Ma'am, these six people are not on the list to see Mr. Ruger."

"Why did you need to see Mr. Ruger?"

"Actually, we're with them."

"Ma'am, they are here for the Sage Comics account." Both groups looked at the other.

"And, you are here with them?"

"Yes, we are." Esther confirmed the union.

"I do not believe there will be a problem with letting them in. Mr. Ruger had a cancellation due to a medical emergency so he will have a little extra time to spare. If you like, I will sign them in and take them up myself."

"Thank you, Ma'am. That would be appreciated." The guard was relieved.

Libra signed in Royal Court and led all of them to the elevator. Lt. Samson exited it when the doors opened. He mumbled to himself that he would get that woman if it were the last thing he would ever do.

"I wonder what his problem is." Erin said to her husband as they boarded.

"Mrs. Sparks, he failed in his duty. He is on leave without further notice. Mr. Ruger had a meeting with a very important client in Thailand. A powerful genetic mutate interrupted the meeting. The lieutenant met her today, here in Miami. Not only did he give away vital information to her, but also allowed her to escape. Because of this, she was able to free an equally dangerous genetic mutate that would have been sentenced to be executed this evening."

"I'm surprised he wasn't fired."

"Lt. Samson is fanatical about his job. Some things you let slide. In his case, he will make it a personal goal to bring her in. He hates to look like a fool. His pride will motivate him well. He won't be on suspension for long."

Suddenly the doors opened. Libra led them to a conference room, where Marcus Ruger was standing at the doorway to greet them.

"Mr. Ruger, this is your three o'clock meeting."

"It seems to be more than expected."

"Yes, that is the case. This is Ms. Anwan and her friends, I have told you so much concerning. It also appears that they are joined together as guests of the Sage Comics group."

"Please join us then and take a seat." He shook everyone's hand as each entered the room. When he got to Psychosis, she dropped to one knee and grabbed her head. Constellation bent over and whispered. "If you ever try that again, I promise you, it will hurt you more than it will ever hurt me." He then helped her up. "Would you like something for your headache?"

"No, thank you." She said weakly.

"Are we sure?"

"Yes sir." Trembling, she moved to a chair.

He continued until he finally reached Tank. As he shook his hand, he tapped him on the chest with his walking stick. Tank passed out.

"Have the twins wake him and take him to the lobby."

He then walked in the conference room and shut the door. When he reached his chair, he did not sit. He stood behind it.

"How do you know who we are?" Adam asked assertively.

"I have your story and so that there are no hard feelings, here it is." He slid an envelope to them. "As I said, we merely wanted to get your attention. We want you to work for us."

"Where is our friend?" Scream tried to be demanding, but she was too nervous.

"And, why would we work for you?" Daemon offered another question.

"Your friend caused a friend of mine to miss his appointment this morning. I am quite upset about it. As for your question, you will be paid well." He tapped his cane and four security guards walk in. Each one carried a briefcase and set it in front of each member of the Elementals then walked out."

What about our book? What's the deal with that?" Tower decided to speak up.

"I do not know where your book is or who has it. Nor, do I care."

"Then where is the original."

"That, too, I do not know."

"Then what do you know?" Tower challenged.

"I know you better lower your tone." Constellation zeroed in on Tower.

"What are you going to do about it, old man?" Tower said standing up.

"I see another example is necessary." Constellation said smiling.

"No, wait!" Psychosis screamed into everyone's mind, including Constellation, which even caught him off guard. She captured their attention. Constellation was impressed by the strength of her mind, although she could barely keep her head off the table. Constellation decided to let her speak.

"He's Constellation. He is the leader of the Zodiacs. They gave us the book so we could bring out the Demon's Claw. It's his cane. It brings…" Her words trailed off as she too passed out. She lay with her eyes open and drops of blood trickled from her nose.

An extremely beautiful woman walked into the room. She brought with her another briefcase. She set it down in front of Mr. Ruger, turned and walked out. Scream felt inadequate in her presence.

"I have a question. Where did the original comic book come from?" Erin wanted to know as did everyone else.

"Truthfully, even I do not know. I just know it exists. We have been trying to track it for some time now. What I know is that it appeared sometime in the last century. It can pop up anywhere in the world. It will change the lives of anyone who enters it, good or bad.

"This is the situation; all of you have been given a gift. I want you to use it for me. If you want the Royal Court on the payroll, take this briefcase, your friend, and go. Make sure you follow the instructions.

"Elementals, I know someone who has an item that can make you a hundred times stronger. It is called the Staff of Nature. All I need to know is will you be working for me or will I be hunting you?"

Blink put her hand on Psychosis' back. "Will she be okay?"

Ruger looked at Scream. "Do you accept my proposal?"

"Yes, we do."

"Then leave!" Constellation became agitated.

Scream had Duncan pick up Psychosis before they left. They noticed there were no other people as they went out of the building. Outside, they saw Tank by the vehicles. Royal Court headed back to the apartment. Blink drove Psychosis' car for her. Inside GemIni let go of their mental illusion and walked away amid the crowded lobby.

In the conference room, Monsoon remembered their adventure in more detail as she flipped through the comic book, while the others continued their conversation. Their quest was to free four elemental beings that held a world together. They were giants in size, standing at least fifty feet tall. An evil wizard imprisoned them. If they had failed, the world would have broken apart.

They needed to bring back the Elementals to the chamber where they began their mission. When they finally arrived to where the wizard held them captive, they thought it was too late. The Elementals of that world were dying. Their last act was giving each their respective power before fading away. They charged them to take the elements back to the chamber. In addition, they would need to embrace the elements to save the world.

It then became a race against time and the wizard. Earthquakes shook the planet without mercy. The waters washed away coastlines. Entire mountain ranges erupted without warning. The winds started blowing so hard in the opposite direction to the point that the planet's rotation was slowing down. The wizard finally met his end outside the chamber. What they did not realize was the closer they got to the chamber, the stronger they became.

After several attempts of trying to return the elements, Adam sat on the platform for the elemental of the earth frustrated. He wished he had what it took to help save the world. Suddenly, he transformed into stone. The others then understood what they meant by embracing the elements. Each stood on their respective platforms and concentrated on becoming that element. At that moment, they knew they had to give up their lives to save the planet. Once transformed, they truly became the Elementals and their quest was complete.

They instantly were transported back to the void where they had originally entered the book. They were greeted by the same individual in a black hooded robe sitting on a throne that rested on a mountain of bones. He said, "Well done, now go with your abilities."

After two and a half weeks, the Elementals left the comic book for the last time. They had searched two months for it. Now Erin was holding the secret all of them wanted. Her husband interrupted her facial expressions.

"So, what you're saying is, we work for you or else. I'll tell you what, if the staff is there, we will work for you. If not, we work for ourselves and you still leave us alone with S.H.A.R.P."

"Perhaps, I did not make myself clear. You work for me whether you find it or not; or you will be hunted down and eliminated. That is the only immunity you will receive."

"It looks like we have no choice." Daemon looked at the others as he spoke.

"I am glad you see it my way. After all, I am only trying to make you stronger. What you may not understand is with the Staff of Nature, you will be able to affect this world in the same manner as the world in that book when the elementals perished. You will be that strong. That is the power you could possess." Constellation got excited at the thought of how much destruction they could cause, he smiled.

"All the information you need is in the briefcases. You may go and prepare yourselves. Tonight, will be the perfect time."

The Elementals left without saying another word. They waited until they were home before they discussed what had just transpired. They also remembered the warning Psychosis tried to tell everyone and what happened with Tank. They were silent again once when they opened their briefcases.

CHAPTER 13
Lt. John Samson

"Jessica, are you sure, you're okay?" Blink held her while they sat on the sofa.

"Yes, I'm fine. I just have a headache. What's in the briefcase?" Jessica was holding her head because she was still trembling from her encounter with Constellation. This hindered her ability to use her powers affectively. It felt like he was still inside her head. She just could not shake the feeling.

"It's our mission." Scream handed Psychosis a picture of Snapdragon, an individual dressed in a tan hooded poncho, and another person that appeared to be Greek or Italian dressed in a white suit.

"Hey, this is the same girl at Let's Eat. She and the guy with her were student reporters asking about us. Why is she our mission?"

"Hey Jess, you want to hear something crazy? That chick, apparently kicked Tanks butt after Chase snatched you up." Traci pointed out.

"What?" Jessicea rubbed the back of her neck.

"Yeah, Chase was telling me about the bruise she left him with."

"That's not possible" Jessica responded in disbelief.

"Apparently, she did."

Esther annoyed continued.   "Anyway, Constellation wants her eliminated as well as the others. Our first mission is to eliminate this guy. Get this, he goes by Charlemagne. I guess he wanted to be the *second* Holy Roman Emperor. Yet, he lives in Madagascar and that's where we are going. The plane leaves in two hours. Here is your ticket and passport. Since you were out, I had Blink pack you some clothes and stuff. We'll have to be at the airport in an hour."

"Thanks. The flight should do me some good. I got a feeling I'm going to need the rest."

While the Royal Court was getting ready, the Elementals were across town going over the plans given to them by Constellation. They received blueprints of Stack Foundation. Their instructions were simple; find the staff and destroy the research building. Each briefcase had a credit card worth two hundred fifty thousand dollars.

"Do you think we can really pull this off?" Quake discussed with the others.

"Quake, what are you worried about? With Tsunami and Monsoon by our side, we can't lose."

"You're right, but I really don't want to do this."

"Neither do I, but if that staff is real; we can use it against him. It's like that old saying, 'a necessary evil', even though we're not."

"Maybe we don't need the staff. Perhaps, hon, we are stronger than we think. Remember, we became stronger the more we focused on who we are. Yes, we all agreed, not to use our gifts because we were afraid of hurting everyone here." Monsoon interjected.

"I agree with Monsoon. Sure, they gave us money, but at what cost? If we succeed, we'll be criminals. If we fail, we'll be criminals. If we do not do this, Constellation said, he'll hunt us down. Either way, we are in a lose situation. However, if no one gets hurt, I'm still in." Tsunami defined her position as well as her sister's.

"Like I said before, what's the point in having what we have and not use it. I also agree, I do not want to see anyone hurt either, but we are about to be forced to use our abilities either way. This could be a good dry run. If no one is there, no one gets hurt. We defend ourselves if they attack us, but if we do not need to use our abilities, we won't. I say let's do it." Quake reconsidered himself, mainly for himself.

"I have a plan. We search for the staff. Whether we find it or not, we will set off the fire alarm to get everyone out of the building. Then, we make the place a pile of rubble, okay?"

Inferno looked to his wife for approval. Monsoon only nodded and held up the outfit provided to her in the briefcase. The others smiled as they held up theirs. The outfits were black steel mesh spandex trimmed down the sides in a color respective to the individual element, as was the logo on their chest, a four arm swirl pattern like a galaxy.

•   •   •

"Allison, I'm leaving now for the fundraiser tonight to help people like us. It's to help pass the Mutate Advocate and Equality bill. It is very important. Best-case scenario is the bill passes quickly and there are no restrictions. Worst case, you have to be registered and your abilities put on public file. Right now, you are a fugitive. If they find you, they will execute you on the spot. However, if this bill passes, you might actually get a fair trial. There is even talk of creating a place to ship people like us, away from 'normal' humanity."

"Ms. Stack, why do people hate us?"

"Because they are scared to accept others the way they want to be accepted. No, it is not fair, but fear is a very powerful motivator. Fear breeds hatred and hatred breeds destruction. People like that are unable to give mercy. It is truly a pity to see lives lost because of willful blindness. Do not worry about that. Get a good night's sleep and I will see you in the morning. Josh will be here if you need anything."

Tetra left Allison with her light on. She left for the fundraiser in her limousine. She was dressed in a black dress with diamonds lining the trim. Tetra tried to relax for the evening, but she was feeling a little stressed about the situation with both Marcus and Constellation. Neither one had created much ruckus late. For her it had been too quiet when it comes to them, but she knew she had to stay focused for the fundraiser in spite of the afternoon's event with John Samson.

·   ·   ·

"Good evening Miami. These are your top stories. Tonight, Lt. John Samson, S.H.A.R.P. officer is on administration leave pending the investigation of his involvement with the escape of a dangerous genetic mutate and this unknown woman. Also tonight, how will this affect the fundraiser for tonight's dinner at the Shepherd's Club hosted by philanthropist and CEO of Stack Foundation, Tetra Stack? She has been lobbying for the passage of the Mutate Advocate and Equality bill. With today's events, that bill may be in serious jeopardy, especially since there is a major protest building steadily

outside the club."

Lt. John Samson was at his neighborhood bar when the news came on. He had eight years of loyal service to Ruger Enterprises and his S.H.A.R.P. unit. He was highly decorated. The mayor had given him a key to the city for saving his life from a gang of mutates while off duty. He simply hated the idea of this tarnishing his record.

Lt. Samson had never married. He was engaged once. Some said his fiancé left him because he chose his career over her. Others said she was sympathetic to mutates or even one of them. Whatever the reason, he has neither confirmed nor denied anything. He simply didn't talk about it. Since then he hasn't looked back. When it came to g-muts, he has shown only contempt.

"That woman needs to be put in a cage with the rest of those freaks. I bet she'll change her tune then, especially when they turn on her."

"John, don't be so hard on yourself. You didn't know she was a mut. You know, it's starting to get harder to tell the difference anymore. Everyone knows how much you dislike those things. You wouldn't just let one get away. Besides, why was she even at the hospital?"

"Ricardo, shut up and get me another beer."

"Watch your tone or you'll be flagged."

"Alright, alright, just get me another beer." He said calmly. "But, you're right. I need to find out why she was at the hospital."

"Look at it like this; you're on a long vacation. Enjoy it. Sleep in. Go fishing, but do something besides sulking."

"It's all her fault, you know."

"How's that? You don't even know her."

"I just know it was one of her freaks that helped that girl escape. And I'll bet a round of drinks that she knows where those freaks are right now. I think I'm going to arrest her for harboring a fugitive, no, two fugitives."

"You're not arresting anybody in your condition. Besides you're on suspension, remember? And you don't know that for sure. If you go messing with her, you will be the one arrested. Besides you have no proof. All you have to do is wait it out and get the proof you need. Then you can get all of them."

"I can make a citizen's arrest."

"Not drunk, you can't. Like I said, you have no proof. So don't go and do something stupid."

"I'm not drunk."

"You will be by the time you get over there."

John was not commonly a drinker. He normally wouldn't tolerate drinking, because of what happened in his childhood. His father was a police officer and an alcoholic. He was very abusive when he drank. His mother died from a drug overdose after his father went on one of his rampages. John thought she did it to escape his father. John always felt like his father hated him for being born.

When he was barely seventeen, his father was drunk one night and walked in front of a train. When he went before the courts to find out what was going to happen to him, he asked the judge to allow him to join the military.

This is when he met his fiancé while on assignment in Cairo, Egypt. She was the most amazing woman he had ever seen. She made him feel whole. He was later tasked with assassinating the head of a local genetic mutate organization. As he went to pull the trigger, she removed her scarf covering. It was his Egyptian beauty. Pulling back tears, he fired. With the feeling of anger and betrayal, he returned to his unit. He never spoke of that night since.

His anger and determination served him well. John was the best sniper in his unit. John was always serious even though others thought he was joking when he said he saw his father as the target. Most of time, he saw himself. He spent six years as a marine sniper, before S.H.A.R.P. recruited him.

In his own mind, Lt. John Samson will always be at war with someone, usually himself. Tonight, however, he had an old target. Tetra Stack was again his prey.

"You know what, you're right. I'm going to go home, get some sleep, and go to Key West in the morning. I'll even book a fishing trip in the gulf."

"That's more like it. Make sure you get home safely." Ricardo bid John farewell. John smiled back at his friend as he left the bar.

• • •

Royal Court made their way through the airport without incident. They were happy to receive first class tickets. To her dismay, Matt sat next to Jessica. However, while they situated themselves, a thousand miles away, Snapdragon had drifted off to sleep on one of Tetra's private jets on her way to Madagascar.

Snapdragon dreamed Pen was with her at the lake. They were sitting on a log and held hands for a long time. As they sat, the lake started to dry up. The water level continued to lower until it was completely gone.

"Chi, you're free to move on with your life. You don't owe anyone anything."

She put her head on his shoulder and began to cry softly. "I miss you so much. I feel empty without you."

"I miss you too, but it's time to let go. You have a future to look forward to. You have cried enough for me. It'll be okay, you will find someone, but for now you must protect this world. You can no longer live in the past. The future is full of danger. You will have to remain focused."

"There are creatures trying to enslave the world and be worshipped at the same time. I feel so overwhelmed."

"Do you remember the day we fought?"

"Yeah, you finally beat me."

"No, I could always win, I just liked to see you get mad, and then I would start to laugh to myself and let you win, but yes, that day."

"What about it?"

"You fought with great determination. Until Master stopped us, you and I pushed our skills to our limits then we just continued. Neither one of us let up. After that day we changed, we were passionate in our training and even more so with the love we had for each other. Now, you are trying to redeem yourself from what you did after my death, that price has already been paid. You have hurt and suffered long enough. Let someone in and find your happiness. I can never come back."

"I wish I died with you."

"But, you didn't and there is a reason for that."

"I feel so alone without you. I hate it. I just can't stand for the disrespect anymore. Everywhere I turn, someone thinks because I'm a woman from Asia, I'm supposed to be submissive and obedient like a common dog."

"You are a rare gem, forged from the pressures of ten lifetimes. Someone deserving will capture your heart again when you're not looking and sweep you away from your sadness. I must say good bye; your life is waiting for you." With that Pen faded from her dream.

She sat on the log alone for several more minutes then walked away in the starry night. Suddenly, Snapdragon opened her eyes to see the night sky through the window as she wiped tears from her face before drifting back off to sleep.

•   •   •

Back in Miami, Tetra felt her fundraiser was a success in the face of continued protest. She was escorted to her limousine through the taunts of the crowd. Once inside, the doors locked and a strange but familiar voice came from the driver's seat as the car drove off.

"Ms. Stack, you and I need to have a little talk about your friend."

"Who are you!?"

"I'm the guy your friend screwed over by helping that little monster escape."

Remembering his voice, Tetra responded. "John? John, I don't know what you're talking about. I'm sorry, but I do not have friends that help monsters. You must be thinking of your employer, Marcus."

"Tetra, watch your mouth!"

"It's not every day I get to meet a patriot so willing to point a gun at the head of an unarmed woman. That must have taken some courage to pull that trigger or does it just get easier. Good thing, you're a bad shot."

The limousine swerved into the parking lot of a closed restaurant before slamming to a stop. He got out and snatched open the back door. John pulled his gun and pointed it at Tetra yelling for her to get out.

He put the gun to her head. "I didn't miss then and I won't miss now!" John screamed becoming very emotional. "You're going to tell me where she is or I will put a bullet in your mutt lovin' head."

Smelling bourbon on his breathe. "Have you been drinking? You're not turning into your father, are you?" Tetra paused. "I'm sorry John that was unfair, all I know is she's out of the country. She mentioned something about going to Africa. And no, I really don't know when she'll be getting back. John put the gun down. You and I both know you are not going to shoot me."

"That wasn't so hard now, was it?" He lowered the gun.

"Why didn't you return my calls? When I got back to our place all your stuff was gone. What did I do that was so wrong? Did you even keep the picture you took? I noticed it was gone off the dresser."

"Damn it, Tetra. I loved you! Why didn't you tell me!?" John yelled still feeling the sting of betrayal.

"John, I couldn't. I'm sorry I was trying to protect those people."

"I was ordered to put a bullet in your head!!" John then pointed the gun to his own head. "You have no idea what that was like for me. Seeing you; of all the people in entire world; it was you in my crosshairs. Had I not wanted to see your face, I would have killed you. I had a clean shot three times. Just imagine the horror for me had I pulled the trigger too soon."

"But you didn't because you are a good man John." Tetra placed her hand on his arm. "You know he only hired you to get to me."

"I know." He looked into her eyes and knew she felt the same. "Look, I can't do this right now. I got to go." Samson got back in the limo.

"You can at least give me a ride home."

"I have a better idea. Why don't you walk and think about what you did to us! Just to let you know, the day will come, I won't have the luxury to miss." With that Samson quietly drove off just wanting to hold her.

"I miss you too." Tetra whispered while she stood, reaching for her phone knowing he was still angry and hurting.

•   •   •

That same evening, at the hospital Dr. Hague was briefing Hong Jin on his son's condition. Ms. Zhu was there also.

"Mr. Hong, the decision is yours. However, my medical opinion is that your son is already gone. We are merely keeping his body alive. I would not want to cause you anymore undo stress. I understand a decision like this is very difficult. So, I want you to take a few days to discuss with your family the options before you. I am sorry you have to go through this. I heard he had a promising future."

Dr. Hague left and Michelle gave Jin a hug to console him. "Jin, I will get a flight ready for Mrs. Hong and Shan Tong."

"Was I wrong for not teaching him? I didn't want him fighting for a living and now he has to fight for his life. He's too young."

"Are you sure she didn't do this?"

"Yes, Jin, she and another young man saved him. She's not your enemy anymore."

"Zufu still wants her dead, which means the enemy of my family saved Jai from death. And the doctors here can't do anything except to let him die."

"They did everything they could and you are an excellent father. You did nothing wrong. I'll go get you some coffee."

Michelle quietly left the room. Jin sat in the chair next to his son. He picked up Jai's backpack the nurse had given him and started to go through it. As he did, he saw Jai's school books, the book he had given to him and discovered paperwork with the keys to Jai's new home. Jin was very proud of his son. And then, he came across the picture of Jai's mother. He started to weep.

"I'm so sorry I didn't protect him." Jin apologized to his dead wife and wept harder. He wiped his tears looking at the picture.

"You knew I was raised to find her. Break that damn curse and avenge Zufu for the sake of the family honor. I thought I would be the one to do it. So I didn't train him. But, if he dies and I fail, Zufu will have to do it. I can't rely on Shan Tong. He's too soft like his mother.

"If Nak had just told me when she rose from her prison, I could've been here sooner. I wouldn't have wasted my night getting nothing from her. I could have prevented this. I just wish you never said you were leaving. We wouldn't be in this mess now."

There was a knock at the door. Jin looked up to see the one woman not to let him down. "Here's your coffee. You might not want to confess so loudly. You never know whose listening." She looked at him, then Jai.

"Have you seen it yet?" He held up the keys.

"It's beautiful. You'll love it."

CHAPTER 14

Change of Heart

Constellation smiled fiendishly as he watched the news. He was accompanied at Gateway Mansion by four of his Zodiacs. Each found humor in the devastation, even mocking Tetra's sadness. The four were quickly silenced as Constellation began to speak.

"I am glad you're all so pleased with what I've done. It angers me to know it took my return to get this simple task accomplished. You've grown weak since the last time I was here. I remember a time when man was weak and mocked the gods because of their jealousy. Now you mock them because of yours. I have the stars of heaven before me fallen weak before man. It's a shame I needed to possess this body because this world cannot contain the reality of who I am. And you; you run around like insects bidding for control with what's beneath you. You have become apathetic.

"Leo, go to Madagascar and help Royal Court. They should arrive tomorrow. Take whoever you want."

"Yes my lord." Leo got up and left.

"Capricorn and Aquarius, I told you to find me another Pandora, innocent and pure. Pandora gifted man with evil. She mourns her action to this day. She was weak because of her naïve curiosity. So have you found another?"

"No my lord," they responded.

"Then why are you here?" Capricorn and Aquarius also quietly got up and left without another word.

"Shall I check on the Elementals to see if they have recovered the staff?" Cancer spoke up as the others left the room.

"There's no need I know how to find them."

"What would you have me do, my lord?"

"Find Pisces and create havoc for the ships on the ocean to keep our enemies occupied." Without saying another word Cancer again got up and left.

Constellation picked up the file stamped Project GODSEND. He looked it over again and mused to himself how Ruger would have implemented it himself. He still contemplated restoring him to fulfill his dream of making 'gods'. Now all he would need is to find a suitable replacement host body. He was very agitated by the complacency of his once mighty Zodiac. He knew he needed to do something drastic to get them motivated again. Perhaps, seeing the success of GODSEND by the real Marcus Ruger would be enough to motivate them, then again, maybe not.

•　　•　　•

Back at Stack Foundation the scene was truly grim. A massive explosion brought down two thirds of the research facility. Four fire departments worked hard at putting out the fire. Tetra stood in tears as she watched a lifetime of work burn away. For her, time stood still as those around her moved in overdrive. Even though more than a dozen reporters were trying to talk to her, not one voice was heard until she felt a hand on her shoulder. It was her father.

"Tetra, I'm here." Ren Lasar hugged his daughter then walked her through the crowd of people to an ambulance. On his way to the ambulance, he waved his hand to put the rest of the fire out. He had a paramedic give her some oxygen to help calm her down.

After a couple of minutes, Tetra started to speak calmly. "How was he able to cause all this damage? I just don't understand why. Why would he do this?"

"Who is that, my dear?"

"It was John, Father."

"Mm, well, I have some good news for you."

"And what is that?"

"John, he didn't do this. It's not his style. By the way, does he even know?"

"Does he know what?"

"Tetra, does he know? And don't play dumb."

"No, with everything going on, no."

"You need to tell him. He has a right. On another note, I may have some new recruits for you. They call themselves the Elementals."

"Really, where am I supposed to put them? There?" She pointed to the building.

"However, I have a feeling they may be partly responsible for this. Although I think they just need a little guidance."

Absolutely flabbergasted by what her father just told her, Tetra could only walk away shaking her head thinking he was insane.

Ren continued as he followed her. "Were there any casualties?" He asked light-heartedly.

Tetra stopped dead in her tracks, turned around and glared at his hood-covered face. "Are you for real? My god, father, I don't know. They're not done looking yet. Why don't you ask your *Elementals*? Maybe, they will tell you how many innocent lives they've killed! After the day I've had, I could just scream. All you can say is, *'you want me to train the ones that destroyed my life's work.'* You are unbelievable. Has senility finally set in or are you just that dense? I don't even know where Josh and Ali are."

"Tetra, we're right here." Josh called out to her.

"Where have you been?"

"Hospital, she has a broken wrist." Tetra looked at Allison, who now wore a cast on her right wrist and forearm.

"Are you okay, sweetie?" Ren knelt down and asked her. She simply nodded. He walked her over to a bench away from everyone. He waved for his aide.

"Yes, my lord."

"I need two cloves of garlic, two mint leaves, one eucalyptus leaf, and one soma leaf. I need that ground together, ready for her to drink as soon as possible. And make it warm."

"Right away." His aide left.

"So why don't you tell me what you remember."

"I was asleep. And then, there were some people arguing outside my room. It woke me up."

"What were they saying?"

"They were upset that they couldn't find something."

"Did they say what they were looking for?"

"They were talking about something called the Staff of Nature."

"Really, did they say why they were looking for it?"

"They said they were supposed to get it to make them stronger and use it to reshape the world."

"Then what happened?"

"I tried to listen and get a look at them. They were in the room across from mine. I could see in because the door was open. That's when I saw them, there were four of them."

"Then what happened?"

"Then I yelled, 'I'm telling Josh.' I went to run and tell, and that was when I was hit with a lot of water. It sent me flying back into my room and hit my hand on the door frame. And then I got really scared and I started crying. My hand and arm hurt really, really bad. When they came in my room I got even more scared. And that's when, my whole body turned into fire. And then the room started to catch fire and I couldn't control it. I panicked and got more scared. I couldn't see them anymore. I was burning up and I just couldn't stop it. The next thing I knew, I saw a flash of white light and then I'm at the hospital with Josh. I'm sorry about my room."

"My lord, here's the drink." Ren took the drink and handed it to the girl. She drank it quickly. Tetra and Josh had walked over to Ren and Allison and listened.

"I'm sorry. I didn't mean to catch my room on fire. Please don't send me away."

Looking back at what was left of Stack Foundation, Tetra realized it was Alison who was the cause of the explosion, not just the Elementals. "I'm not, Allison. We're going to teach you how to use your extraordinary gifts."

"After this incident, the doctor said she isn't showing any sign of having abilities anymore. He said it may have burnt out her system." Josh responded.

Tetra said as she put her arm around her and let out a sigh. "Right now, we just have to find you a safe place to sleep. Josh, we need to get her out of here before the media sees her. You should take her to your mother's house for the night. It will give me a chance to get some other accommodations for her." Josh left with her quickly and flew her to his mother's home.

"I have to go and take care of something as well. I will return shortly." Ren stated as he walked to a limousine. Again, Tetra was left alone reaching for her phone.

•   •   •

"What happened?" Inferno demanded from the rest of the group.

"I don't know what went wrong. Everyone was supposed to be gone. Where'd that girl come from?" Tsunami tried to defend herself.

They found themselves confused by the evening's events which now had them fighting amongst themselves. What the Elementals didn't know was how pleased Constellation truly was, in spite of the fact, they were arguing on a beach. They didn't understand the true ramifications of using their powers outside of the comic book; what chain of events that could be unleashed.

"Why would you react like that?" Monsoon yelled at her sister.

"She startled us and I was trying to make sure we weren't caught. I didn't realize she was a kid. I just reacted."

"It's a good thing we got outta there when we did. Did you see what that kid did? Aren't you able to do something like that?" Quake interjected looking at Inferno.

"Yeah, but I never used it. What were you thinking?" He asked Katie again.

"I WAS SCARED, ALRIGHT!" Tsunami screamed and ran into the water.

Monsoon encouraged Quake to go after her sister. When he reached her, he put his arms around her.

She turned and cried inconsolably on his shoulder, "I don't want to do this anymore."

"I know, but right now we have no choice."

As they reflected on the night's events, Inferno made up his mind that he didn't want to be a part of Constellation's game anymore. He also knew the others felt the same way. They sat quietly for almost an hour when he began to speak in a softer tone.

"We were entrusted with these abilities for some reason. We saw firsthand inside the book what we could do. Now, we are acting scared because of what we've done. There is no reason for it. In the comic book, we were heroes. And now, we're villains. I don't know about the rest of you, but as for me, I will not be a part of this any longer. I am Inferno! I am an Elemental!" With that, he stood and embraced his elemental power; transformed and exploded into living fire then continued. "We must go to make atonement if we can."

"But what if we can't?" Tsunami challenged.

"Then, we do what we can. Either way, Constellation and his Zodiac must fall." He extinguished his flame and began to walk towards the road. The others slowly followed. Before they reached the road, a limousine pulled to the side a short distance away.

As they came to a stop, Monsoon spoke. "Do you think it's Constellation?"

"If it is, be ready." Inferno commanded as they cautiously walked forward they all transformed preparing for a fight.

The chauffer got out and casually opened the door. A single man got out. The Chauffer closed the door and stood by the car. He was dressed in a tan hooded poncho and pants. The hood covered half his face. Growing from his right hand was a staff with lightning surging through it. He walked toward the Elementals and stopped about twenty feet away.

"I heard you were looking for me. A little birdie told me you felt the need to get my attention. Now that you have it, what do you want?"

"I'm not sure if you know who you're dealing with, mister, but we are the Elementals and we have the power to destroy you." Inferno proclaimed as he created a fireball in his hand. The others followed suit with their respective abilities.

The lone individual started laughing. "You, you are elementals?" Suddenly, he stopped and drove the staff into the ground. Enraged he proclaimed, "I AM REN LASAR AND THESE ARE ELEMENTALS!!!"

Before they realized what was going on, four elementals appeared behind them standing about thirty feet tall each. Shock and awe caught them off guard and they were immediately overtaken by their respective elements.

"You will be held in the plane of your element until I decide what to do with you."

Their cries and struggle to be heard fell upon deaf ears as Ren turned and walked away. Just as quickly as the elementals appeared, they disappeared taking their captives with them. Ren took his staff and returned to the car.

"My lord, what will you do with them?"

"Train, they are misguided. They need to be punished for their crime, and then trained to understand the full potential of their power. I will give them a second chance." Ren looked back at the beach. "It shouldn't take too long, unless they enjoy suffering."

"It appears we will miss the conclave again this year."

"So, it seems. Take me back to Tetra."

"Yes, my lord."

· · ·

'RING… RING… RING…' A phone rang on the nightstand next to a picture of John with his ex-fiancé Tetra.

"Hello."

"Lt. John Samson?"

"Yeah, who is this?" John responded with a slight hangover.

"I would like to know if you like what you do?"

"What!? Who is this!?"

"I am a doctor, Dr. Seba, from the hospital. I am also funded by a corporation called *Gene*Tech. I saw your story on the news this evening. I would like to know while you're on suspension, if you would like to make some extra money."

"Doing what?"

"My colleagues and I have discovered a way to give real humans extraordinary abilities. We would like to offer this opportunity to you in your fight against the unnatural. It's, kind of like, leveling the playing field as it were."

"What kind of abilities are you talking about?"

"It will depend on your specific genetic makeup and how receptive your body is. You will be the ultimate soldier."

"Knowing who I am, why would you call me?"

"Lt. Samson is it merely by chance that the little monster that escaped from your custody today came in this evening to get a broken wrist reset. As I said before, my colleagues and I have concluded it would be advantageous for you to be equipped. You need to handle these types of monsters without a need for bulky armor or extra ammunition. Unless that's the type of limitations you desire for yourself." He was silent as he took in the information. "Lieutenant, are you still there?"

"Yeah, I'm still here. I'm just thinking about your proposal. By the way, how much money are we talking about?"

"We would be able to offer you up to two million dollars for your assistance. What do you think about that Mr. Samson?"

"Did you just say two million dollars?"

"Yes, Lieutenant, we are offering you up to two million dollars for your assistance. We figure it would help fund any operations you may desire. Should you not wish to continue in your current position, you may feel the need to hand out justice as you see necessary."

"So, what is the probability of something like this going wrong and I need the money for medical expenses."

"As with any procedure there is always a small percentage of risk, but I assure you sir, there is even less of a risk in your case."

"And why is that?"

"*Gene*Tech is also a storage facility for DNA samples. When you give blood, it gets stored here. When I saw the report on the news I decided to test a sample of your blood with our formula. It's a good match. Remember, it's just a test. The results may vary on full scale, but the thought of what you can become is electrifying. We foresee a complete success and you will become *the* top agent in your field. The best part is, it will be government sanctioned and you will be given immunity to do your job as you see fit. You will be able to go after any criminal and execute judgment at your leisure."

"What happens if I choose not to do this?"

"You will never hear from us again. And any attempt to find us will not end well for you. Then again, I think you will be happier to be able to do your job without restrictions. It is still your choice Lt. Samson. If you like, I can call you back in the morning to give you some time to think about it.

"I don't need the time to think about it. I'll do it."

"Are you sure?"

"Yes."

"Very good, Lieutenant, be at the hospital in the morning by ten. Ask for me. By the way, turn on the news. You may like what you see." Then

Dr. Seba hung up the phone.

He watched a grim scene on the news. It was a live report of a fiery explosion at a local research facility.

> *"Yes, this is Roja Domingo here. I'm here at Stack Foundation near South Beach where I spoke to Tetra Stack, CEO and Founder of Stack Foundation. This is truly representative of the adage, 'No good deed goes unpunished'. After a successful fundraiser for the Mutate Advocate and Equality bill; an explosion has destroyed over half of the research facility here at Stack Foundation. The normally stoic Ms. Stack was very emotional when I had chance to speak with her earlier. Ms. Stack commented tearfully, "It is truly sad when the ignorance of a few can impact the future of so many." Again, this is Roja Domingo, at a quieting scene here live near South Beach."*

John sat on his bed with extremely mixed emotions looking at the only person with the ability to see him as he truly was. In his heart, he knew he could never hate or harm her no matter how much it hurt. Even in his current state, he thought he caught a glimpse of the very fugitive he's been put on administrative leave for in the background, but wasn't sure. He thought about the phone call. It made him angry knowing there are people so eager to betray humanity. The only thing that infuriated him more was they may actually be right. After a while, he drifted off to sleep with thoughts of Tetra.

CHAPTER 15
The Morning After

The following morning Jessica went to the bathroom to make a phone call. "Hello, Ms. Zhu, how's Jai?"

"Jessica, right, I'm afraid I have some terribly sad news." Michelle quietly answered the phone with a stretch and yawn.

"What happened?"

"He's still alive, but shortly after you left he went into cardiac arrest and they had to cut him out of his cast. However, because of that, his ribs were re-broken. His father is waiting for his wife to arrive later tomorrow before any decisions are made concerning Jai. Are you coming back in the morning?"

"In the morning, it's already morning." Jessica looked out the window to see the sun up in the morning sky.

"It's 2 a.m. here."

"Oh, I'm so sorry. I forgot about the time difference. I had an emergency trip out of the country. Our fight will be landing in Paris in about an hour, so I won't be there in the morning. However, I will be there as soon as my plane lands when I get back. Hopefully, Jai can pull through or at least hang in there until I can return. Is Mr. Hong okay?"

"Would you like to talk to him?"

"I don't think now would be a good…"

"Hello, is this Jessica? I'm Hong Jin, Jai's father."

"Mr. Hong, I'm so very sorry we have to speak for the first time in this manner. Your son was very honorable and respectful to me for the short time we knew each other. Hopefully, I will have a chance to see him again when I return."

"Where are you going, Ms. Jessica?"

"I have to take care of something in Africa. I should be back in a couple days. I'll talk to you later, okay? Bye." With that she hung up and returned to her seat. Feeling a little mischievous, she decided to have some fun. She read everyone's mind to see what they were dreaming about. Then she planted the idea all of them had to use the bathroom. She started laughing as everyone began to wake in a rush to the bathroom.

•   •   •

Royal Court and Snapdragon's flights both landed approximately the same time, one hour apart; Royal Court in Paris and Snapdragon landed in Cairo. Each was encouraged to see their respective city because of the long layovers. Royal Court only had a six hour layover while Snapdragon had ten.

Two hours later, two alarms went off in Miami; the first for Tetra Stack and the other for John Samson. Surprisingly, they continued the same routine they had done since when they were together. The difference was Tetra's home had an indoor track and gym, John's did not. He ran his neighborhood and worked out in his backyard, lifting weights and pounding a body bag.

Both were tired. Both could not stop thinking about their last days together. Tetra remembered going home finding him gone. Nothing was left of John except his scent on the pillow. She searched weeks to locate him. After three months, his number was disconnected. She lost touch for a couple years until she heard he was in Miami. She quietly moved there.

Tetra walked to her jewelry box. As she looked over her small treasure, she changed her mind. She went to her safe and opened it. Staring in, Tetra reached for a small box. She knew she had no other choice. Nothing else would do.

For John, it was the happiest and most destructive time in his life. He found the perfect woman. Tetra was smart and beautiful. He thought she was amazing, without any flaw. Friday night he was engaged. They celebrated though Sunday morning. She had come from the bathroom beaming when he got a call for an assignment. She wasn't too upset because she had something to do as well. By the end of the day, he was being told to take the shot. He was so devastated. The heartache was just as real in that moment as it was ten years prior.

•   •   •

In Paris, the Royal Court made their way to the Eiffel Tower. After their meal they went to the upper observation deck. Duncan noticed some photographers taking pictures of Esther. Duncan and Matt approached one.

"Hey buddy, what do you think you're doing?"

"I'm sorry, but the mademoiselle, she is so beautiful. I must have her model for me. She is so exquisite."

"You take one more picture and I'll throw you over the side!"

"Is this guy for real?" Esther asked Jessica.

Jessica started laughing after she looked around. "This idiot thinks you are glowing like a goddess. It's almost like he's obsessed with you. He thinks you're none other than the Egyptian goddess, Isis."

"Girl, you are looking radiant." Traci interjected.

"Duncan, sweetie, let him be. He will print these pictures and they'll all come looking for me. I'll be paid."

Duncan walked to the railing with Matt and Chase. He was angry for being dismissed as he was. Suddenly, an explosion at the base of the tower caught everyone's attention. Scream yelled for Blink to get them down to the ground. Blink grabbed her and Psychosis and teleported safely to the ground. Sprint ran down one of the legs. Tank and Tower jumped over the side.

Once on the ground, the scene was clear. A local deputized mutate was trying to apprehend some criminals. He was walking over to the crashed vehicle. Scream ran over to the Mutate and started yelling at him for ruining her perfect day in Paris.

"Mademoiselle, if you will pardon me, I need you to step back. I have a job to do. These are dangerous criminals, again if you will excuse me."

Scream was so irritated because she was ignored; she spun him around, grabbed him on both sides of his head, and screamed a sound blast directly to his face. Her scream ruptured all the capillaries in his head. She threw his limp corpse to the ground. She looked around to crowd. With a booming voice she yelled to them.

"This is what will happen if you defy the Royal Court."

"You know these people don't speak English, right?" Jessica yelled back at Esther.

"Oh yeah, you're right. Come on guys, let's get outta here."

Blink grabbed Sprint and told him to go to the airport, off he went. Blink then teleported each of the other members back to an airport bathroom. Chase met them as they came out.

An hour east, Snapdragon was slowly enjoying her tour. She was relaxed and kept to herself. The tour was doing her some good. She climbed the pyramids, petted the Sphinx, and sailed the Nile. She was having a great day.

Meanwhile, in Thailand, a woman and her son were going to the airport. They began their journey to America and left Master Cea in charge per her husband's request. After they realized the true danger they were in, Guo and Kwan made a hasty escape. Unknown to them, they were spotted entering the woods.

"Zufu, Commander Tahaan has left taking the one called Kwan with him." Lahan proclaimed as she approached her grandfather.

"Tam, take some men and go after them. Bring them back. If they resist, kill them." Tam left immediately. "Lahan, gather the rest in the courtyard then make sure the women have the meals ready."

• • •

"Look, there's a cottage." Kwan spoke up.

The two men quickly reached the cottage. As they knocked on the door, an angry young man stained with blood answered. They saw a dead woman on a bed. They instantly accused the young man of killing her.

"I didn't do this. She's my sister. I came home to surprise her for dinner. I found her hanging from the ceiling with animals eating off of her." He looked at the two men angrily. "Perhaps you're the ones that did this to my sister." Zeng Sun, Nak Kian's brother, challenged and attacked Guo and Kwan without mercy or restraint.

After several minutes, Tam Lai and four men arrived on the scene. He ordered the men to use their bows and fire on all three men. One of the men fired early. His arrow flew between the three men, warning them of their imminent doom. All of their attention was drawn to the line of fire. Kwan's quick thinking allowed him to push back Zeng and cover Guo. All the arrows hit Kwan.

"Kwan!!!"

"Go help Chi…" Upon hearing this Zeng realized he was fighting potential allies. Seeing the others coming, he pulled Guo behind the cottage for cover.

"Are you trying to help Zhe Duan Chi?" Zeng Sun questioned Guo. He nodded in response. "Follow me." Zeng went back to face his attackers grabbing an arrow from Kwan in the process. Guo followed.

Zeng and Guo confronted Tam Lai and his men. The four archers were already drawn.

Tam smiled. "Do you really think you can win?" He then stared at Zeng.

"Who are you to presume my defeat?" Zeng countered.

Guo answered Zeng. "This is Tam Lai, Lord Chai's chief lieutenant. He collected the tribute for Lord Chai."

"You know who he looks like?"

"Yeah, the resemblance is uncanny. However, I don't think you have a chance, this time." Guo calmly responded to Tam's question. "Let us go. They won't say anything. By the look on his face I think he just realized who you really are; the decisions yours." Guo Tahaan stepped back away from everyone only to lean against a tree.

"Kill'em both!"

·   ·   ·

"Luna, what am I going to do?"

"Tetra, you know what to do. Your father is right. Come clean. Tell the truth instead of hiding behind your secrets. It will be better that way. It won't be easy, but it will be better."

"You sound just like your father."

"No, he would have said, 'Always tell the truth, life's more fun that way.'"

"You right."

"Promise me you will call him when we hang up."

"Fine." They said their goodbyes and hung up.

Across town, John didn't recognize the number calling his phone. He thought it was Dr. Seba's office confirming his appointment but he was wrong.

"Please, don't hang up."

"What do you want, to hurt me some more."

"No, to explain, can we meet this morning?"

"I can't. I have an appointment at the hospital at ten."

"What's wrong?"

"Not your concern."

"Fine, there's a diner three blocks from the hospital. If we leave now, we can meet there. I only need twenty minutes."

"I'll be there in fifteen."

"See you then."

• • •

Royal Court happily escaped Paris in route to Madagascar. Snapdragon was back in the air. She too was happy. She saw Egypt, or at least Cairo. Her day was very relaxing until she went shopping in the market. Some kids tried to rob her. She laughed to herself as she thought back.

"Excuse me miss. Is this yours?" Snapdragon was caught off guard as a young man pointed to the chair next to her.

"Uh, no, you may have it."

"Good, I thought someone as beautiful as you would've had an army to protect you."

Snapdragon surprised herself because she wasn't angry and actually enjoyed the compliment. She smiled and said thank you. She then asked who he was. His answer made her burst with laughter.

"Right, Mr. Right."

While Snapdragon was laughing, his accomplices stole her bags. She invited him to stay for a bite to eat. He declined and said he really needed to go. She said bye. The boy walked off in the other direction.

When the waiter got back he warned her to check her purse and packages. He said 'Mr. Right' and his friends were thieves and to be careful. Snap quickly became aware she had been robbed. They didn't get her satchel because it was over her shoulder resting on her lap. However, the rest of her bags were gone. Angry she paid for her food and left.

Snapdragon searched an hour for Mr. Right. She eventually found him ducking down an alley with several other young men. When she entered their hideout she caught everyone off guard.

"May I have my stuff back?" She asked politely.

"I don't know what you're talking about." Mr. Right responded.

Snapdragon smiled and walked up to him. "You said you're my Mr. Right, right?"

"That's right, Baby."

Snapdragon smiled lovingly at him as she tightened her grip around his waist. "Can I please have my stuff back?"

'Sorry, Baby' was all he got out before Snapdragon flew straight up in the air with him. She counted to thirty and stopped.

"I can fly. Can you?" Snapdragon let him go. For ninety seconds they freefell two hundred feet per second together. She never felt so free. She had asked him again. He screamed she was freaking crazy. Her rebuttal was that she asked nicely.

"Okay, okay, you can have your stuff back, just don't let me die."

Snapdragon said thank you, brought him to a safe stop three feet above the ground, and then let him go. He was screaming even after he hit the ground. She landed while he backed away trembling in fear.

"He said I can have my stuff back." Everyone scrambled to get her stuff. After getting her bags she left for the airport thinking, he was definitely not Mr. Right.

CHAPTER 16
Second Chances

"Are you sure you want to start without Tetra?" Josh inquired of Mr. Wilson.

Lawrence A. Wilson, Esq. was the winningest attorney in Florida history. He is also the most expensive. His reputation for integrity is unrivalled. Prosecutors fear him, even his clients are afraid to lie to him.

"I've already spoken to Ms. Stack. Everything is going to be fine. She mentioned a medical report from last night."

"Yes, right here." Josh handed the report to the attorney. "Mr. Wilson, as you can see, the report says Alison doesn't show any more traces of mutated genes. According to the doctors, whatever happened last night gave her genetic code a clean slate. It's as if it's been burned or purged out of her system."

"That will still have to be verified."

"What's going to happen to me?" Alison Burns, the eleven-year-old escaped prisoner, requested of the lawyer.

"Now, as for you, Ms. Burns, what we have to do, is turn you in. You will be arraigned and either be sent to a juvenile detention center or a home for wayward girls, to wait for trial. I am going to do what I can to get you placed at Blue Wings Orphanage. Since your mother signed you over to be a ward of the state, I will not need parental consent to represent you. Therefore, I will be by your side the whole time. So there is no need to be afraid."

•   •   •

John saw Tetra standing outside of the diner as he drove into the parking lot. He thought she looked fidgety and nervous compared to her normal stoic and calm public demeanor. He admired her as if it were the first time he saw. He parked the car, took a deep breath, and got out.

"So what is it that you want to talk about?" John challenged Tetra as they walked toward each other.

"I just want to explain what happened."

"Alright, start talking."

"Not out here, come inside. You will understand better." Tetra pleaded with John.

"Tetra, I don't have time to take a trip down memory lane with you. I have things to do."

"Please John, it's important." Tetra reached for his hand because she was afraid he would walk away.

"Fine, lets' get this over with."

John snatched his hand back and walked into the diner. Tetra followed nervously behind him.

"Alright, so where are we sitting?"

"Down here."

Tetra moved passed John toward the table. Once they arrived, John saw a young girl sitting there. She was flipping through a photo album with newspaper articles and clippings. He noticed he was in most of the pictures. Suddenly, the girl got up after she saw John. She stood and saluted John with a big smile on her face. This caught both John and Tetra off guard.

"Abi, sit down, hon." Tetra said to the girl to encourage her to sit quietly.

Abi refused expecting to be saluted back. Tetra looked at John in desperation. He took a breath. He looked the girl in the eye and saluted her in return. Afterward, they all sat. Abi's face beamed with joy.

Angrily, John looked at Tetra. "Is this the reason why you called me here? To play soldier to one of your …"

"JOHN! She's …" Tetra quickly interrupted him before she herself was interrupted.

"Mommy says you're her favorite hero. She said you saved her life once. And you're a really good man and I should look up to you. She also said not to believe the reports on the news yesterday. They lied on everyone." Abi leaned in and whispered to John as she covered her mouth from Tetra. "I think mommy has a crush on you." She sat back giggling.

"Mommy? What's going on here?" John was confused as he looked at Tetra and the girl. Tears rolled down Tetra's face.

"Her name is Abinatu Lynn." She wiped her tears then continued.

"Lynn, that's my …"

"Yes, John, it's your mother's name. She is the reason I called for the meeting that night and this morning. I wanted to let them know why I was leaving."

John leaned back and quietly listened. The realization of the conversation slowly sank in. He briefly reflected back to when he first met Tetra. They were at a bar in Cairo. He was on leave. He had been watching her dance all night. She was out with her girlfriends. Every guy in the place tried to talk to her except for him. He was nursing his third beer when he felt a tap on his shoulder. When he turned around, John saw a very drunk Tetra standing there saluting him, wobbling and giggling. She asked the soldier boy to salute her back or dance with her. He did both after his buddies gave him a hard time. The rest was history. Now he was looking at the same glimmer in Abi's eyes.

Tetra continued as she put a small box on the table. "I found out two things that weekend. This ring told me how much you loved me. The morning after, I found out about her. I knew in that moment, I was the happiest a woman could be. You were going to be my husband and I was going to have your baby. Please understand I was walking away from them, not us. I had no choice; I had to get out so we could be a family; you, me and her."

Tetra grabbed John's hand and held it tightly as she also put arm around their daughter. She was afraid John was about to storm out in anger when Abi suddenly started screaming.

"You're my daddy! Mommy, he's my daddy! OH! MY! GOD! You're my daddy!"

Abi screamed again as she slid under the table to John's side. Aibnatu hugged her father for the first time. Any anger he was building up melted away every second she hugged him. He slowly hugged her back and began to weep as it sank into his soul that he almost killed her too. Tetra was relieved he didn't reject her. Applause erupted in the diner.

After a couple minutes, John pulled Abi away from him. "Ok, ok, we'll have time for a proper reunion later. I really must be going. I have something I have to take care of." He looked at Tetra. "I'm sorry I didn't stick around long enough for an explanation. When I got back, I was informed you were still killed. I wish you would have told me sooner."

"Well, as you know, once you took your shot, we were invaded. Your mole almost got the job done though. He was one of my advisors. I didn't think anything of it when he said to follow him so we could escape. As we reached the door, he turned and stabbed me several times. That bastard knew why I was leaving. Before he left, he knelt down and said things that were so cruel. When he heard the others coming he left. But yeah, I really almost died. The only thing that kept me going was my faith in this ring and her. I was so scared I was going to lose her. Instead, I lost you."

"That jerk came back bragging. He said you were begging for your life among other things. He actually helped me pick out the ring. He never once let on to me who you were. I found out later almost everyone else knew. I felt like such a fool."

"I'm so sorry you had to go through that."

"I felt a lot better after I broke his jaw and put his head in the soda machine. He was in the hospital almost six months. My record saved me from a court-martial, but I was immediately sent home. I know it's going to take some time, but will you give me a chance to make things right between us, that is, if there is no one else?" John reached for the ring and put it on Tetra's finger. The crowd waited with anticipation for her response.

• • •

In his persona of Marcus Ruger, Constellation decided to visit Jai at the hospital. He was greeted by Hong Jin and Michelle Zhu. Michelle spoke first after she recognized Marcus.

"Mr. Ruger, what brings you here?"

"We shared a flight from Thailand. We spoke of you Mr. Hong, and the fact that I made a lot of money betting on your fights. I also told him that you must be very proud to have such an intelligent son. He has a bright future ahead of him. I even offered him a job once he got settled. It was brought to my attention I was the last person to speak to him on the phone. I had set up an appointment with him to come in. He didn't make it. So, Ms. Zhu, why am I here? I'm here to check on a friend. As a business man, I'm here checking on an investment."

"Thank you very much, Mr. Ruger. It is very kind of you to take time out of your busy schedule to visit my son. However, he may not have much time left. When his mother and brother get here, we were talking about taking him off life support."

"Nonsense, I am so confident Jai will survive this, I brought a gift for him. It will make it easier for Jai to get around when he wakes up."

"Again, Mr. Ruger, you are too kind, but it was not necessary." Hong Jin replied to Marcus.

"It's my pleasure."

Marcus then walked over to Jai and placed his gift into Jai's right hand. It looked as if Marcus was examining him when he opened his eyes. "Everything is going to be fine." Marcus smiled.

Suddenly, Marcus stood straight. He slowly looked around the hospital room and left quietly. Michelle followed him to the door. She watched him get on an elevator before going back into the room.

"That was very strange." Jin said to Michelle as he moved to his son's side.

•   •   •

Halfway around the world, Tam and one surviving member of his team returned defeated. They knelt before Master Cea.

"Master," Tam spoke as he looked to the floor. "Commander Tahaan has gotten away. I believe they saw us coming and ambushed us. On a brighter note, Kwan was killed by this one."

"How can two men ambush five?" Lahan mocked Tam.

Tam glared back at Lahan before continuing. "Commander Tahaan, was somehow able to recruit the brothers and someone else. It's funny; he bears a striking resemblance to Tufei."

"Cowards run and the dog comes back pulling his tail between his legs." Lahan looked down on Tam Lai in disgust.

Tam Lai stood and faced her. "What's your problem?"

"I was bored, so I read the scroll in the lobby. Guess what I found out. I found out what triggered her and caused her to slaughter us. It was YOU! You deserved what happened to you! We didn't! I DIDN'T!"

"Enough!" Master Cea commanded capturing everyone's attention. "We will find Zhe Duan Chi in the land of America. I will put an end to her. She will suffer far greater than when she was in the lake. She... Will... Die..."

Tam Lai looked around as he noticed the people of the school started to drop to the ground dead. Once the dying stopped, there were seven men and three women still alive. Through it all, Master Cea and Lahan remained calm. The rest were scared. Of the survivors, Master Cea, Prince Thi Tai, Tam Lai and Lahan, two women personally chosen by Cea and the prince, and four men. One of which was still loyal to Chi.

•   •   •

"The time has come to separate ourselves. Constellation was right about one thing. In time past, the gods themselves prayed to us for power. No matter where someone was in the universe, all looked up to us, without fail. Before life, we were. When it ends, we shall remain. Man will learn what the gods fear. Nothing exists without us. We bring to light what is in the dark and when we remove our light, darkness is the master at our will. It matters not to me, whether this constellation has a place in our universe or not. We gave Ophiuchus a place to be, because we took pity on him. He knew this and manipulated his way to a throne too great for his small mind. I say, we put an end to the façade of his rule and remove him from his space.

What say you?" Aries expressed his discontent with Constellation to his fellow Zodiacs after he called for a meeting.

"I agree with Aries. He's the smallest of us. He's even betrayed us to the gods and devils alike, allowing them to ignite their own legacies amongst us." Taurus proclaimed.

In unison, Gemini declared they couldn't make up their mind yet. However, Scorpio was all too eager to continue the rant. "Precisely, he's been trying to wedge himself between us for eons and all he has among us is his foot."

"Because of that, he thinks he's above the rest of us. My bow is ready to take him from amongst us." Sagittarius raised his bow and fired a new comet into the night sky.

Aries spoke again. "That's four, who desire separation with one undecided; what about the rest of you?"

Virgo smiled. "He loves me."

Aquarius interrupted Virgo. "But he prefers me."

"That's because you prostituted yourself to him. All the while, he steps over you to me."

"Prude!"

"He doesn't care about either of you. He only cares about that serpent of his." Libra weighed against both; Virgo and Aquarius. "My vote will balance with the majority."

"Why are the two of you even bickering over him? He's betrayed each of you with the other as he has done with the rest of us as Taurus has already said. Besides, every time he is around we somehow become lesser than what we were." Leo roared in.

Capricorn quietly speaks to Aquarius. "I think Libra has a point. As you know, he wants us to find another Pandora. All he wants is his weapon free so he can try to keep us in line. If Megoon Dracul is free, I fear the worst, not for us, but our followers will get caught in the middle. I'm sorry I believe it's time for him to go. He has proposed himself a healer however his type of medicine is a venom to us all."

All attention turned to Cancer when she said, "Why don't we use his own pet against him?"

"There will be two ways that could go." Pisces answered. "First, we are able to successfully beguile the serpent and use it against its master, but the problem may come when it's time to put it back to sleep. Second, we can't beguile it and he uses it against us. Will it really be worth the risk?"

"I believe we can cast a vote now." Aries announced. "Stand if you are in agreement." Aries was the first to stand. After looking around, others stood as well. Slowly, all stood, understanding the truth was greater than any personal feelings. Unified they condemned Constellation to become a void.

CHAPTER 17
Order in the Court

"How can we help you?" A nurse questioned the frail older man in front of her.

"I'm here to see Dr. Seba," the man responded softly.

"Do you see that lady with those guys over there?" The man turned slowly to look. "Go over there and have a seat. Someone will be out shortly.

"Is there any paperwork for me to fill out?"

"Sir, just go over there and have a seat. Someone will be out shortly. Can I help the next person?"

After a few minutes the old man was able to sit down. When he got comfortable a young woman came out to get the four of them. As John got up, he told the woman something has come up and now wouldn't be a good time for him. However, she insisted he still talk to Dr. Seba. John hesitated, but then agreed.

•   •   •

"All rise. The court of the Honorable Lyda Justice is now in session." The bailiff barked to the gallery. After sitting, the judge told everyone else to sit.

"Bailiff, what's first on the docket?"

"Well, you remember the fugitive that escaped the other day?"

"Yeah, what's your point?"

"S.H.A.R.P. agents are bringing her up now."

As he finished his statement a door opened. Two agents were leading a twelve-year-old girl into the courtroom. One, lead her by a rod attached to a collar and the other was in the rear rushing her with an electric prod to the back. Even with a cast on her arm her hands were locked inside an iron box. She moved slowly because her legs were shackled in iron boots. The other accessories she had on were the neuro-collar to block any special abilities she may have, a gag ball strapped to her mouth to prevent her from speaking, and finally blinders so she couldn't see anyone.

A woman in the gallery started screaming monster as she held a young woman wrapped in bandages. This led to the crowd to become unruly to the point they were throwing things at the girl and demanding the court to execute the demon child.

The gavel hammered down several times to restore order. "Order in the court, I will have order in this court or I will clear this place out." The judge then turned her attention to the bailiff. "Is all this really necessary?"

One of the S.H.A.R.P. officers spoke up. "Yes, Your Honor, its' victims are here as you can see. They are scared and have reason to be. We took the utmost precautions to make sure you and the rest of us humans are safe."

"Very well, proceed. I was informed she had an attorney. Where is he?"

"I believe Mr. Wilson realized he is going to lose this case and decided to jump this sinking Titanic." The prosecutor exclaimed mockingly as he pointed to the defendant.

"Well then, the young lady still needs representation. We will have to postpone until she has proper representation or someone who can speak on her behalf."

The same woman that called the girl a monster stood to speak on her behalf to condemn her. "I can do that Your Honor, and she would like to plead guilty and receive a punishment befitting something like her for her crimes against real human beings."

The people in the courtroom erupted again. The judge slammed the gavel several times. "I am not going to repeat myself. Ma'am, how is it you call this girl a monster and then proclaim to be able to speak on her behalf?"

A man slipped in the courtroom as the woman started to speak. "My name is Connie Burns. This is my daughter. I can therefore speak on her behalf."

"Actually, no ma'am, you can't. You gave up the right to your fraudulent claim the moment you made her a ward of the state. Now, if you like, I can talk to the prosecutor on your behalf and work out a deal concerning your guilty plea for perjury. You did after all just lie to this court. Or, would you like to recant your testimony as to your claim of being the mother of my client?"

"Mr. Wilson, are you done with your theatrics?"

"No, Your Honor, I want to know why my client has been brought into this court bound up like some kind of rabid dog or gimp. What are you trying to push to have her executed as a sacrifice on your bench!?"

"Mr. Wilson, that's enough!!!"

"Is it? Or is the pending lawsuit against you and everyone else in this building for obstruction of justice and deliberately endangering the welfare of a minor enough, starting with you!" He pointed directly at Connie Burns. She quickly and quietly sat down holding her bandaged daughter again.

"I said that's enough or do you want to be held in contempt." Mr. Wilson remained silent as he approached his client with a smile. "Bailiff, remove the restraints."

"I object. What about the safety of the people of this courtroom?" The prosecutor challenged the ruling.

"Sustained, take everything off except for the collar. Dogs still need to remain on a leash. So, will that make everyone happy?"

"Thank you, safety first." Wilson mocked the judge and the prosecutor. After a few minutes the courtroom returned to normal. L.A. Wilson., Esq. was now ready to represent his client, Alison Burns. When she returned to her seat she thanked her lawyer.

"What was so important you were late?" The judge demanded an answer.

"My apologies, Your Honor, I was securing a sworn affidavit concerning her medical report she received from the examination of her broken wrist which claimed she was not a genetic mutate."

"So did you get it?"

"Yes, Your Honor, right here." A copy of the report was given to both the judge and the prosecutor.

"As you can see, Your Honor, with all the genetic mutates popping up all the time now, there rose a need to create a standardized test. That test is to check to see if a person is a carrier or mutated by the genetic marker. This report clearly shows my client; Ms. Burns is clean and clear of any such marker. Therefore, my client is NOT, and I repeat NOT a danger to herself or anyone else. It further shows a 0.0001% chance of her ever being able to develop any kind of special abilities in the future. I would almost dare say she was framed if it weren't for her own confession. That being said, as far as the charges go, my client does understand people were hurt. However, she had no part in her escape other than being a scared little girl being helped out of a scary situation by someone who had compassion for her. Since Ms. Burns came in of her own free will, I believe it is in the best interest of justice those charges be dropped. And still, with my client willing to except responsibility even at the age of twelve; says multitudes for her character; especially seeing how she was deliberately and brutally mistreated this very morning, even within the last half hour in your courtroom. So much for innocent until proven guilty, this is more like a witch hunt for the circus. And everyone here wants to burn her at the stake without knowing any facts. Honestly, I'm surprised this courtroom isn't handing out torches."

The judge slammed the gavel again on Mr. Wilson. "Watch yourself! I suggest you get to your point real soon or you might find yourself next to your client." Libra was instantly irritated.

"My point is my client, Ms. Burns, is willing to plead no contest on the condition of probation until she is sixteen. Furthermore, since she doesn't have any living family to go home to or with, it is recommended she be emancipated and placed at the Blue Wings Orphanage. And to also please the court, she will also agree to be genetically tested twice a year until she is eighteen. Should no other occurrences happen between now and her eighteenth birthday; her record be expunged. This is so she may be able to enter the world of adulthood with a clean slate."

"Do you understand what's going on young lady?"

"A little." Alison responded timidly.

"What Mr. Wilson is saying or proposing is you are excepting responsibility for what has transpired. However, with the evidence he brought forth, he's asking for mercy. You still confessed to committing a crime. Do you understand you still have to be punished for what you've confessed to?"

"Yes, ma'am."

"Does the prosecution have any objections to the recommendations by Mr. Wilson?"

"In light of the evidence, no, Your Honor." The prosecutor was clearly upset that he had to eat his words.

"The court accepts the plea of no contest and the following order to be carried out: four years of probation; genetic testing every six months until the age of eighteen; and on Ms. Burns' eighteenth birthday with no other occurrences with the law, Ms. Burns, your record will be expunged. So as

Mr. Wilson so eloquently put it, you get a clean slate." Judge Justice hammered the gavel once to put the order into motion. Alison started crying because she was happy.

"As to the matter of emancipation, the one thing you and I agree on completely is that Ms. Burns has no definition of family in her life. Upon completion of your probation, Ms. Burns, you will be legally emancipated from your past." Libra looked over at Connie Burns. "Mrs. Burns, you are despicable human being. I am embarrassed to call you a mother, or even a woman for that matter. To hate your own child the way you have demonstrated is unfathomable, but you somehow made it reality. Mr. Wilson, have you contacted Blue Wings to see if they even have a bed for her?"

"Yes, Your Honor, they said they were going to send over a representative to help Ms. Burns with her transition."

"Bailiff, see if the representative has arrived."

The bailiff left for a few minutes. Connie Burns with her remaining daughter left with him. When he returned, the patron and founder of the Blue Wings Orphanages entered the courtroom. Adanore Cromore was a powerfully built man. He wore a black silk suit with a blue sapphire silk tie. He had light brown skin, blue eyes, and long white hair. His appearance and stature was both foreboding and intimidating.

Adanore looked directly at Libra. Judge Justice looked terrified. Seeing the expression on the judge's face; everyone look to the door. The bailiffs and the two S.H.A.R.P. agents went to intercept him, suddenly they stopped with the realization of suffering was at the end of their decision.

No one heard the exchange of words that passed between Lyda and Adanore.

"Guardian, what are you doing here? It wasn't necessary for you to come. The situation really isn't that important. She's fine. Look, she's fine."

"I've come to see the Scales of Justice are truly balanced and to remind you and your kind of who hung the stars. And to inform you an example has been decided."

Fear overcame Libra, as Adanore took one step forward; Judge Justice quickly called for a recess and left the bench stumbling. Adanore smiled as he walked over to Alison to introduce himself.

"Do I want to know?" Lawrence asked.

Adanore simply smiled and continued his conversation as he walked Alison out of the courtroom.

•   •   •

Meanwhile in the skies above Madagascar, two planes were trying to land. The first to land carried the Royal Court. About forty-five minutes later Snapdragon landed. Unbeknownst to either, their final destination of the night was going to be under the same roof.

Having rested on the flight Jessica decided to go see if the hotel restaurant was still open. To the back of the restaurant was a bar with one customer. The bartender rushed to greet her. He sat her at a table near the bar and handed her a menu.

"What would you like to drink?"

"I hear the water is good." The man at the bar interjected.

"That actually sounds good; ice water with extra lemon."

"Very good ma'am, I will be right back to take your order."

Jessica was surprised she wasn't able to look into the mind of the man at the bar. She became very angry at the thoughts of the bartender concerning her. To retaliate, she mentally tripped him as he brought her drink. He got up apologizing and quickly refilled her drink. When he brought out her sandwich and fries she did the same thing.

"You don't like him much do you?" The voice at the bar spoke again as the bartender went back to fix another plate.

"He's very disrespectful."

"I know, much like your friend."

"Yeah, but he got a beat down for his lack of respect. I didn't do it, but he is getting better. How do you know that and why can't I read you?"

"I'm not letting you."

Jessica had quickly grown tired of having a blank conversation and decided to go up to the bar.

"Who are ... you?" Jessica stopped cold when she realized who he was.

"A friend, maybe an enemy; you choose. My friends call me Charlie. Why don't you call me Charlie and toast to new friendships." Suddenly, a glass of lemon water appeared in Jessica's hand.

Jessica drank the water and asked her *new* friend a question. "If you know we're here to kill you, why? No, how does that song go? Oh, yes. Why would you offer your throat to the wolf with the red roses?"

Charlie smiled as he felt the blade of a knife pressed against his throat. Instantly, he disappeared and reappeared beside Jessica, holding three red roses.

"I should ask the same, but I'm not here for that." He then threw the roses to Jessica's table. "I'm here for something else. First, to let you know I'm not afraid of you or your friends. Second, offer you a gift, but I warn you, it comes with a cost. And it is painful."

"And what is it?" Psychosis turned to face her adversary.

"Before we get to that," Charlie handed her a yellow snapdragon flower. "You and she have the same desire. The rest, don't. You might want to help her out, just saying."

Charlie started to leave the restaurant when he flicked something over his shoulder and into her glass. He continued walking as he spoke once more. "Here's a little something for you if you're willing to accept the cost."

He stopped for a moment and held out his hand. The cane resting against the bar vanished and appeared in his hand. Jessica thought it reminded her of a unicorn's horn with a pearl the size of a golf ball on top. It had a silver cap with veins of silver running in the valleys of the horn up to the pearl.

Jessica looked in the glass to see a ring. When she looked up Charlemagne was gone.

"I'm so sorry miss, here's your meal and don't worry there's no charge."

"I think the guy at the bar forgot to pay his tab before he left, because we were talking so I'll take care of his if you like so you don't get into any trouble for a ditched check."

"Miss, you must be seriously exhausted from jet lag. You've been my only customer since two."

Jessica sat with her glass and placed the flower on the edge of her plate. She ate her food quietly staring at a ring in the bottom her glass given to her by a man who wasn't there. The ring was a silver band with a solid black diamond encircling the band. On three locations equally spaced was the Greek letter Psi embedded with gold in the black diamond.

"Jessica, there you are. Are you going to get any sleep? I've set up an open air jeep rental for our trip tomorrow, well today. We leave in a few hours at eight-thirty."

Jessica watched Esther come in. When she got to the table she thought Jessica looked like she was about to pass out, the truth was she was seriously distracted by her encounter. Before going to her room Jessica casually drank the rest of her water while grabbing a napkin. She wiped her mouth and put the napkin in her pocket.

As the elevator doors closed, Jessica kept to herself that she saw Snapdragon walk into the hotel. Her thoughts went to the flower lying on her plate.

•　　•　　•

"Calm down. You have a right to be upset. There is no need to be hysterical, okay? We'll talk later. Get some rest." Capricorn hung up the phone.

"Who was that?" Aquarius perked up with the hope of gossip.

"That was Libra. She had a surprise visitor in court this morning and she is freaked out. Although after talking to her I've got a sheepishly perfect idea."

"Do tell."

•　　•　　•

After getting help from the Burazai brothers, Zeng Sun decided to help them in return. He, himself, was going to Japan, so he decided to help them get home as well. Zeng took everyone to a hotel while he got the proper papers for all of them. While out, he contacted a friend in Japan. Soon Ye was a professor at the University of Kyoto. She studied the history of warfare in Asia. She was always on the hunt for rare artifacts.

"Kyoju Ye, have you found it?" Zeng inquired.

"What are you talking about? What was I supposed to find?"

"Hyaku Atama."

"I told you before that sword is a myth. How many times do I have to tell you it is not real; it does not exist." Kyoju Ye rebuffed Zeng.

"Fine, one can hope. Anyway, I'm heading back to my sister's place. She was so full of life when I saw her. Everything here is so easy going. I have to stay a while."

"I'm so happy for you. Well I got a few things to handle here at the school. Take your time and I will talk you later."

"Ok, later." Zeng hung and turned to his friend. "Hey Papers, how much longer?"

"Three days. What's the hurry? You wouldn't rush Van Gogh or Di Vici. Art takes times."

"Fine, but I got a blow torch on both ends of this candle."

"Don't worry my friend, I gotcha. Sorry about your sister."

"Yeah, thanks." Zeng Sun left quietly. He went to the market for food then back to the hotel.

CHAPTER 18

Didn't See That Coming

"John, please pick up the phone. I'm worried about you." Tetra stared at her phone after she ended her call. She worried he had rejected them, or maybe something happened. She didn't know.

"Ma'am, your father is here." The housekeeper announced.

"What does he want now?" Instantly irritated, Tetra wiped her tears. She composed herself and put on her game face. She took a deep breath to release her emotions before seeing her father. Tetra thought about how he was so immature with his nonchalant attitude toward everything.

"What can I do for you today, I'm busy?" Tetra responded to her father's surprise visit.

"I came to see how you were, and to see my granddaughter."

"She's on a school field trip to a museum. Besides, I have a lot of work to do today. So, what do you really want?"

"Like I said, I've come to see you and Abi."

"Oooh." Tetra stopped what she was doing to look at Ren. She went to her bar and poured herself a double of whiskey, drank it down, and slammed the glass so hard it broke.

"I know why you're here. You're leaving, AGAIN! You just stopped by to see how I'm doing. Bull! At least you're willing to see me before you just up and leave." Tetra poured another drink then continued her rant.

"Where are you going this time? South America, Asia, perhaps your precious Conclave? Nooo, I know where you're going, Antarctica to the South Pole. You'll finally have a conversation at the bottom of the world with someone who actually cares." Tetra poured again.

"There's no one living at the South Pole."

"That's my point, Father. God, you are the definition of dense. You stick around long for someone to care then poof, you're gone. Like I said, at least you come to tell me."

"What's that supposed to mean?"

"None of your business."

"You're the spitfire of your mother." Ren smiled as he watched his daughter.

"Oh, hell no," Tetra said under her breath as she threw her glass at her father. He casually caught the glass saving the whiskey. "Leave my mother out of this. You don't have the right to bring her up. It's because you she's dead. I have a question, actually two."

"What's that?"

"Of all the children you've had, how many of their mothers survived birth? And how many of those children did you abandon, when they needed you most."

"Tetra, we've talked about this. It's not something I talk about with my children."

"ANSWER THE QUESTION!" Tetra screamed at her father.

"I haven't seen you like this since..."

"Don't you dare!"

"John, you saw John? Did you tell him?" Ren completely changed the subject as if nothing previously was said.

Tetra sat down. "Yeah, I saw him. I took your advice and did one better. I introduced John to his daughter."

"He fell in love with her instantly, didn't he?" Ren smiled.

"I don't know. I haven't seen or heard from him since. He said he had to leave for an appointment. He left and now he's gone. If it weren't for Snapdragon and her drama, I'd still have Stack Foundation up and functioning. Now, if it weren't for listening to you, my daughter wouldn't have to grow up wondering if there was something she did wrong to make her father not love her enough to stay. I guess the old saying is true; like mother, like daughter." Tetra glared at her father fighting back tears.

"Well, at least she has me. I didn't have a mother remember." Tetra was broken. She grabbed a pillow from her sofa and sobbed hard into it.

Ren sat beside Tetra and hugged her. "Don't worry I will take care of this."

"What goes on with John and I is none of your business? You never cared about anything before, no need for you to start now."

"Sweetheart, I care very much for you and you are always going to be my business." Ren got up to leave.

"Where are you going?" Tetra looked up at her father wiping the tears from her face.

"Something, I should have done ten years ago; have a talk with your boyfriend about breaking my little girl's heart. After I deal with him; I have to go to Africa to look into something that's come up." Without missing his stride out the door, "By the way, it's for one of my many children I've abandoned. I'm going to go watch over your sister."

"Don't you; what, I have a sister? Where? Who is she? Who's my sister? How can I find her?" Tetra ran after her father with more questions than before.

• • •

"Alright everyone, I know it's early but all of us are being treated to a football game by Mr. Cromore. We are flying to Jacksonville in an hour. I have the itinerary. Once we arrive, we'll be going to a candy factory, the InterActive Children's Museum, and then we'll have lunch. After lunch we'll be on our way to Dolphin Playground and swim with the dolphins. When we are done there, we go back to Jacksonville and watch Miami kick their butts. One more thing, our seats are on the fifty yard line and to top it off, all of us are going to be on the field calling the coin toss before the game. What do you think about all of that?"

Every kid raced to their room to get ready. Two hours later they landed in Jacksonville. They were greeted by Miss Hapi. She held a sign that read 'Blue Wings'.

"Good Morning. Everyone, I am Miss Hapi. That's one 'P' and an 'I' no 'Y'. I'm with Comet Tours; in a fast moving world, we help slow you down. My associate Miss Capri is at the InterActive Children's Museum preparing something special for you guys. So she'll join up with us there. Until then who's ready for some candy."

The kids screamed and cheered. Two staff members from the orphanage helped to get the kids on the bus Mr. Vince and Ms. Parker. Once on the bus Miss Parker spoke to the kids.

"Alright everyone, Mr. Cromore wants us to be on our best behavior. He also wants you to have as much fun as you can. You bigger kids should look out for the little ones. Remember what Mr. Cromore always says, 'Family is more than blood, more than who you choose to grow up with, its loving and caring for those that don't know they need your help. Alright everybody, let's do this." She quickly took her seat and off they went.

•   •   •

"Hello, is there anyone here?" A young man slowly opened his eyes to a blurred scene in his room. He struggled, a little, as he realized he was in a body cast.

"Jai, can you hear me, son?" Hong Jin rushed to his son's side.

"Father, she's real. She saved me."

"I know son. Just relax and I will get someone." Jin quickly left the room in search of a nurse. Jai smiled as he felt something in his hand and gripped it tight.

Ms. Zhu walked over to Jai. "I'm glad to see you awake. Your father was worried. I reassured him you were strong and would pull through. You had another visitor. Mr. Ruger stopped by to bring you something to help you get around once you got home. Speaking of which, I have the keys and paperwork for your new home. So, you have nothing to worry about."

Jai weakly smiled back at her.

•   •   •

In his office at *Gene*Tech, Dr. Seba was interrupted from his research as the intern, Dr. Marci Athene, entered.

"Dr. Seba, we have the last of the subjects ready."

"Very good Dr. Athene," Dr. Seba looked up from the paperwork on his desk.

"Dr. Seba, are you sure we have the right test subjects?"

"Of course, the key is looking for who can fill the parameters for each experiment. For the project to work we have to be willing except whatever 'X' factor we come across. In this case, it's our subjects. All we have to do is trigger the right genomes and release the '*DNA of the Gods*'."

"Have you calculated if the bodies reject perfection?"

"Yes, should any of the subjects reject the procedure then they are replaced with one more suitable. Do we have any back up supply?"

"Yes sir. We've had a few volunteers. Plus, we should receive a new shipment in the morning. That would make about seventy or eighty potential subjects including those including those that didn't make it."

"Good, we can start again when Marcus arrives."

CRASH!

"Dr. Seba, did you hear that?"

Yes, I did." He responded while reaching for his handgun in his bottom drawer.

CRASH!

The next thing they knew, a twelve foot creature pushed through the walls. Its appearance was that of an earthen-stone creature on fire. It had hands and feet of water. Its mouth and eyes crackled with electricity. It made its way to the labs and storage areas. It released the subjects and destroyed the process.

The guards with Dr. Seba fired upon the creature to no avail. Dr. Athene grabbed a fire extinguisher and tried to put out the fire in the office and labs as well as the creature. She was smashed with a table in response.

•   •   •

"We can hold your room for another night, if you like? And will you need a car rental?" The front desk clerk asked Snapdragon since she was leaving for the day.

"No, I think I will just fly up to Antisiranana."

"Would you like a driver to take you to the airport?"

"That's not necessary."

"Very well ma'am, enjoy your day out."

"Thank you." Snapdragon said goodbye to the clerk and left.

She flew north as soon as she walked clear of the hotel. She loved flying. For her it was freeing. People looked like ants, where the cars and buildings looked like toys.

Meanwhile, on RN4 a couple hours away, the Royal Court was already on the road to Antisiranana. Everyone was enjoying the trip. The temperature was perfect with a light breeze. They had the top off. They could see for miles. They thought Madagascar was beautiful. They had casual conversation along the way, talking about their desires and dreams. Everyone participated except Jessica.

Jessica was busy meditating on her new keepsake, truly oblivious to everything going on around her. She thought it strange, even though she was holding tightly to the ring; it was like it didn't exist at all.

"Anybody notice Jessica seems to be sleeping a lot more lately?" Matt asked the group.

Duncan smiled as he answered. "That's because she's tired, man. You know, aside from school she's got a fulltime job. Yeah, it's bad. You've got her working double and triple shifts. It's GOT to be exhausting rejecting you."

Everyone erupted with laughter and poured extra salt on the wound. Duncan had embarrassed and burned him good. It made Matt red in the face and very self-conscience because of the way he had been treating Jessica lately. He knew he deserved it, but thought the issue had died when he and

Jessica last talked about it. His encounter with Chi gave him a major dose of humility. Matt struggled with being alone.

"Pay no attention to him. She's just meditating. It's what she does now. Because she's psychic, she meditates to calm her mind." Traci explained to Matt about what was going on with Jessica. Matt nodded quietly.

While deep in meditation, Jessica didn't realize she slipped the ring on her finger. When she stopped, the ring was activated. Chase swerved to a stop before passing out as did everyone else within a thousand feet because Jessica screamed out in pain both mentally and physically.

The Psi-Ring locked itself onto Jessica's finger by burning through to the other side, crossways. Mentally, her mind expanded outward in a mind burst. She had been thinking about Jai when she put the ring on. To her horror she saw Snapdragon with Jai.

"I need to get out of here." Jessica struggled to remove her seatbelt. Flashes of her friends exploded in her mind as she looked at each of them. She knew their thoughts and their futures all at once.

Jessica climbed over the side of the jeep and ran into the field beside the road. Suddenly, she fell to the ground unconscious as well. After several minutes everyone started to come to except Jessica. They got to her side. A few minutes later she came to also.

"Jess, are you okay?" Traci questioned her friend.

"Yeah, I think so. I feel a little dizzy, but I think I'll be fine."

"What the hell was that? You really live up to your name, more *Psycho* than Psychosis but whatever. Why did you attack us like that? And it better be a damn good reason." Esther demanded an explanation from Jessica.

Matt helped Jessica to get up. She looked around at each of them before she began to speak. "I saw him die. We need to get back to Miami before she does."

Duncan was irritated and got in Jessica's face. "We got a job to do so you better start making sense or you'll be lumped with the rest and dealt with properly."

"Yeah, I'm kinda with them. What's the deal?" Chase, rubbed his head, chimed in more out of curiosity than anger.

"Yeah, I don't cosign any of that but I would like to know what just happened. That hurt, I still got a headache." Traci found it hard to concentrate.

Jessica angered by the interrogation kept the information about the Royal Court to herself, but pointed to the south while walking back to the vehicle. "Her; she is going to kill Jai. That woman has to be dealt with first." She was now more determined to fulfil her mission. She reached for the handle of the jeep then turned around and marched straight to Esther. Duncan attempted to step in front of Esther but was pushed aside without being touched.

"You think one more time for him to die is a good thing and it will be the last thought you have. Yeah, I wouldn't try that either." Psychosis glared into Scream shaking her head before turning her back to Esther.

CHAPTER 19

Stardust

The scene was grim. A caravan of ambulances was carting nearly a hundred men, women, and children away from *Gene*Tech. Police and fire departments were working hard at bringing order to the area by closing it off to everyone when a reporter was injured.

Jhaz Lee was a young African-American reporter doing her first live report when the incident happened. She had replaced Roja Domingo who was on special assignment.

While Jhaz was live; one of the fire trucks knocked down some power lines which fell and whipped around striking the young reporter. She was electrocuted instantly. The firemen scrambled to free her from the current. The cameraman continued to film the scene from a distance.

Not seen were the microscopic chemicals in the air around the building. Chemicals breathed in by Jhaz when she was electrocuted, it had an instant reaction. As her body hit the ground, Jhaz watched in horror. Her mind had somehow separated from her body.

Things felt different for Jhaz. After several minutes, she was able to gather her life energies to one location. If someone saw light in the right wave length, they would see a very weak and faint electrical form of Jhaz Lee. She tried to communicate with her camera man; however he couldn't see or hear her. Once Jhaz got her bearings she noticed her body was being placed with other dead bodies laid out on stretchers.

Jhaz saw Dr. Seba beside his assistant, Dr. Athene, as she was being placed into an ambulance by paramedics. At the same time, S.H.A.R.P. was hindering the police in their investigation. They claimed the police were out of their element and league in the investigation. Suddenly, Jhaz felt like she was fading and dying for real. She raced back to her body before dwindling away to nothing. She prayed as she lay down.

•   •   •

"Was all that really necessary?" Tetra pointed to the news report.

"You wanted to find him. So, I found him. And you are still not happy." Ren laid John on the sofa. He walked over to Tetra.

"I don't often have the luxury to stick around the way I'd like, so I do my best. I more than understand what means to be crazy about someone, one lifetime at a time; to hold your child's hand as he or she takes his or her last breath; generation after generation. Of the children given to me, four are still living. One is asleep because he couldn't fully control he was; another is imprisoned because she could. The third, she feels like you. She thinks I abandoned her. Yet, whenever she truly needed me I was there for her even though she didn't know it was me. Right now, she needs me. I'm here with you because you're my baby girl and you need too. For you, you will have a long life. You will watch him grow old and die and Abi, well, you will learn to understand what it's like to bury a child. Life diminishes with each progressive generation. Speaking of which, where did you say Abi went?"

"She went on a field trip with her class to the InterActive Children's

Museum."

"I really have to go. Take care of John. He needs you now. I promise we'll talk when I return."

"Father."

"Yes, dear?"

"Thank you."

"Yes, dear." Ren left quietly.

•   •   •

"Hello, Ms. Parker, can I help you with something." A young man at a small comic book shop around the corner from the IAC museum addressed Parker.

"I'm sorry, how do you know who I am?"

"The name badge is a dead giveaway." The clerk smiled at Parker.

"Oh dah, I forgot it was there."

"That's okay. What are you looking for?"

"I work at an orphanage. Bobby is one of the boys at the orphanage. He will be leaving soon. He collects comic books. I wanted to give him something special, something different."

"Do you know what kind he likes to read?"

"He just likes comics; I don't think it will matter to him. Maybe something knew, like hot of the press." Parker tried to sound witty with a cheesy smile.

"We did just get a shipment in. If you like, you can look through the stack and see if you see something he might like."

The clerk walked Parker over to the new comics. Flipping through she saw something that looked familiar.

"Hey, wait. My, well, ex-boyfriend talked about these."

"He and his new ho-bag girlfriend, Raven; they apparently loved these books." Parker's face got red as she rolled her eyes.

"You're a ho-bag?" The clerk snickered.

"What, NO, Raven's a ho-bag. I'm not a ho-bag. Are you calling me a ho-bag?" Parker babbled quickly.

"No, you said 'new ho-bag' as if you were the 'old ho-bag'."

"Oh, no, I'm not, but Raven is still a ho-bag."

"I tell you what. I'll sell you one to give to the Bobby. And, I'll give you the other one to rub in your ex's face."

"Deal, I have to get back to the museum before Vince loses one of the kids or they start to worry I got lost. I told them I had to use the bathroom. Now I really have to go." Parker paid for the comics. The clerk laughed as he showed her to the bathroom.

Meanwhile at the museum, Miss Hapi and Miss Capri walked the kids around the museum. They encouraged the kids to interact with the exhibits.

Miss Hapi slipped away to prepare the final exhibit.

"Alright children, let's gather together. We have a special surprise for you guys. We are going to the Dinosaur exhibit. And yes, it too is an interactive exhibit. That means we get to play with bones." Miss Capri was enthusiastic about the exhibit. She got the kids excited to go.

"Now when we get in here, Miss Hapi will have a challenge for you guys. Is everyone here?"

After looking around, only Ms. Parker was still missing. Miss Capri led the group into the exhibit. The doors were closed. A sign on the door read 'Exhibit Closed to the Public'.

"It looks like we're not able to do it today kids." Miss Capri was saddened by the sign.

"I knew we wouldn't see the dinosaurs." Kenny was heartbroken. He wanted to see the dinosaurs more than anything.

"I know it's not fair, but look how much fun we've had so far. Remember, after lunch we'll play with the dolphins and after that we're going to see a football game." Bobby gave Kenny a pep talk to help him feel better.

Miss Capri smiled mischievously as she spoke to the group again. "Does anyone know what the sign says?"

Bobby raised his hand. "It says 'Closed to the Public'. We're orphans not stupid."

"That may be true, but do you understand what that means for you?"

Miss Capri countered.

"Yeah, we're locked out."

"Nope, it means it's closed to the public. This is not a public tour. This is a private tour. Special arrangements were made so you guys will be the first to see the exhibit. That's what closed to the public means; a private showing. And you, Kenny, get to be the first one in." Miss Capri rejoiced with Kenny and gave him a high five.

She had Kenny knock on the door. Miss Hapi opened the door wide to let everyone in. Inside the room was a single dinosaur. It stood more than fifty feet tall and about a hundred and twenty feet long. The strange thing about this dinosaur was the bones; they were all black except one of its horns at the center of its forehead which was bright white. This particular dinosaur even had a skeletal structure that expanded out like it had wings.

Miss Hapi walked over to a portable elevator and got on. She raised it a few feet then began to speak.

"I want to tell you a very special story about this dinosaur. This skeleton has been classified as *Mávro Astéri Drákos* in Greek and *Stella, Nigrum Draco* in Latin. In English, it translates to the Black Star Dragon. Which means it is not a dinosaur at all, but a great dragon. It's one of a kind.

"According to legend, it was birthed when a quasar collided with a black hole, within the constellation *Ophiuchus*, collapsing both instantly. The energy released from it is what created Megoon Dracul. It's said the remnants of the black hole formed the serpent and the quasar formed the Nova Star. That's the white horn. As the story goes, Megoon Dracul drifted asleep for eons until Ophiuchus pulled the white horn from him tossed it across the sea of space. When he was free, he wreaked havoc in the universe at the command of his charming master.

"In a time before the Titans, Ophiuchus heard tell of a little blue planet where the indigenous people lived in fear and superstition. The people of this planet worship Ophiuchus and his council of twelve for fear of destruction. The council of twelve stretched forth their hands to rule the universe in the stars.

"Over time, champions searched for a means to stop the reach of Ophiuchus and his dreadful serpent. They came from all over the universe to meet their end at the hands of Megoon Dracul.

"There is an expression, 'When gods go to war; worlds get destroyed.' That being said, the earth was ravaged and tired. Ninety percent of the population fought and died. Before the pyramids were, a human was born empowered by the four elements rose to the challenge. Without interruption, the two warred against the other. The Grand Canyon was not created by a lazy river. It's the result of that epic battle. As the battle went forward, the human grew stronger and was transformed. He became the fusion of the four elements. Frustrated, Megoon Dracul changed from the humanoid form he had grown accustomed to back into the mighty dragon.

"Then one day a quiet individual came armed with his own serpent. He aided a rebellion against Ophiuchus from a distance. He found the Nova Star and brought it to Earth. Watching the battle he decided to through down the Nova Star between the two combatants. The human was able to wield it after returning to his human form. Instinctively, he knew where to strike. After many attempts, he struck home and sheathed Nova Star into the forehead of Megoon Dracul, the Black Star Dragon. It killed him instantly.

"As the story goes, each generation has stood as a protector of this world. His children had fought against Ophiuchus until he was banished from the earth. The legend says whoever can remove the Nova Star will have Megoon Dracul to command. The belief in this is so strong even one of the children of that human tried to free Megoon to destroy her father and failed. Does anybody have any questions?" Miss Hapi asked the group.

Bobby raised his hand again. "Has anyone ever been able to pull that thing from his head?"

"Not yet, but that's why we're here so each of you get a chance to try and be a real archeologist." Miss Capri spoke up.

"I have another question, is it true that thing will come back to life?"

"Of course not, remember it's a myth. Just something to scare you guys. Alright, who want to go first?" Miss Hapi asked.

"I'll go first." Bobby decided.

He rode the elevator up with Miss Hapi to the top of the skull. Nervously he pulled and shook the horn to no avail. Half way through, Parker managed to find way her back to the kids. She leaned against the door as she watched. She laughed when the other house attendant flex his muscles as he took his turn.

Miss Hapi smiled devilishly. "Hey kids, I bet I'm stronger than this hunk of muscles. I can lift him up with one finger." She said this as she squeezed Mr. Vince's bicep coyly.

"But first, let's see how strong you are." Miss Hapi asked if he was ready. She wrapped her hand around his arm and pickup her feet. As she swung on his arm Hapi squealed like a little girl.

Miss Capri yelled for her to get off his arm and the kids roared with laughter. Miss Hapi composed herself.

"Hey Ms. Parker, wanna go for a swing?" Vince flirted with Parker. The kids cheered on Mr. Vince.

"You might be strong, but there's no way you're strong enough to handle all this." Parker posed as she rebuffed Vince. The kids cheered Ms. Parker and jeered Mr. Vince.

Not happy being ignored, Miss Hapi spitefully interrupted the kids. "Are you ready to see me pick up this big galoot with one finger?"

Miss Hapi turned to Vince twisting his shirt with her index finger, she yelled to the kids. "Are you ready kids?" The kids cheered. She turned back to Vince. She whispered. "Are you ready? And I thought you were a keeper." Miss Hapi tugged his shirt and pushed the button to the lift at the same time. Everyone erupted except Vince who looked a little worried.

Capri felt like time was running out. "Before we go to lunch has everybody taken a turn?"

Bobby pointed out everyone took a turn except Kenny and Ms. Parker.

"Kenny, you go and then I'll go. Then we can all go to lunch."

"I don't want to."

"Come on buddy, everybody gets turn. Even the new girl Alison took a turn. I think you're the one to master that thing." Bobby encouraged Kenny. He conceded and went up.

Being the smallest, Kenny had to climb onto the head of dragon. As he put his hands around the horn it started to glow a bright white. Everyone stood in awe. Kenny became empowered to pull the horn. As he did, a rush of energy escaped. It knocked everyone down including Miss Hapi and Miss Capri. It slammed the door closed on Parker hard enough to knock her back more than twenty feet. The sound of the slamming shut echoed throughout the museum.

After a few moments, Parker got herself together. She ran to the door trying to force it open. She could hear the children screaming trying to get out.

Inside the room, Hapi snatched the Nova Star from Kenny. She pulled a sheath out to cover the Nova Star. With a blink she stood to the side of the room next to Capri. The two women smiled because of the cries for help in and outside the room. Poor Kenny was stranded on the lift panicking.

The room got quiet as parts of the structure holding Megoon in place started to fall. Parker could still be heard crying for help trying to get in.

The skeleton began to speak. "Who has released me?"

"We have and we present to you a peace offering. Behold a meal to restore your flesh."

Megoon saw Kenny pushing buttons trying to get down. He ate the boy quickly. A heart began to grow within its ribs. A minute later, Megoon

Dracul was fully restored. He roared and blew a cosmic blast at the rest of the children turning them to stardust.

Outside the room, Parker did everything she could to get in. She knew they were gone when she heard the screaming stop. Weak, she sobbed uncontrollably as she slowly slid down the door. Footsteps race down the hallway. Security guards tried to open the door, but it wouldn't budge. A small crowd grew when a crashing roar could be heard again.

Suddenly, the door opened, Parker got to her feet. Out came Hapi and Capri, Capri had what looked like a horned long sword strapped to her back as they moved through the crowd. When Parker looked in the room she saw a large hole in the ceiling and one of the walls. Upon entering, they saw perfect black statues of the children. She walked over to Vince who tried in vain to protect the kids. She touched his face and he started to collapse. Not realizing what happened, security pushed the door completely open; bursting through half of the children. A strong wind blew into the room. It stirred the air blowing through Vince and the remaining children into a black cloud of stardust.

The moment was surreal, time froze for Parker. The orphans were gone. She was led out of the room to the director's office. She sat quietly until someone came to pick her up.

However, upon exiting the museum, Hapi and Capri were blocked from leaving by bluish-white lightening striking the steps in front of them. They were surprised when Adanore Cromore showed up.

"What do you think you're going to do? They're already gone. So much for being a 'Patron of Orphans' you couldn't even protect them, what a joke; ain't that right, Hapi."

"Yeah, so you might want to flap away before we make you stardust like your precious orphans. It's not like they had any family that cared about them anyway." Hapi stepped closer. "Sooo…, if you don't want end up like them, MOVE!"

"I going to make this as simple as possible that fools such as yourselves; may have an inkling of understanding. I am here for the sword." Adanore mocked Capricorn and Aquarius.

"Or what? You know you can't win against us." Capricorn challenged.

"Sword, now, or you will not survive to your self-imposed banishment. I will not ask again. Besides, you know who I am." Adanore bypassed Aquarius and stepped straight to Capricorn and glared into her. "Do you really want to test that theory?"

Adanore held out his hand. Slowly and fearfully, Capricorn trembled as she surrendered to him the sword. Adanore left in the same manner to which he came.

Aquarius was furious. "What was that about? WHY WOULD YOU GIVE HIM THE SWORD?"

Capricorn stood speechless as a tear crawled down her face. Aquarius shook Capricorn. GemIni raced up the steps.

"Why are you here?" Aquarius looked down at GemIni.

"We felt you were in danger." Gem replied. Gemini touched both sides of Capricorn's head. They look at each other; then at Aquarius. Quietly together, "It's not good we need to gather the others."

CHAPTER 20

Double Header

Later in the day in Madagascar, Chi was flying north over the country side. She started to get hungry and decided to land for a bite to eat. She chose a spot outside of a small town. Chi landed in a wheat field. Walking out a few cars passed her.

Up ahead Chi saw an abandoned jeep parked partially in the wheat field. When Chi reached the jeep she noticed a man jogging towards her. He was carrying a red gas can. He stopped about forty feet from the jeep.

"Can I help you with something?" The tall man eyed her suspiciously.

"Is this your vehicle?"

"No, it's a rental that's out of gas." He approached holding up the gas can.

"I'm not from around here. I'm hungry. I thought you might know of a place to eat."

"Yeah, I know of a place in town. My friends are there waiting for me to get back. Let me fill up and I will take you there."

"Thank you."

The man filled the gas tank. He faked his attempt to start the vehicle, and pop the hood.

"Hey, come take a look at this."

Chi got out and walked to the front. "What's wrong?"

The man started laughing. "My friends thought we were out of gas. All it was; was a spark plug had vibrated loose. See?" He pointed to the engine.

Chi walked around see. As she leaned in the man slammed the hood down on her several times. Tower grew to his full height with Chi lying under the hood. Chi slowly slid from under the hood shaking off the attack. She barely turned around when a twenty foot Tower struck her to the ground. As she tried to get up he struck her several more times.

Tower started laughing over Chi. Chi became enraged, grabbed the grill of the jeep and swung it around hitting Tower square in the side. As he staggered to the left she swung around the other way and hit him again.

In town, Jessica started counting. "One... Two... Chase you need to get back to the jeep, the third one is really gonna hurt." She then continued to eat her fries.

Esther instantly looked worried. "Chase, go! Traci, get us there."

Jessica put down her burger. "I swear I can never finish a meal. Oh, well."

Back with Tower, Snapdragon not seeing Chase, she jumped up and slammed the vehicle onto Tower's head. Sprint rammed Snapdragon at full speed. It knocked the wind out of her sending her flying and tumbling backward more than a quarter mile. Sprint raced past her and came back for another strike sending her back toward Tower. He went full throttle at her. She was able to move fast enough to grab the jeep again with a full wind up smashed Sprint with a power swing. Upon contact, the jeep exploded into a thousand parts. With his forward momentum, Chase burst through making him tumble and bounce another mile before stopping.

Suddenly, a bruised and battered Snapdragon was surrounded by the rest of Royal Court. She looked around, when she saw Tank Snapdragon's eyes turned crimson and she let out a terrible roar. Before she could go after him, Scream snatched her to the ground by her hair. Psychosis tried to penetrate her mind but was unsuccessful. Scream jumped on top to hold her down and screamed with all the power she could muster to blast Snapdragon directly in the face. But, nothing happened.

Snapdragon was able to easily power through and pushed Scream up about fifteen feet before hitting her in the face with an energy blast of her own. It was so intense; it caught Scream's burned away her hair and melted portions of her face. She quickly scrambled to her feet to face Tank again when Blink touch her and sent her a thousand feet in the air not knowing Snapdragon could fly.

Snapdragon soared down to Blink. As soon as she landed she punched Blink with the same intensity as she hit Ba and Tank with. She broke the right side of her face and skull caving it in completely. Blink was hurdled limply into the field. Snapdragon stopped. She stared at Tank catching her breath.

"You will pay for what you have done to my champion."

"You will pay for what you've done to my friends."

As Tank charged Snapdragon, Psychosis was finally able to tap into her mind. With each successful strike Tank landed, Psychosis found out more information about Chi. She learned Chi was the statue Jai was thinking of while he was in his coma.

Tank struck and pounded away on Snapdragon. She realized quickly he hit almost as hard as she did. After about a half hour of battling back and forth, Tank was running out of gas. Psychosis did what she could to slow Chi down, but her mind became closed off again. At that point, she beat Tank unconscious. Psychosis hid herself away in the wheat field. Battered and bloodied, Chi staggered toward town. She looked at the decimation of the area. She felt pretty good about the fact that she hadn't had a fight this good in a while, she thought it was nice to be able to let loose. Chi actually appreciated the fight being able to work out her frustrations. Chi walked through the growing crowd.

Psychosis followed from a distance. She thought to herself, 'Yep, that's pretty much how I saw it.' She almost felt bad not telling the Royal Court, but she knew they needed a dose of reality, especially Esther. She thought about it, the court was technically finished. Chase would be in traction for about a year if he survives at all; Matt should survive as well as Esther. However, she knew Duncan and Traci wouldn't make it. Chi split Duncan's head wide open. Traci never stood a chance. She would miss Traci though. She will have to avenge her and hopefully prevent Snapdragon from killing Jai.

Once in town, Chi stopped at the same café as Royal Court had previously. She ate quietly. Jessica followed in and watched quietly from a distance as did the rest of the patrons. It felt like déjà vu to Chi.

Back at the battle sight, two friends talk about what they just witnessed. "Wow that was a great battle. I could've sold tickets."

"I told you my little girl was awesome."

"Are you going to offer any help for her next fight? You know she's not a hundred percent."

"She has to overcome on her own. If I interfere now, it may push her away from the fight to come. I might have something on standby, just in case. So, are you going to help them?" Ren pointed to the fallen 'Royal Court'.

"Well, her outside is finally as ugly as her inside, I'll let her be. That one's pretty tough. He should recover from his wounds just fine. The one down there, he needs to slow down."

"What about this one here?"

"It's not going to matter much; he was just a mindless follower anyway even if he finds her hideous. She can get others. No, it's not going to be worth it. That one, however, was a good friend. I will help her."

Charlemagne stretched forth Uni-Horn over Traci. After a quick incantation Traci's face started to restore and pop back to its former structure. Ren suggested they get something to eat.

Ambulances and police dispatched to the scene were at a loss. They didn't know where to start after they got Chase to the local clinic. The police called for a scrap company to pick up the pieces of the vehicle. Everyone, injured and dead was taken to the clinic.

Chi left after she ate. The waitress had told her not to worry about the meal. Jessica was about to leave when she was blocked by a familiar face.

"Do you like the ring?" Charlemagne asked. "Was it worth all you could see?"

"Knowing, I am going to kill you, why are you helping me?"

"Because you're not and you need it. You want to save Hong Jai. So does she?"

"You're full of it. I saw her kill him. Why is she even here?"

"She's looking for me to heal the Hong Jai. You're here to get paid. You and your friends want to kill me, her, and even her father. You saw first-hand, you and your friends couldn't even handle her. You think you can do it by yourself? No, pride, ego, and greed has brought you to this point. Those aren't even your characteristics. Those belong to your 'beloved queen'."

"She's not my queen anymore. The court is finished."

"No, it's just been motivated."

"What are you talking about? I just watched them get their butts handed to them. Tank would've been the only one to survive that massacre, but I'm quite sure they are all dead."

"Nope, only, what's his name? Duncan, he's the only one still dead."

"That's not possible. Traci's face is crushed in."

"I fixed that. The rest I left as they were."

"Why would you do that?"

"It's simple because I can. The funny thing is they might be a little upset you're not beside them."

Why is that?"

"They are going to figure out you knew this was going to happen and didn't tell them, then what are you going to do with that target? Treason is hard to get past, even among the closet of friends. Sometimes it hurts more. You know what the problem with young people is? You never seem to see past your own reflection. Well, see you later."

"Wait, if you know she's looking for you, why don't you reveal yourself to her and help Jai?"

"Let me ask you a question. Do you believe in a god?"

"What?"

"Do you believe in a god?"

"Not really, but I suppose with everything that's happened I suppose anything is possible. Why would you ask a question like that?"

"I've heard people say too many times if God was real this or if God was real that. Why doesn't God just show up and fix everything and shut me up? In the journey of life, if God just showed up every time you stubbed your toe or broke a nail, you would not have a chance to grow. You would be no better than some animal or pet. Since you have a conscious mind, you need to experience life so you can grow. The most important part of anyone's journey for truth and answers is the journey.

"In her case, she has to go through some things so she can grow and become stronger in order for her to be ready to deal with what's coming. If I just showed up and helped Jai; where would you be; a slave to Esther's ego who in turn coddles herself to Constellation. No, you would have eventually left and been hunted by your 'friends'. They would have been able to kill you in a blink. Now, you have experience, power and understanding. When they come for you and they will, you will know what to do. Then again things might be a little different if you didn't block her power. Just saying."

"So what am I supposed to do now?"

"Come with me, I want to show you something."

Charlemagne held out his hand. Slowly, Jessica placed her hand into his. They were instantly transported to a field about fifty miles north. They were sitting in Adirondack chairs, with a small table between them with popcorn and iced tea.

"What are we doing here?"

"Some events that have recently transpired have dictated Snapdragon must overcome what's about to happen as a response to a message that was sent earlier. If she fails, the earth will be plunged into a war it's not prepared for.

"Look at it like dominos. Had your friend not attacked Jai, she wouldn't have come searching for me. Then once she got here, she was attacked by you guys. After committing regicide on the Royal Court, she is now mentally ready for what's about to happen. Should she survive this, she will be strong enough to deal with a cosmic threat. Dominos, first you line them up, and then you knock them down."

"Fine, is there butter on this popcorn?" Jessica reached for her bowl of popcorn and her drink.

Meanwhile, Chi was flying overhead. Suddenly, a lion's roar broke the silence. Chi came to a stop and looked around. Not seeing anything she went to continue when Sagittarius appeared with his bow drawn. He fired. It looked like a small white meteor pulsed out of his bow at the speed of light. He fired quickly in rapid succession. Chi was continuously hit on the way down.

Taurus appeared at the end of her trajectory with a large studded club in his hands. He measured her as she came in. As soon as she was in range, he swung for the fences. He hit her square in the center of her chest sending her flailing backwards. It sounded like bones shattering for a couple hundred feet.

"Man that had to hurt." Jessica stuffed her mouth with more popcorn. "This is good popcorn."

As Chi was about to hit the ground again, Scorpio appeared and caught her with a stinger to the back. Snapdragon's eyes shot open, eyes crimson bleeding down her cheeks. She barely took in a deep breath and roared softly even as Scorpio locked his claws onto her arms as he continued to stab her in the back.

Leo finally appeared, slashing and clawing Snapdragon's face body and chest. Leo was actually trying to scratch the dragon from her flesh. She cried weakly as she struggled against her attackers. Chi started to fade. Sagittarius trotted over as did Taurus. They took turns striking her methodically for several minutes, one after other. She was beaten limp near death. Blood oozed from her many wounds.

Sagittarius fired one last blast at her, when out of nowhere a white tiger slowly walked on the scene and roared. It captured the attention of everyone. They turned to face the tiger. Scorpio slung Snapdragon to the side and stepped forward.

After the Zodiac turned to face the tiger, the earth began to shake. Suddenly, a stone man rose from the ground on the right side of the tiger. On the left, a gravity well of humidity formed drawing in the moisture from the air creating a body of water in the shape of a woman. Above them, floating in the air, another man and woman also appeared. The man exploded on the scene as if stepping out of the sun. Regardless of her feminine form, the woman was the living embodiment of an F10 tornado with lightning coursing through her body.

"That's what he meant." Charlemagne whispered to himself."

"Oh my god, now that's how you make an entrance. Things are about to get real." Jessica sat up quickly enthralled by the scene before. She held her popcorn tight to her chest as she watched the drama unfold before her. Charlemagne, on the other hand, casually sipped his iced tea.

With what little life she had left, Chi's mind remembered her life. Her mind's eye opened. She gingerly got up. She saw Pen.

"I failed."

"No you didn't. You're going to get up and beat respect into them."

"You are so funny. They won. I'm dying."

"Who are you?"

"What?"

"Who are you?"

"I'm nothing; nobody."

"I think you need to be reminded of who are. When I first met you, you were just as scared as I was. You were the finest warrior I ever fought. Then I died. Yes, your life was like the hills of home. Then it happened, Tufei and his men showed up and you woke up. You know he loved you. Then Chai sent Tahaan again. You killed more than a hundred of his men."

"I got tired and lost. I carry those scars even now under the dragon."

"Yes, the dragon, Long Tian Di empowered you. And you set everything right. Before that though, you were in that restaurant and you had enough and you demanded respect and got it. Then you commanded it because you knew who you were. Who are you?"

"I'm just Chi."

"No, who are you? Until you fell into the Pool, you never gave up. Long Tian Di called you Snapdragon. You wear his image as a symbol of the power you have. You are Zhe Duan Chi. You are Snapdragon. You are both. You are one and the same. You are a fighter. You are the yellow dragon. You are Zhe Duan Chi. You are Snapdragon."

Chi found herself back in the courtyard fighting Pen for her heart and her life.

"WHO ARE YOU?"

"I'm Chi."

"WHO ARE YOU?"

"I'M CHI!"

"WHO ARE YOU?"

"I'M ZHE DUAN CHI THE SNAPDRAGOOOON!!!" Chi fought Pen until he was gone.

Charlemagne and Jessica watched as the Zodiacs marched toward the tiger and his entourage. Then they noticed Chi's body started to glow yellow. The Zodiac stopped when they heard something behind them. As they turned, they heard Chi mumbling and saw her slowly stir. They were stunned as was Jessica. Mesmerized, she got up from the chair dropping her popcorn and slowly walked forward to get a better look.

She mumbled slowly as she stirred. "I am Zhe Duan Chi. I am Zhe Duan Chi. I AM ZHE DUAN CHI." She got to her knees, "I... AM... ZHE... DUAN... CHI..." She stood the Zodiac in a fighting stance. "I!!! AM!!! ZHE!!! DUAN!!! CHI!!! AND YOU WILL RESPECT IT!!!"

Oblivious to everything, Chi lunged forward and attacked the very surprised Zodiacs. The Zodiac had to revert to using their cosmic powers to defend against her. However, it still wasn't enough. Chi ripped out one of Taurus' horns and stabbed Leo with it. Then grabbed his club and broke it on Scorpio. Remembering Pen inspired her to use Sagittarius' bow to lock his arms by bending the bow behind his back. With the others beaten unto submission, Chi jumped up, locked her legs around Sagittarius' neck; twisted and slammed him to the ground. With his arms locked behind him, the impact dislocated both of his shoulders.

Charlemagne walked up beside Jessica. "Looks like that little yellow dragon just snapped."

"That's not even funny. How the hell did she do that?"

"That's who she is. Still want to kill her?" He handed her another iced tea. Jessica didn't hesitate to drink. She watched the four individuals with the tiger revert to their human forms. Jessica recognized them right away as the other group from the comic book; the Elementals.

After her mind settled some, she caught her breathe, Chi dropped to the ground still weak from her wounds and started crying uncontrollably. The tiger walked over to her. Quake raised four small pillars of earth for himself and the others Elementals to have a seat. The tiger had lain down beside her and nuzzled her to get her attention.

Chi scrambled back quickly. She thought it impossible. She thought to herself that this could not possibly be the same tiger she knew centuries before and yet she was at peace with him there. She slowly reached out for the tiger. She petted and played for a few minutes with the tiger hugging and scratching him behind the ears ignoring everyone else there. Chi felt better even with her wounds and blood loss.

"I wish I knew why you keep following me."

He knew it was time. The tiger stepped back and slowly changed into a man. He looked at his little girl with pride as she started to cry again. Ren hugged his daughter and whispered to her.

"I'm sorry I couldn't reveal myself to you sooner. I had to honor my agreement with Long Tian Di. I am so proud of you."

Suddenly, Aries walked through a portal. He looked around. Snapdragon and Ren turned to face him. He recognized the situation for what it was. He took his fallen comrades and left without an incident. Ren walked while Chi limped over to the Elementals. After introductions, Ren informed the Elementals, they were free to go home once they were back in Miami.

Ren pointed to Charlemagne and Jessica. Ren talked to Chi on the way over. The Elementals were relieved to be home; on earth. Daemon and Erin kissed as did Adam and Katie. They greeted each other with joy and tears before they follow Ren. For what was just a couple days on earth felt like years for them in the dimension of their respective element.

Charlie spoke as Ren and Chi approached. "I here you're looking for me. My name is Charlemagne. This is Jessica. Before you do to her what you did to them, hear me out."

Chi looked at them. "I'm too tired. Are you able to heal Jai?"

"Would you like me to heal you first?"

"Sure."

"Why are you going to kill Jai?" Jessica blurted out.

"What are you talking about? I could never harm him. He's my champion. He freed me. I owe him my life."

"But I saw you kill him." Now it was Jessica's turn to be upset; still afraid of losing Jai.

To change the subject, Daemon asked a question. "How are we getting back to Miami?"

"I will take care of that too, once I'm done with Chi. Chi when you get back, you need to get cleaned up. You look like you've been to hell and back. Yes, you've been restored, but you still need some rest." Charlemagne reassured everyone. When he was finished healing Chi he opened a portal to Miami. He helped everyone get through except Jessica.

"I'm not going. You have the capabilities to help Jai. What better way to show someone you care than to help them find their way home. Go get him."

"What about the others?"

"The Royal Court's path had change from ego and pride to ugliness. The friends you knew are not the same. But you shouldn't have to worry about them for a while. I'll see you in a little bit."

Jessica thanked and hugged Charlemagne before going home.

"That was fun. I should get out more often." An old man walked away from his projection mirror. He sat in a wooden rocking chair to sip on his iced tea as he watched the red sun lower to meet the horizon.

CHAPTER 21

That's Just Wrong

Meanwhile, back in Miami, Abi finally made it home. She stayed after school with some friends laughing about their day.

"Bye, see you tomorrow."

"Abinatu Lynn Stack, get in here right now!"

"Yes, mom?" Abi ran to the living room.

"Where have you been?"

"I was at school."

"Why didn't you call me?"

"My phone died."

"How is that possible? That phone carries a seven day charge. Are you that irresponsible, you can't plug in your phone at least once a week? Give me your phone!"

"But, mom!"

"NOW!!!"

"Fine." Abi handed Tetra her phone and ran to her room crying.

"Hey Tet, don't you think that was a little harsh? Besides, what did she do wrong?" John walked in the living room with a cup of coffee.

"Don't think you're going to waltz in here and tell me how to raise my daughter. I've done fine so far." Tetra glared at John.

"Ok, Clay, you raise your daughter anyway you want, but you better start treating MY daughter better. Poor kid doesn't even know what she didn't do wrong." John set the coffee down. "You know, you keep treating her like that, she'll turn into me. I got to admit, your father definitely taught you something."

"One, I am not your father. And what is it my father taught me?"

"How to push people away." John grabbed his jacket. "You know, you should be up there right now telling her your glad she's okay and wasn't in Jacksonville today. Nope, you're down here sulking because you didn't get your way. So what, she forgot to charge her phone. Big deal, when you were her age, you wished your father was even here to yell at you. Oh wait that's it." John paused for a moment.

"You're mad at her because of your father and me. He left you alone when you were young. You felt I abandoned you. You're upset because you thought she was leaving you too. Tetra, that's just wrong. Don't punish her because of us. Abi needs you."

"Your right John, I'm sorry."

"Not me, her." John threw down his jacket and took Tetra by the hand up to Abi's room.

Tetra apologized and Abi got animated as she talked about her field trip to the InterActive Children's Museum in Miami. She learned about farming. They were shown how to make cars, movies and cartoons. They pretended to be doctors and scientists. The class even helped put a T-Rex together.

Suddenly, John started to shake violently and dropped to the floor. Abi began crying and screaming. Tetra raced for her phone.

•   •   •

"How is Dr. Athene? Is she going to be okay?"

"No, Mr. Ruger, she did not make. She died about forty-five minutes ago."

"Too bad, on another note, when were you going to tell me you had started 'Project Godsend'?" Ruger's tone changed quickly, becoming irritated.

"You said to begin." Dr. Seba charged Ruger.

"Did I? Was I in front of you when I told you?"

"No sir. You called."

"How many times did I tell you when it came to *Gene*Tech and the project nothing is done unless I'm present?

"Once, you called this morning, said you were on your way over and to begin. So I did."

"Dr. Seba, when I tell you to something, my expectation is for it to be carried out in my presence not carried out over the phone. You're a brilliant doctor, I am confident you will not make this mistake again. Are we clear?"

"Yes sir."

"Now that's out of the way; how were the results?"

"Well, Mr. Ruger, before that creature attacked us, we had about eighty percent inoculated."

"How soon will it be before the experiments start to take effect?"

"That will depend on how receptive each specimen is. The genetic reconstruction should have started about twenty minutes ago."

"What is the projected mortality?"

"I do not expect ninety-two percent to survive at all."

"That's better than expected. I thought we would lose more if not all."

"And I expect gods to be reborn over the next few days. The best part is they will be under your complete control."

"That's the best news I've heard in ages. Since the project has already started, keep me informed of any changes to the specimens. Once everyone has died call me? If you will excuse me, I have something I have to go take care off."

"Me too, I've got rounds to do. Remember the reporter? Well, she was put with the dead after she was struck by the power line. Come to find out, it didn't exactly kill her. She is, however, in a coma. She's definitely worth examining."

"Sounds intriguing, but I really got to go. Keep me up to date. We need to be able to fight every enemy, no matter where they're from. Remember they need to be extra strong and mentally pliable to my commands.

The two men shook hands and both departed the coffee shop at the hospital. Marcus left for home and called his daughter on the way.

"What do you want?" Jessica Ruger answered her phone. She had been angry with her father since his return.

"Button, that's no way to answer the phone when I call."

"It is when you throw me out of the family business."

"I haven't been myself lately. I'm sorry. To make it up how bout I pick you up and take you out to dinner, your choice."

"Sorry, 'Daaad', but I have other plans."

"Like what?"

"I'm taking the jet to Jacksonville. Parker's a wreck and I'm going to pick her up. Right now, she needs me more than having dinner with your ego. Maybe, I'll ignore you when I get back." Jessica then hung up her on her father.

• • •

The room was quiet with the exception of a soft beep and a mechanical lung. A young woman slowly woke. She was relieved to be awake. 'I survived' she thought to herself. Her body tingled. She struggled to get up at first because she had to use the bathroom, then she focused.

She got up and stretched before looking for the bathroom. When she looked back at the bed she froze. She was still lying in the bed. Jhaz Lee stared for a moment. She went to the bathroom to look in the mirror. What she saw left her speechless. She saw herself.

An electrical form of her body stood against her reflection. It was like she was an electrical ghost with a physical form. Jhaz thought it was pretty cool to be able to do that. She learned she could move easily through almost anything that was a conductor of electricity. She practiced firing an electrical charge.

Then Jhaz remembered her body. She went back to it. She noticed her breathing was much shallower than before. She felt amazing. Suddenly, Dr. Seba walked in. It startled her. She instantly became completely translucent.

Dr. Seba checked her vitals. He noticed Jhaz's vitals were much lower. He observed them for several minutes. He saw she was stable. He used the intercom to call for a nurse.

"Yes, Doctor."

"Order a full blood panel. And did we pull a vial for testing the genetic marker on this patient?"

"No, sir, the physician in charge at the time didn't deem it necessary. So the test was skipped."

"Go ahead and draw for the marker. I got a feeling this one may surprise us."

"If you say so." The nurse made a note on Miss Lee's chart and left.

"I may just be superstitious, but you should be dead. It might be a fluke. However, I need to make sure you're not one of them." Dr. Seba held Jhaz's wrist to check her pulse one more time before leaving.

Jhaz decided to follow Dr. Seba. He went to the emergency room to make his rounds. His first stop was to the nurse's station. He looked over the charts of six patients. The charge nurse briefed him on the specifics of each patient.

Upon entering the first room, a man was with his wife. She was going home from work when another vehicle struck hers. The woman was eight months pregnant. The accident induced a premature labor. She was also injured a broken leg and wrist. On a brighter note, the baby was going to be fine. Dr. Seba had the attending nurse check on the status of a delivery room for the woman, and order for her to be prepped for surgery after the delivery.

In the next room was finishing up on a code blue in progress. It was the driver of the other vehicle. He was in his early twenties. Dr. Seba recognized his name. He was one of the test subjects cleared an hour before and released. He left with his girlfriend. The young man didn't make it.

Next to him was his girlfriend. According to the accident report, the boyfriend was driving when he slumped to the right, shifting his weight onto the accelerator. The girlfriend had undone her seatbelt so she could try to steer better. She had attempted to switch sides when the accident occurred. She slipped between the air bags going through the windshield at ninety mph. She flat-lined as the doctor walked in. The doctors and nurses slowly looked up to the clock to confirm time of death.

Dr. Seba met with the EMT's outside of the next room. They informed him the patient was DOA and they needed him to sign off on the paperwork to make it official. Dr. Seba was also informed the next of kin were up front in the waiting room. Dr. Seba smiled when he saw Tetra Stack and a little girl waiting up front.

He moved on to the next room. It was a mom with a couple of sick kids. However, in the last room, Thea Garrah, a beautiful woman in her thirties waited impatiently for her release papers. Dr. Seba told her she didn't have any side effects from her experience. She snatched her papers and walked out. She claimed she was going to own *Gene*Tech. The woman stormed down the hallway ranting for twenty feet before the drop-dead gorgeous woman simply dropped dead.

Dr. Seba had the charge nurse get some orderlies to move the dead to the hospital morgue and put Tetra in a small conference room. He then changed his mind. He wanted Tetra to see Samson. He wanted to see her reaction.

Jhaz was too caught up with her journalistic instinct to notice she was getting weaker when, "Ouch!" Jhaz cried out as she felt a sharp pain in her arm. She suddenly realized her outburst was heard by everyone present and for a brief moment visible. Jhaz quickly made her way back to her body. As she arrived, she saw a nurse walking out of her room carrying a vile of her blood on a tray. She tried to knock the vile loose, but shocked the nurse instead. The nurse dropped the blood anyway. Jhaz returned to her body. She knew she needed to practice as much as she could and figure out a way to get her body to a safer place away from the hospital.

Meanwhile, Tetra and Abi were led down to the morgue. Dr. Seba had waited outside for them to arrive.

"Miss Stack, I'm surprise to see you here. Why are you here at the morgue with this little girl?"

"I was asked to identify John Samson. The nurse told us he was DOA and we could meet with his doctor. You just happened to be down here."

"How are you related to the deceased?"

Tetra spun her ring from John. "He is my daughter's father."

"Isn't that an interesting curiosity? I didn't know you had any children."

"It's not something I make public."

"I understand. So, are you ready to see you daddy?" Dr. Seba smugly asked Abi.

Abi started to cry. Tetra was ready to rip out his spine for being heartless. She hugged her daughter instead. Dr. Seba led them in with a smirk on his face.

•　　•　　•

Across town surfboards lined the beach. A large group of surfers were preparing a bonfire. Only a few of the many surfers were locals. Some pitched tents on the beach. The early morning report promised ten to fifteen foot waves with swells up to a possible twenty-five feet. Everyone was excited. They laughed about who would leave with broken boards and egos. Many challenges were made over who would become 'Wave King of Miami' when a portal opened.

Seven individuals came through the portal and closed immediately. They were all happy to be back in Miami. After looking around it dawned on them they had crashed a beach party. Their arrival startled everyone there. One surfer thought it was so awesome he approached them.

"Duuude! That was like totally awesome. Yo, those are some sick wets. Wicked logo, who's your sponsor?"

Ren walked away. Chi followed. Jessica was a little over whelmed by all the minds she was being bombarded with. She took a deep breath to clear her mind.

Another surfer strolled up to Jessica. "You want me to catch you next time?"

"What?"

"When you fall from heaven." The others listened intently for Jessica's response.

Jessica looked at him and shook her head. She put her thumb and pinky to the side of her head and feigned a phone call. "Hello... It's your mommy. She said before you come home, stop by the store and pick up some better lines." Jessica walked away snickering and thinking what a loser.

"Quick, somebody grab a life guard, cause this dude just..."

"WIPEOUT!!!" The crowd erupted.

The Elementals laughed and talked amongst themselves. They decided to stay with the surfers. When they asked for some beer, they were told it was a 'Spuds Free Zone'. They were disappointed but stayed anyway and had a great time.

•   •   •

Ren went to Tetra's as Chi and Jessica made their way to the hospital to see Jai. Upstairs, Dr. Hague visited Jai one last time before releasing him. With him were Jin, Morra, Shan Tong and Ms. Zhu.

"You are truly a miracle of medicine. We had even tested you for the marker. You were clean. Since you woke, you made an amazing recovery. It's like you were never wounded. So I conferred with a colleague of mine. He recommended retesting for the marker again. You were still clean. I have your chariot in the hallway waiting to take you downstairs." Dr. Hague gave Jai a clean bill of health with a smile.

Chi and Jessica rode the elevator up together. No one else would get on because of the way Chi smelled and looked.

"We should've stopped so you could've gotten cleaned up. Not only do you look like a hot mess; you smell like one too. You need a shower bad and some fresh clothes."

"My champion needs to know I have avenged him and he's going to be okay, thanks to you."

"Suit yourself."

Ding. The elevator doors open. Coming off the elevator, the girls turned right for Jai's room. They saw him being pushed in a wheelchair by his doctor, Dr. Rasa L. Hague. The only person Chi recognized was Jai, while Jessica remembered Ms. Zhu, but neither knew the rest. To Jai's right was his father. Behind him, was wife Morra with Shan Tong to her left. Finally, on Jai's left, Ms. Zhu noticed the girls first.

"Jessica, you're back. It's so good to see you. See, Jai is all better." Michelle moved quickly to greet Jessica and bring her over to Jai.

"Chi!" Jai exclaimed. Curiosity and jealousy got the better of Jessica. She looked into Jai's mind to see who Jai was happier to see. Jai slowly stood and looked at Jessica with the Demon's Claw in hand.

"I warned you to stay out of my head."

Jessica grabbed Chi by the arm to stop her. "Chi, Ru..." was all she got out when Jai held out his hand and pulled her the twenty feet between them. He wrapped his arm around her.

"*I missed you. Did you miss me?*" Jai said to Jessica's mind as she struggled to be free of him. Jai touched her forehead with the Demon's Claw. Within seconds, Jessica started to age.

"No!!!" Jessica screamed.

"Hell has a special place for those that commit treason against their friends." Jessica screamed again in fear. Her mind was opened to hell. She experienced a lifetime of torture in just a few seconds.

Snapdragon for a moment fought herself and her heart to do the right thing. She felt her inner rage boiling within. She remembered the painful words once again. 'You may see him die' and 'I saw you kill him.' Before her mind vanished Psychosis projected the image of Constellation into Snapdragon's mind. Tears of crimson flowed heavily down her face. Trembling, filled with remorse, regret, love, hatred, betrayal, rage, and an overwhelming, demanding fire for justice; Chi screamed out her pain as she fire a blast at Constellation and Jai, her champion, to save the one who wanted her dead. She blasted him with everything she had.

Jessica dropped to the floor like dead weight. Jai flew backwards almost fifty feet only to be stopped by the plate glass window at the end of the hall. It fractured on impact. He knocked Dr. Hague down in the process. Unfortunately, Shan Tong was caught in the blast burning through a third of his body. Both Morra and Michelle fell backwards away from the blast screaming hysterically. Snapdragon slumped to her knees when she was done and cried regret and self-hatred again.

"I should have killed you when I had the chance!" Hong Jin screamed.

Jin ran to Chi and struck the side of her head. He continued to kick Chi as she lay against the wall, over and over again. She finally had enough. She grabbed his leg and punched his knee. It snapped instantly. He yelled out in pain as he stumbled backwards. Both slowly got up. They stood facing each other. Jin slowly pulled a knife from inside his jacket.

"Does it look familiar?" Chi looked on in surprise. Chi remembered her Pen. It was the knife he was killed with and the knife she used to kill Lord Chai.

"Where did you get that?"

"It's kind of ironic. It was used to kill your Pen, and then you used it to kill my grandfather, the grandmaster of Paed Cud Tay School, Lord Cea Chai. When the school was raised from the lake, it was laying on a table in the central hall. Now I'm going to kill you with it."

Forcing himself to surge pass the pain, he faced a very angry Snapdragon. They fought with the intensity of their respective training. Jin was no match for Chi. Her skills and strength were too great. He dropped the knife when Snapdragon shattered all of his major joints. Completely broken he could only lean against the wall, when Snapdragon kicked him through it.

Chi noticed Dr. Hague had helped Jai up. She ran down the hall charging at him. "Get away from him!"

"No Chi STOP!!!" Jai screamed as Chi kicked him through the window. Jai flew halfway across the parking lot when he smacked a truck before hitting the ground.

Chi leaned against the side of the window and wept for Jai. Morra cried over her son. Michelle cleared her mind, saddened by her loss she grabbed the knife and made a quiet retreat to the elevators with thoughts of revenge.

Dr. Hague slowly moved away from Chi. "You know he had a bright future. Then again no he didn't."

Chi turned in surprise to the doctor's comment. "How can you say that?"

"What is your name young lady, Zhe Duan Chi or is it Snapdragon? It doesn't really matter because… You missed!" Dr. Rasa L. Hague quickly pointed the cane directly at the center of Chi's chest and hit her with a blast of energy straight from the pits of hell, Hell's Fire. It sent her flying across the parking lot and into the building across the street.

Constellation walked to the window to watch Chi bounce as she hit several objects before coming to a stop. He then turned and walked to Morra who was wailing over the loss of her husband and sons.

"You're giving me a headache." Constellation touched her with his cane. She erupted in flames. The shock killed her almost instantly.

Then he turned his attention to Jessica. He smiled as he knelt down to the now eighty-year-old woman. Jessica appeared to be dead, yet alive, barely, but alive. Her eyes were dark and sunken in; her hair was white and her skin old and shriveled.

"Where were we? Oh yes. You were telling me how much you missed me. Well, I have some bad news. I'm not into backstabbing old hags. So, I'm breaking it off. Enjoy the last twenty one seconds of your life."

Jessica attempted to get up. Her breath was short and she had a dry wheeze. Constellation stepped on her frail hand and crunched her boned in the process. He saw the ring on her finger. He reached down and ripped off the finger with the ring. Constellation snatched the finger out of the ring and tossed it to the side. Immediately, the ring began to crumble and turned to silver dust and vanished. He shrugged it off and moved on.

Constellation casually walked with the Demon's Claw to the elevator after wiping his hands. Jessica groaned as she laid her head down as she breathed her last. Witnesses coward and hid in fear. Constellation stepped on the elevator with a smile. He turned around to watch those hiding. Suddenly, the eyes of all those who saw what happened ruptured within their heads. The elevator doors closed.

CHAPTER 22

When the Stars Go Out

Angry and hurting, Tetra walked out of the hospital to her car in tears with Abi. She was also crying. As they reached the car, a man crashed through a window from the seventh floor down to the parking lot. A few seconds later, fire blasted through the opening spitting out someone else into a building across the street. The person looked to be engulfed by the flames.

Frantically, Tetra fidgeted with her key fob to unlock her car doors. Abi was frightened and started to scream hysterically as she too struggled to get into the car. Once inside Tetra sped off quickly not paying attention to what was in front of her.

"Mommy, Look Out!" Abi yelled as an Asian woman darted in front of them also not paying attention. Tetra slammed on the brakes stopping just short of striking the woman. Michelle Zhu froze for a moment as she grabbed the hood of the car releasing the knife. Tetra and Michelle stared at each other before Michelle looked up to the seventh floor window and ran toward her car taking the knife with her. Tetra drove forward as soon as she was clear. She was still scared for her daughter's safety. Michelle also raced out of the parking lot once she reached her car almost running over the people trying to flee the hospital themselves.

Tetra reached for her phone to call for back up for the hospital. She called Placer and Steel Hawk. Desperate, she wanted to contact her father but she thought he was still out of the country and not at her home getting something to drink.

Jhaz Lee, two floors below, was disturbed by the commotion. When she got to the window she saw a man lying on the ground and people fleeing the hospital. Her instincts guided her to help the man. She made her way through the wall and surged to the ground next to Jai. As she looked over the burned man she noticed he was alive but fading quickly. She used the little energy she had to recharge his heart and sent a jolt to his brain. She did what she could before she had to return to her body. It was enough to stir Jai, but that was it. He had received additional broken bones from his fall and couldn't be moved at the moment.

After several minutes, Dr. Rasa L. Hague had made his way to the lobby and out of the hospital. He noticed an energy being over by Jai for a brief moment. He saw it weaker as it left him and attempted to fly up toward the upper floors of the hospital. Annoyed by this he blasted it with Hell's Fire from his walking stick. On the fifth floor a monitor flat lined. He casually walked toward the building Snapdragon smashed into to make sure she was dead.

As night crept with her shadow, across the street a very distraught Chi sat on the floor wailing for what she had done. She never thought in a million years she could or would've been the one to kill her champion. And yet by her own hand she fulfilled Long Tian Di's prophecy. The thought of being tricked to kill him enraged her to the point she started trembling. Her crimson eyes stopped shedding tears. She roared out her pain and rage with the power of Long Tian Di himself. Her roar exploded the very building she was in; shattering windows and walls alike. It left her floating in the air. It shook every building within a mile. She was heard more than ten miles away. Car alarms were going off all over Miami.

Everyone and everything that heard stopped what they were doing; from Constellation to Tetra. Even Steel Hawk came to a stop and he was already flying to the hospital after he talked to Tetra. The Elementals paused from their conversions. They rushed toward the sound of an explosion and roar. They had been talking about the hurricane off the coast that was supposed to churn up some killer waves the following morning, as some of the surfers got rolled into the ocean. And over the darkened skies of northern Miami, Placer stopped momentarily with his battle against the Black Star Dragon as did the dragon. Megoon recovered quicker and devoured Placer before he raced to his master.

Meanwhile, on the seventh floor of the University Hospital a lone individual walked from a portal. He looked at the carnage and coming death. He felt the power surge behind him. Quietly, he walked to Jessica.

"Looks like you dropped something, old girl." Charlemagne knelt next to Jessica. He shook his head. "You have so much more to do." He rolled her over and placed the top of the Unihorn by her heart. The pearl glowed for a moment and a pulse of life was shot into her heart and removed the curse of aging. Charlemagne stood and walked back over to a pair of Adirondack chairs with a table between them. He poured two glassed of iced tea and sat.

As soon as Snapdragon's roar subsided she shot through the dust cloud from the building back up to the seventh floor when she noticed Dr. Hague/Constellation on the ground. She went straight at him. She fired her own blast of energy at him. As is the cliché, he parried with his own Hell's Fire. Inching closer to one another, they remained relentless in their mutually desired destruction.

Upstairs, a young woman slowly made her way to her seat. She picked up her glass and drank until it was gone.

"Dehydrated I see."

"Yeah, something like that. It was like I was dead and in hell."

"You were."

"How am I alive?"

"It doesn't matter. You're alive and have work to do."

Charlemagne got up and handed Jessica her ring. As they watched the standoff below, he asked her a question as she put the ring on her restored finger.

"Do you enjoy being a spectating bystander?"

"What is that supposed to mean?"

"Are you always going to watch life happen or are you going down there and make the world see you? Otherwise, I've wasted my time?" Before she could answer, he shoved her out the window. On the way down in mid fall her mind opened and her ring locked itself on again. After her initial scream, she was able to calm her mind and overcome the pain of a second death to safely stop from being smashed into the ground.

Jessica's scream was enough of a distraction to Constellation for Snapdragon to penetrate through and blast him into the marble pillar at the entrance.

Jessica looked up to Charlemagne and yelled, "You Asshole!" In response he toasted her with his iced tea, then opened a portal and walked in. She turned her attention to Snapdragon who was now pummeling Dr. Hague. Satisfied, she ran to Jai. She saw he was badly hurt yet again. She knew she had to keep him safe if she was going to heal him. Even though Constellation had to be dealt with first, she refused to leave Jai's side. She mentally created a domed barrier to protect her and Jai while she worked. Psychosis placed one hand on his head and the other on his heart then began to meditate.

Suddenly, Constellation was able to push Snapdragon off of him and struck her again with Hell's Fire. With pride, he stood. Limping, he walked forward. "Do you think you are going to stopped me? It's my fate to rule the universe."

Out of nowhere Steele Hawk swooped in for an attack. Constellation waited for Steele Hawk to get closer and opened a gateway to hell. He was not able to pull out of the way in time.

"Like I said, it's my fate to rule..."

Looking down on Constellation, Inferno interrupted him. "Hey Doc, Fate just called. She said you application for a beat down has been processed and approved. You're not ruling a damn thing!"

Constellation started to laugh at Snapdragon. "I see you have more back up ready to die, now meet mine."

Megoon Dracul, the Black Star Dragon, dropped from the night sky and landed in front of Constellation. He had already transformed into a human/dragon hybrid. He stood ten feet tall. His hide became his armor.

In his hands appeared a black claymore. And on his forehead was a four-pointed white star. He blocked Snapdragon and the Elementals from getting to Constellation. His landing shook the immediate area and broke Psychosis' meditation.

Psychosis stood and looked around. She sent a message out on a psychic wave to inform everyone one to get to safety. Seeing the Elementals, she told them the doctor was actually Constellation. She told Snapdragon and the Elementals to draw them away from the hospital to protect the rest of the people in the hospital. The Elementals moved closer.

"Chi, do you think you can handle that thing?" Psychosis was concerned that Megoon may be more than she can handle.

"Yep."

"Good, 'cause I'm about to do brain surgery on this bastard."

"Fine, if that's how you want to play. Megoon, I want them extinct. Kill her slowly. Consume the rest! I will take care of these fools."

"Yes Master."

With Megoon's sudden arrival, Snapdragon was able to see past red and realize her environment had changed. The sea of witnesses gave her a greater understanding of the level of destruction the two of them would cause wasn't worth the loss of life. There were people already hurt, injured and afraid. Others were ready to see this fight regardless of the potential danger.

With her centuries of experience she knew how to draw him away. Without hesitation, Snapdragon charged at Megoon. He put away his sword and took a fighting stance. As she was about to strike, Megoon literally beat her to the punch. He sent her flying backwards toward the Everglades.

Megoon surprised Snapdragon by his strength. He flew after her and reached her again before she recovered. He struck her again and sent Snapdragon further into the Everglades. On his next attempt, she was able to maneuver out of his way and took the fight to him.

Meanwhile, Constellation found himself in the middle of a two front confrontation. He was fighting a physical battle against more seasoned Elementals. Whereas with Psychosis, he fought both a physical battle on the surface, but in their subconscious, it was a psychic war of wills. Constellation was surprisingly agile and quite competent in doing both.

Over the next several minutes, S.H.A.R.P. arrived as did the police and fire departments. S.H.A.R.P. attacked both sides per the orders of Marcus Ruger. The police and fire departments did what they could to help the injured where they could. More than that, everything was being recorded and televised. There were several news organizations in helicopters reporting live.

The Elementals were mindful of the growing crowd. Because of this, they reframed from using their more powerful abilities. Constellation on the other hand didn't care who was harmed. Between psychically hurdling cars back and forth with Psychosis and fighting the combined strength of the Elementals, he was forced away from the hospital.

In a higher level of consciousness, Psychosis and Constellation delved deeper into their psychic battle. At first, she was intimidated into believing she was fighting space itself. As each level of consciousness eroded away she was able to penetrate pass his illusion of greatness; the cosmos, until she was standing among the highest clouds touching space.

For the first time in eons, Ophiuchus' true self was exposed to someone else. As he stepped forward, he appeared to look like a very young and timid Dr. Rasa L. Hague. He wore pale green pants with no shirt or sandals. In spite of a snake slithering over his shoulders and around his body, Jessica thought he was beautiful. He had crystal blue eyes, soft blond hair, and a smile that could charm anyone's soul.

"I'm impressed to see you were able to break through." Ophiuchus complimented Jessica.

"Is this really who you are?" Jessica felt oddly at ease.

"There is no need for hostilities here. We do not have to fight anymore. You are safe. If you will allow me, I will explain." Ophiuchus casually walked over to Jessica and took her by the hand. As if traveling through time, he continued.

"Long before time existed as you know it, there were thirteen clusters of stars in the universe divided into twelve regions. Each Zodiac was set watched over their own region of the universe and me to watch over them. And in the midst of all this was a little blue planet. For some odd reason we were not alone anymore, because the Great Consciousness deemed it fit to create life. Then you became the center of his universe instead of me. So I decided to make you love us instead of him. I blocked your view of him by hanging my own stars. I then allowed others to do the same until your people were so confused, you didn't know where to look. Now, you are here; challenging me in a fight you are so under equipped to win. The greatest illusion your people are convinced of, is hope. My greatest achievement besides blocking your view of the Great Consciousness is the implosion of the human family; brother killing brother and all that."

Feeling the seductive words penetrate her soul, Jessica was unaware of the serpent gliding over her body as she was captivated by Ophiuchus' voice and appearance. The serpent slowly coiled around her body and began to squeeze once it encircled her neck.

In the Everglades, Snapdragon had turned the tide in her battle with Megoon Dracul. She used everything she had to fight against him. It shocked Megoon that a mere human was besting him. Frustrated, he created a gravity well on Snapdragon. She began to slow down as Megoon increased the well. Soon Snapdragon struggled to fight or fight back. She was no longer strong enough to move nor was she able to scream out in pain. Sound and flickers of light were being drawn unto her.

Almost broken, Megoon smugly drew his sword and slowly backed up to watch gravity take its' course. Things were flying into Snapdragon. Birds were pulled from the sky and gators drug from the swamp. Trees were uprooted. Even the water was drawn to her.

She was being crushed under her growing mountain of debris. The pressure squeezed out the last breath to escape her mouth before she blacked out with a single faint, barely breathed word, 'help'.

As Megoon felt the tug on his sword he smiled and let go. The sword raced to her heart. Suddenly, a streak of light struck instantly from the heavens into the hand of Snapdragon. The force of impact negated the gravity well and exploded outward with the force of a nova in a Planck of time.

Megoon didn't know what hit him. It knocked him back several miles.

Snapdragon's eyes opened with a deep inhale. She slowly rose to her feet wielding the Nova Star.

Holding the Nova Star, Snapdragon stood. The blade's glow was a bright white which illuminated the area. She flew straight for Megoon. Flashes of her life raced in her memories as she approached. Like light, she burned through the night sky, sword in hand ready to strike, but Megoon was able to parry the strike at the cost of his blade. Nova Star sliced through the Edge of Darkness eclipsing any hope of victory.

Cut after cut, Snapdragon wore down the great warrior. Valiantly, he fought until he dropped to his knees. Then suddenly, she jumped up and locked her legs around his neck with a twist, flipped backwards slammed him to the ground, braking his neck instantly. She jumped up again and drove the sword down into Megoon's heart.

Snapdragon slowly caught her breath leaning on the sword when she noticed a tear gliding down the face of the Black Star Dragon. Compelled, she knelt beside his face and wiped the tear and put it to her lips.

She slowly got up to fly back to Miami. What she didn't notice was the sword had been absorbed into Megoon Dracul. Without warning, the Nova Star and the Black Star Dragon, in the heart of the Everglades, fused together and created a reaction that exploded and consumed everything within a twenty five mile radius. Just as quickly as it happened, it and they were gone.

Just as suddenly; as the serpent was squeezing the life from Psychosis, turned to stardust, releasing her from the clutches of death once again. This made Ophiuchus freak out and panic. He attacked Psychosis as he screamed obscenities at her. She did the best she could to defend herself.

Ophiuchus had a psychotic break from the spiritual and mental separation from Megoon Dracul. He dropped to his knees and sat on his heels. He began to wail the loss of his serpent. His loss was greater than he could accept.

After looking into his mind, Psychosis was able to loop his memory so he would be forced to relive the moment when Megoon died. She created a cage around Ophiuchus seven fold. She then set his mind adrift at the event horizon of a black hole before she left his mind and returned to hers.

When Psychosis came to herself she saw the destruction. She saw Dr. Hague kneeling in the street. He was motionless and blank. The Elementals were about to continue their attack when the shockwave hit from the everglades. Dr. Hague fell over as did most people.

Psychosis went over to him and smiled. "Welcome to your *psychosis.*"

S.H.A.R.P. rushed over to seize the moment. They even tried to arrest Psychosis and the Elementals. Psychosis used her power of persuasion to convince the S.H.A.R.P. agents to let them go.

•   •   •

After a couple hours, things were getting back to normal. However, at Gateway Mansion, the mood was sad and grim. The Zodiacs gathered to witness the fulfillment of a promise. As they were in their stations, they looked up to the snake charmer to see every star, both great and small, that represented the entire region of the serpent go supernova and go out. They knew all life in that region of space was extinguished as well.

"This is what the Guardian showed me. We will be put to the sword and become void if we do not leave this world behind." Capricorn became desperate to convince the others to leave.

But we can't leave without him." Aquarius continued as she pleaded for Constellation. "I know he is still here because his stars are still intact. GemIni, are you sure you can't sense him."

"Yes, we're sure. He is nowhere to be found. It's like his mind is gone."

Everyone conceded it was time to leave. The Zodiacs left Gateway Mansion to their homes among the stars. A few mourned; others rejoiced, but all left.

At the hospital, in a small padded room, Dr. Rasa L. Hague sat on a bed in a straitjacket slowly rocked back and forth. He kept mumbling about the death of his snake.

CHAPTER 23

Coffee at Jo's

The following morning a woman was arguing with Dr. Seba about the care and safety of her daughter.

"Mrs. Lee, your daughter needs to be here. It's the safest place for her."

"Are you kidding me? Safe? This was a warzone last night no one is safe in this hospital. I'm taking my daughter out of this hospital today. I will take care of her at home where I know she is safe."

"Ma'am, our staff saved your daughter's life last night. Her heart gave out. We were barely able to save. She's in a coma. If you move her, what you will be risking is taking her to the morgue not you house."

"I don't care, I want her home."

"Fine, before I release her I have to test for the genetic marker."

"Don't you touch my daughter! She's not a freak, their freaks. It's because of them my daughter is in here. I saw the news." Mrs. Lee pointed across the fifth floor waiting room to the Elementals.

Ren and Tetra returned to the hospital after dropping Abi off to her friend, Luna de Terra.

"Why is it always the hatemongers that are the loudest?" Tetra asked her father.

"They can't help it. They are motivated by fear. And fear, as you know, is a very powerful motivator."

Erin, trying to change the subject, asked if anyone had heard from Chi.

"Sorry, I don't sense her anywhere." Ren answered. "Sadly, I don't believe she survived. With the amount of energy released, it was like a small star touched the earth. I don't think anyone could've lived through that."

Just then the door to Jai's room opened. Jessica looked exhausted and drained as she pushed Jai in a wheelchair.

"How are you doing this morning?" Adam enquired.

"Honestly, I feel like a new man. Have any of you heard from Ms. Zhu? She'll know what to do."

Jessica intervened. "How bout we call her when we get in the car. Remember I told you your phone is in the bag with your stuff. Plus, she should be able to answer some questions about your family."

"Oh yeah, that's right. Well anyway, I was going to have a pool party at my house this weekend. However, it will more likely be funerals instead." Quietly, they walked Jai to the elevator.

As they reached the elevator doors Tetra was tap on the shoulder. As she turned to see who tapped her, she was met with a full swing slap in the face by Mrs. Lee. Then she spit in her face.

"I knew I recognized you. That's for my daughter! You need to die with the rest of those damned mutts and freaks."

Orderlies and the Elementals immediately got between Mrs. Lee and Tetra who was still in shock by the assult. Mrs. Lee was restrained until Tetra was guided onto the elevator.

"I hear you have a kid, do you feed it 'Puppy Chew'." Mrs. Lee continued.

"Wow, what was that about?" Jai asked.

"Don't worry about it, sweetie." Jessica replied. "Some people are just crazy."

•   •   •

At that same moment, eight hours east in Madagascar, Esther Anwan was slowly waking from her induced sleep. The remaining members of Royal Court have been awake for some time. Chase was bedridden in a full body cast. Matt and Traci were up and about. They called for the nurse.

"How can I, oh, I see you're awake. Let me get your vitals real quick and I will get the doctor." The nurse was able to understand her mumbling under the bandages that covered Esther's head.

"You have really nasty burns to your face. We did everything we could." Esther mumbled some more.

"Who's Duncan?" The nurse asked Matt and Traci.

"He's her boyfriend." Traci responded.

"I'm so sorry dear, he didn't make it." The nurse turned back to Esther.

Esther started crying and demanding to have the bandages removed so she could see her face.

"I'm sorry dear, but you will have to wait until the doctor returns from supper."

"Please nurse can't you do something?" Traci pleaded with the nurse.

"I will look to see if the doctor has returned, but that's the best I can do." A few minutes later she returned and said the doctor decided to make a house call while he was out. She also mentioned he would not be back until morning. The nurse then left to check on other patients.

Angry, Esther demanded Matt break the cast away. Traci helped where she could. As they removed the wrapping, fear grew on their faces as they looked upon Esther. Slowly they backed away. Traci grabbed a mirror and handed it to her.

Esther raised the mirror to her face. She stared in awe and fear of her own face. She was severely deformed. Portions of her face had melted away leaving holes. Her left eye socket was completely exposed, her nose burned off, and she had no flesh where her lips should have been. The rest of her face was bubbled and blistered.

Outside, the wailing scream Esther let loose blew out the wall and crippled the next two buildings. Traci was able to quickly teleported her and Matt to safety. Unfortunately, Chase wasn't so lucky. He didn't to survive the scream with his other injuries.

"I'm going to kill her!!!" Esther screamed again.

•　　•　　•

Later that night back in Miami, three friends sat together to celebrate Jessica Ruger's nineteenth birthday. Sarah Pennington and Parker Madison had dinner with Jessica Ruger, their longtime friend. Parker wasn't really in the mood, but it was her friend and she did have a present for her even if it was meant for someone else. She handed her two comic books, 'Terror by Night'.

After going through the books they realized what they actually had, proof of who and what Max, Raven, Ron and Joe have become. So when midnight came with some liquid courage they took up the challenge and entered the comic book.

Meanwhile, Raven Kali, a young woman of Indian descent, had prepared a means to understand the whispers she was hearing from a demonically clawed scepter. She found it after the battle at the hospital. It kept whispering 'free me'. She had prepared a spell to find its owner. It pointed her back to the hospital.

•   •   •

A week later, Miami was able to take a deep breath. Tetra Stack stood at a podium in front of City Hall.

"My fellow Miamians, we are here today to remember 'Heroes'. These heroes lived and breathed among us. These heroes strove for the peace of all mankind. These heroes stood up with courage against the enemies of peace and goodness. And even though we have our differences, we all have the same desire; Life…, Liberty…, and the Pursuit of Happiness.

'We were all threatened. Man and woman, human and mutate; were all threatened. And we all; Man and woman, mutate and human came together to fight against an enemy seeking destroy us all. I would like to personally thank the S.H.A.R.P. agents and the law enforcement agencies involved for keeping a clear head. And I would like to personally thank all of the genetic mutates for not succumbing to the fight or flight mentality and not resisting the help of S.H.A.R.P. agents.

"We must remember; we are all children of the earth. And should any decide to have the courage to defend another, even if just one; is a hero of all humanity; both human and mutate alike. Let us rebuild together. Thank you."

Tetra returned to her seat next to Marcus Ruger.

"Thank you Ms. Stack. Tetra Stack everyone." The mayor began to speak. "Before we continue, all the honorees, please step forward."

The Elementals and Psychosis came forward with S.H.A.R.P. They were all presented with a key to the city. Both Snapdragon and John Samson received the honor posthumously. Both recognized as heroes fighting for a safe earth. Tetra received the honor on behalf of Snapdragon and Abinatu received her father's. Afterward, all the names of those who died or still missing were spoken aloud. Of those mentioned, Steele Hawk, Placer, the Hong family, and the children of the Blue Wings Orphanage among others were honored with a twenty-one gun salute.

•   •   •

In a café named Jo's, in Key West, a young Asian woman sat at a table by the window overlooking the Caribbean. She held a small yellow flower with one hand and the other she held her head with her fingers in her hair.

A waitress walked over to the table. She noticed the young woman weeping. She quietly sat down.

"Are you okay, honey? Is there anything I can get for you?"

The young woman slowly shook her head no and spoke softly as tears fell from her eyes. "My life back."

Over the next couple of hours, Jo listened to her and gave her some food to eat. She decided to offer her a room and a job until she was ready to leave.

• • •

The room was cold and dark. The only light came from the door signs that said exit. Twelve gurneys were in the room. Five of which held a body. Suddenly, one by one, those five bodies started to rise from their eternal slumber. The sheets fell from them to reveal two women and three men. Lightening surged through the body of the last to rise. His toe tag read, John Samson.

Made in the USA
Middletown, DE
11 November 2022

14544586R00166